Welcome to Clarence Bay!

Oh, Canada. Home of moose, beaver, and Tim Horton's coffee. Of the world's greatest supply of gold, fresh water and the two Ryans (Gosling and Reynolds). You can find all that in Clarence Bay. (Well, maybe not *those* Ryans, or gold.)

Clarence Bay is my fictional take of the real small town of Parry Sound, located about two hours' drive north of Toronto on Georgian Bay, smack dab in the heart of cottage country, where my own cottage is located.

What's cottage country, you ask? Sure you did. It's where hordes of Toronto's 6-million people head on the weekends, tying up traffic on all the major highways for hours until, finally, you arrive at your place in the woods (could be a century-old cabin or a private island compound), to relax with a cold one and listen to the loons. Better lock up your trash at night, though. If the raccoons don't get it, the black bears will.

Sight for Sore Eyes is the second book in the Clarence Bay Chronicles. It's three years since Emma and Asher met. Life had put up major roadblocks to a relationship, but now a pair of scheming seniors have matchmaking on their minds.

Next up is *Stormy Wedding*, a collection of five inter-connected short stories that all take place on the same four days. Four friends, a wedding, and an ice storm. So stay tuned!

Visit my website at www.joanleacott.ca to find the link to my newsletter, discover more about my small town and its gossipy citizens. I love to hear from my readers. Connect with me on Facebook or Twitter.

Come meet the neighbours and find new friends in Clarence Bay!

Sight for Sore Eyes

CLARENCE BAY
CHRONICLES
Book Two

JOAN LEACOTT

WOVEN RED PRODUCTIONS
Toronto Canada

Cover and Interior Design by Woven Red Author Services, www.WovenRed.ca
Edited by Kristin Anders, www.TheRomanticEditor.com

Sight for Sore Eyes/Joan Leacott—1st edition, revised January 2019
ISBN ebook: 978-0-9920028-4-8
ISBN print book: 978-0-9920028-5-5

To my mother Tove and my father Magnus
Together Forever

To my wonderful Victor

Acknowledgments

Endless thanks to my brainstorming buddy
Gina Grant.

Making sure I got the India details just right is my
friend and TRW chapter mate
Roopindar (Randi) Kang.

Helping me with my musical selections for Asher,
my friend and piano teacher
Ann Edwards.

Table of Contents

CHAPTER 1

Porcelain Lady

The bell chimed over the entrance door of Finn's Fine China and Gift Shoppe. Emma Finn closed her satisfying financial report and left her small office. The glass shelves of china, silver, and crystal gleamed in the grey light of the cloudy mid-April day. "Good morning, Dahlia."

Emma's friend held her special-order Royal Doulton figurine, checking every delicate curve for imperfections. With a sigh of deep appreciation and avid possession, she smiled broadly. "She's perfect. I've waited a long time for this little lady to come to me."

"I found her in Hawaii. And now I have a new dealer contact."

"You're a genius."

Emma accepted the accolades with a smile. "Thank you. She's a lovely lady."

"Just like you, with shining chestnut hair and brown eyes."

Emma took Dahlia's credit card and slid it into the reader.

"Myra always said she'd leave the shop to you." Dahlia ran a fingertip over the gold embossing of the white box waiting for the figurine.

"So she said." Emma hid her grin while she teased the matriarch of the Gossiping Grishams, leading nurturers of Clarence Bay's grapevine.

"And did she? Leave you this shop?"

Emma dragged out the suspense a little longer. "Yes, I inherited the shop and Grady was left the marina." Emma clipped her lips together. No need to mention Gran's instructions to sell the shop to fund her abandoned dream of becoming a world-class photojournalist. Emma still took photos, but her goal was to manage Gran's shop for future generations.

"Well, she left her treasure in capable hands," Dahlia said. "Finn's is practically a historic site."

Emma tilted her head. "Historic is a stretch. But I'll give you vintage." Apart from her computer and the cash register, everything remained as Gran had modernized it back in the nineteen-fifties.

"Vintage works. Tourists love it. Just look at my salon. Women come just to take pictures of themselves under my old bonnet dryer. Lots of them come back for updos for the Fifties Bandstand Dance on Labour Day."

"You're right. This place could use an overhaul." Emma continued to tease her friend knowing she wouldn't alter a thing.

Dahlia's face creased in worry. "Don't go too far, will you? Change isn't all it's cracked up to be."

"Amen to that." Change had never been a friend to Emma, destroying her family and friends. Emma drummed her fingers, waiting for the receipt to print. "Maybe just a thorough cleaning and a fresh coat of paint."

"Paint is all you need. Have you been to see the new homes

Ryan is just finishing up?"

"Uh huh. Melody and I checked them out. They're gorgeous.' The mixed-income eco-friendly neighbourhood on the shores of Mill Lake was a recent, and closely watched, development in Clarence Bay.

"You should buy one. Get out of your cramped space upstairs." Dahlia rolled her eyes. "Jump start your life after spending the last two years caring for Myra."

Emma shook her head. She'd been sorely tempted to move into the small bungalow beside the one Melody had purchased. "Why change? My apartment's big enough for me and you can't beat the commute."

"Well, there's change for the bad and change for the good. Speaking of which, have you been on anymore dates?" Dahlia inspected her perfect manicure while peeking at Emma.

Breathing deep for patience, Emma handed over the receipt. "You know as well as I do, I have dated every appropriate guy in town and none of them do it for me. I'm happy as I am."

"What about the delicious Dr. Asher Stockdale?"

Emma hid her blush by gathering a sheaf of tissue paper from the shelf under the cash register. "It's been two years since I had my last appointment with him." Well, twenty-one months and a bit. But who's counting.

Dahlia replied with a loud doubt-filled *humph*. "What about that kiss?"

Emma gusted out another sigh. "Enough with that ancient rumour. He's my eye doctor. He's not my boyfriend, or my significant other, or whatever." Dream guy, perhaps. But that didn't count either.

Dahlia tapped the back of Emma's hand. "Well, my recent observations of Dr. Stockdale are impeccable. Fact is, whenever you happen to be anywhere near him, he only has eyes for you. And your eyes are equally sticky."

Emma reared back in mock disgust. "Eww."

Eyebrows crimping, Dahlia paused and visibly replayed her words. She chuckled along with Emma, and then pointed a finger at her. "Don't distract me. No matter how long it's been, the delicious doctor wants to get in to your pants. And you want to let him in!"

Emma's jaw dropped. She didn't know what shocked her more, Dahlia's audacity or her accuracy. Emma clacked her teeth together and turned to shove the charge receipt in the cash register. She pulled the Royal Doulton catalogue of figurines from the shelf and offered it to Dahlia. Her friend's eyes lit up as she reached for the precious pages. Diversion accomplished, Emma made a nest of tissue paper and picked up the china lady.

A flash of bold warm pink beneath a battered brown leather jacket snapped her attention forward. Her belly contracted with a gasp. Her hands dampened and trembled. The shop bell chimed, and the china lady slipped from Emma's grasp.

Dahlia shrieked.

Emma gasped.

A slow, horrified moment ticked over.

The figurine landed with a rustling *pooff* in the tissue-lined box.

Dahlia snatched up the figurine, inspected it minutely.

Emma peered over Dahlia's shoulder, her cheeks prickling. She dared not risk another glance at Asher's handsome face and his warm smile.

"I'm a doctor. Any first aid required?" Humour twinkled in his dark eyes.

"She's fine." Dahlia nestled her treasure back into safety. She glanced from Asher to Emma's pink cheeks then slid the remaining sheets of tissue from beneath Emma's nerveless fingers. "I'll do it, Emma dear. You look after your doctor."

Emma's hand rose of its own accord to invite Asher forward. He stepped towards her and took her hand in his, bent his head and kissed the offered palm. Blood whooshed through her smitten heart, filling her with a soft warmth. She stared into the dark depths of his eyes, where a strong heat burned.

A romantic sigh escaped Dahlia, and she gave a sly smile. "I'll see myself out, shall I?" She gathered up her self-wrapped purchase and the catalogue, winked and walked towards the door. She paused on the swooping Finn's logo inlaid into the oak floorboards. "Whatever you do, don't touch this tribute to the long history of your family and this shop."

Emma had no intention of altering anything. She had decided to be content with her life. Change wrecked lives. Sameness might be boring, but it was safe.

Yet she still couldn't remove her hand from Asher's clasp.

Reluctantly, Asher lowered their joined hands to the cash desk. The glass cooled the back of his hand. He should let go of her. He didn't want to.

The shop bell tinkled into silence as Mrs. Gossip left.

"Hello, Emma."

An awkward pause writhed among the dust motes. He would not apologize for his spontaneous gesture, no matter how presumptuous. The rewards of her floral scent in his nose and her softness on his lips were too good to regret.

"Afternoon, Dr. Stockdale," she said to his hand. Emma dipped her head further and slid her hand from his, leaving an achy emptiness.

"I'm sorry I didn't make it to your grandmother's funeral last week. I had emergency surgery. Did you get my flowers?"

Her smile wobbled, and tears glinted in her eyes. "Yes. Thank you, and thanks for your donation to the Heart and Stroke Foundation. We all expected her to go, but it still shocked us when the stroke took her."

He wished he knew Emma well enough to offer her a comforting hug. She stood just the right height to rest her head on his shoulder. Because of their separate dramas, words were all he could give. One day, if things went well, he hoped to offer his whole self. "It was the same with my grandmother. I still miss her, even eight years later. How are your brother and his family holding up?"

"Grady's hanging in there. The kids are having a harder time. Teenagers aren't into change they don't originate." She blinked back the unshed tears. "Is your patient okay?"

"He will be."

She nodded.

Another awkward pause. Damn, he used to be much better at talking to women. He cleared his throat. "Anyway... I did come with another purpose in mind."

"Yes?" Did her smile show a little anticipation?

He gestured around the place. "I need some dishes."

"Oh." Disappointment showed in her face.

Hope whispered in his ear. Please let it not be too late. He'd done the right thing, deliberately avoided her temptation, until he'd recovered his equilibrium after the battering of divorce and custody dispute.

She mimicked his sweeping gesture. "Well, this is the place. Are you looking for something specific? China, pottery, stone-ware?"

"Plates. And cutlery. And glasses." And a date, for starters. Natural and unsophisticated, Emma was so different from his ex. He wanted her in his new life.

"For special occasion or everyday use?"

"Special?"

She smiled kindly, like one does to a confused kid.

His gaze snagged on her upper lip pulling crooked over a short pale scar on the right side. Another thin scar lay on the crest of her cheekbone. He'd noticed them at their first meeting in Emergency, had wanted to soothe the phantom pain. He clasped his hands at the small of his back.

Her tongue brushed against the scar from the inside. "A car crash, a long time ago."

He paused, inviting her story, but she said no more. He nodded. "My family is coming to town and I have to serve them dinner. I only have the cheap unbreakable stuff. My mother would not be pleased."

"Why not take them out to a restaurant?"

"My mother insists. She wants to put her stamp of approval on my new home."

"Okay. Mom-pleasing is a good thing. Can you cook?"

"My specialty is roast beef and mashed potatoes. Most of the time." He gave her a self-mocking smile.

She stared at his mouth.

He smiled even more.

She blinked and looked away.

His rising hope protested that she protested too much.

"Impressive," she said. "My brother's lucky enough to have a wife who cooks incredibly well." She waved off her sidetracking. "Did you have any particular colour in mind for your dinner service?"

He scanned the shelves and cases. "White? I guess?"

"Patterned?"

"Sure. Why not?"

Her indulgent smile came with a metaphorical pat on the head. "You and your wife never shopped for china?" She glanced at the floor. "Sorry, none of my business."

"My ex-wife chose everything. It was easier to go along with her." He straightened. "Haven't a clue what I want, but I like looking at the designs."

"Lots of men do." She flicked her eyes at his pink shirt and smiled archly. "Even the straight ones."

"Hey!" He laid a defensive hand on his chest. "This is my favourite shirt. Most women like it." He got a strong kick to the memory; flirting was fun.

She laughed with an intriguing hint of bawdiness and a suggestive twinkle in her brown eyes. His pulse stuttered at the naughty pictures in his mind.

"Do you have a budget, Asher?"

"Depends on the set." He loved hearing his name in her slightly husky voice.

Leading him over to a display of white plates grouped in graduated sizes with matching cups and saucers, Emma chatted about china, porcelain, and pottery.

Who knew there was so much to know about something so basic?

"Not square. And not all white." He rejected the bland selection; the epitome of his ex's taste. "I want something old-fashioned." A bold pattern caught his wandering eye. "Like this.' He picked up a plate and ran his fingers over the raised gold flowers on the glossy black band circling the plate.

"Excellent choice," Emma said. "It's discontinued, which doesn't mean unavailable. How long before your dinner party?"

"Three weeks."

Her brows drew together.

"Not enough time, I assume?"

She tipped her head from side to side. "Hmm, might be okay. I'll call around and see what I can find. I seldom buy everything from one place. How many guests are you expecting? And how many place settings would you like in total?"

"Mother, Dad, Granddad, my sister Tenley," he counted off on his fingers. One more finger popped up, but he re-folded it. "And me, making five."

Curious. Who would be missing? "I assume you want serving pieces as well? Coffee pot, teapot, platters, bowls, etcetera."

He nodded.

"Okay, I'll start immediately and keep the deliveries here at the shop. Then you can pick them up all at once."

"Would it be all right if I picked them up as they came in?" Then he'd have plenty of excuses to see Emma.

"Sure. Now, what about silverware and glassware?"

Asher held up his hands in surrender. "Whoa, I freely admit an interest, but I hit my limit for today. Why don't you pick something that works with my choice and we'll call it a day?"

"That would be my taste, not yours." She slid a tray out from behind the counter and laid down his chosen plate. "See if anything catches your eye?"

"Do I have to?" he teased.

"You do. Now come over here and look." He pretended to drag his feet while he took in her rear view. Nice.

She opened wide shallow drawers of silver place settings and scooped up a few in varying styles. Then she escorted him over to shelves laden with wine glasses.

An easy decision—clear and intricately cut, sparkling even on a dull day.

She added a pair to her stash then took everything to a table in the center of the room. A silver candelabrum centred on the white tablecloth held five white candles.

"Now comes the fun part." Her confident smile encouraged him to join in. She laid a place with the china and glasses then tinkered with the various silver patterns. "You could go with something very simple as a contrast." She stepped back to show a precise placement.

A quick glance sufficed. "No, thanks."

"I didn't think so, but I like to cover all the options." She moved those aside and spread more cutlery.

"Nope."

She set another grouping.

"Hmm, almost."

Those were gone with a soft clinking and she placed the final set.

"Yes." He crossed his arms and gazed with satisfaction at his selection. An image gelled in his head of a long table, fully dressed, crowded with people large and small, Emma at the far end.

Crossing her own arms, she tilted her head. A brilliant smile declared her satisfaction with his choice. "Now, was that so painful?"

He shook his head and smiled down at her, giving it his all. "Not with you to help me."

Instead of smiling back at him, she stared, her eyes a little wide, her lips parted.

No matter how out of practice he might be, he remembered this look. He'd shared it at least three times in the past hour. He arched his eyebrows in question.

Giving herself a little shake, she came out of her trance. "You're welcome."

"Thank you." Damn, she took his breath away. "Will you come to dinner, let me cook for you and serve you on my new china?"

"You're cooking? Is that a promise or a threat?"

His bawdy angel returned, and he couldn't be happier. "Very much a promise."

Emma drove along Waubeek Street towards Asher's home. A heavy box, loaded with his second and final order, a tea service, sat in the passenger seat, just in time for his family dinner.

Last week, she'd sourced a dinner service for twelve from a single vendor in California, an unusual stroke of luck. Thanks to previous dealings, she'd been able to buy direct without going to auction. In return, Emma had shipped off an equally rare Belleek collection found in Hamer Bay.

Asher had dropped into the shop a couple of times bringing her small gifts. She smiled to herself. His last visit had been for the actual shipment and he had come bearing flowers. A thrill ran through her at the memory of their near-kiss. Sometimes, customers were a pain in the butt.

She parked a little way down the street from what had once been an ordinary red brick house with white trim. Wow. Asher had made the house his own; restored the deep scrollwork around the pillars, painted the door and shutters indigo and the window frames taupe.

She'd been to the house countless times in her childhood when it had belonged to the Rossettis. Cathy Rossetti had been one of her best friends since childhood. Then she left for university and all but disappeared. Until the summer before last, when she returned with her daughter Hayley and stunned the whole town with a double whammy of secret identities. Now, Cathy was married to Hayley's father, Ryan, and Hayley was over the moon with her newfound family.

Was the playhouse still in the backyard to echo back their girlish giggles? Did the porch swing still creak on its chains? All the hideous flowered wallpaper had to be gone.

On the sidewalk in front of Asher's house, Miss Pentland stood transfixed, listening to the solo piano performance spilling from his open windows. Eyes closed, the piano teacher swayed, her trench coat moving against her slim legs. She seemed so familiar with the music that she anticipated its tune. Given her world-renowned career, it wasn't impossible.

Emma got out of the car as quietly as she could. Too bad she needed to slam the door to make it shut properly.

The teacher pressed a finger across her lips in a silent shush.

"Sorry, Miss Pentland, I didn't mean to interrupt your pleasure of the recording."

Miss Pentland shook her head. "This is the real thing, played on a real grand piano, by a man with a deeply passionate soul."

"How do you—"

She raised her hand in a stop-sign gesture. "Shh. He's just be-
gun. I must hear it all."

The wonderful music carried on. Emma's arms strained beneath the weight of china in her hands. Moving cautiously, she
bent her knees and lowered the box to the sidewalk with a quiet
groan.

"Close your eyes, open your ears, and let the music fill you,"
Miss Pentland said in a low-voiced command. Her hand beat time
with graceful movements, compelling Emma to join her.

The sun heated Emma's head and shoulders. The music con-
jured thunder, lightning, a false calm, the wind cavorting in the
treetops. A last soul-stirring cascade of notes hung in the air for
an eternity.

Emma opened her eyes, expecting a storm's aftermath in the
cloudless sky.

Miss Pentland sighed. "Perfect. Lovely soft landing on the final chord. It takes a very talented amateur to play Beethoven's
Pathétique without going overboard." A sheepish smile lit her
features. "Please don't tell Dr. Stockdale I was here. If he thinks
a stranger's eavesdropping, his future practice might be compro-
mised."

"Yes, Miss Pentland."

The teacher nodded and walked off briskly, leaving Emma
staring after her.

A closet audience. Huh. She glanced at her watch, astonished
almost twenty minutes had passed. She hefted the box off the
ground and strolled to the front door between gorgeous gardens
overflowing with tulips and daffodils. The local businesses were

very happy with all the money Asher had spread around to transform the place.

As she crossed the porch, she couldn't resist a detour to give a slight push to the freshly painted dark-blue swing. She smiled at its soft creak. Good thing the swing couldn't talk. She rang the bell with her chin and waited. A slow flutter of anticipation spread from her chest to her belly. Footsteps echoed behind the door. She tightened her grip on the box.

The door opened. Dark hair, dark eyes, muscles in all the right places. *Wow on legs,* as Cathy had once said.

"Emma. Hello." Asher's smile stalled her heartbeat.

Did he really have to do that to her every time they met? "Hi, Asher." She stood there like a dummy, staring way up into his handsome face.

His smile kicked up on one side, creasing his cheek. "Come in."

She shook off her store-window dummy act and stepped up into his hallway. He took the box from her and set it on the floor. The sun shining through the stained-glass window on the landing laid precise squares of colour over walls stripped of paper and painted sage green, and oak floors restored to their original golden hue. The delicious smell of roasting beef wafted from the kitchen.

"Do you like it?" His gaze skipped around the refurbished spaces.

"Very much." She pulled her attention off the sleek, navy leather couch and massive TV in the front parlour, perfect for cozy nights and movies running without being watched. She went through to the back parlour, where a gleaming Steinway grand piano took pride of place. Funny, she hadn't actually believed the teacher. "You were playing?" Remembering Miss Pentland's words about ruined practice, she said, "I only heard the last bit, but I enjoyed it. It moved me, made me imagine things."

He played a few notes with his right hand, the movement of his fingers sure and quick. "Thank you. That's my goal. My piano is more than a prop for picture frames." He pressed a group of keys at the low end. "I love the music. I never performed well enough for the world stage, but I have to play." He met her gaze, and she swore she peered into his very soul.

A deeply passionate soul.

A chord of longing, hidden deep within her and seldom played, vibrated through her, disturbing slumberous dreams of home and family. Her throat tightened, and tears threatened. Biting on her scarred lip to counter the emotion, she cast about for something, anything, to break the charged silence.

"You're getting more furniture, right?" Stupid, but effective

There went that crooked-grin heart-stall thing. "Yeah, I know the place is kinda bare. I'm taking my time about buying exactly what I want." They went back to the front hall. "But I do have a complete dining set I found at a farm auction in Bracebridge."

"Beautiful." She strode forward and ran her fingers over the smooth curve of the armchair. The black-and-white service glowed darkly on a gold tablecloth laid with white-and-gold napkins. A sixth place setting implied an extended guest list. Is this what he meant by his promise to cook for her? How disappointing.

"The table looks amazing. I would never have thought of this combination, but it works. I love the gold finish you put on the walls." Her gaze met his beautiful dark eyes. "You have very elegant taste."

"Thanks. You helped me get there."

They stood staring at each other, awareness sparking in the

space between them. He leaned towards her, his head bent, his gaze on her mouth. He was going to kiss her. She was going to kiss him back. Sparks started going off like fireworks.

Rhythmic fireworks, like chimes.

He shut his eyes and uttered a soft groan. "The oven timer. I have to take the roast out. I'll be right back."

Emma sagged with disappointment and relief. His family would arrive at any moment and she did not want to be caught in a flagrant lip lock.

When he returned, she tapped the box to redirect the conversation. "Here's the final shipment. The tea service—coffee pot, teapot, creamer, and sugar bowl. It arrived this morning, so I checked it out and brought it over."

"Excellent. Thanks for your message." He unpacked the pieces to the sideboard, stroking the embossed patterns. He had a delicate touch as an ophthalmologist, which she knew from personal experience. What would it feel like if he stroked her bare hip so gently? Hot tingles ran up her spine. She discreetly rolled her shoulders.

"I washed it for you, expecting you'd want it today." Special service for a special customer. She sucked in a breath. *Please tell me I didn't say something so fatuous out loud.* A quick glance at Asher showed him focussed on the last item. The pent-up air sighed out. From force of habit, she checked the place settings for the correct positioning of cutlery and glassware. "Who taught you to set a perfect table?"

"The housekeeper who thought my sister and I should know how to do things for ourselves. She also taught me to make my bed. I'm fully housetrained." He grinned and bowed with his hands at his waist. She laughed along with him and returned his bow with the elegant curtsy learned in long-ago dance classes.

"Would you like to stay for dinner?" He gestured towards the head of the table. "I set a place for you right beside me, hoping you'd say yes. And no, this isn't the dinner I promised you."

Emma stared down the table at the extra setting, surprised at the invitation. Some classy woman from the city should be sitting down with his family, not her. "Why do you want me to stay?"

His crooked smile charmed her. "Would you believe me if I said I wanted you to meet my family?"

Whew, those eyes and that smile were some powerful charm. "Uh... no."

"Would you believe me if I said I wanted protection from my family?"

She cracked a smile. "Nope."

He sighed dramatically. "Okay, fine. Believe me when I say I want your company."

She had no answer for him other than a single jerky nod. His gleaming smile stalled her stupid heart again. She tidied her yellow sweater down over her pleated green skirt, glad she'd dressed up a bit for Asher.

"Do you want to see what else I've done with the Rossetti place? Everyone in town still calls my house that when I give directions for delivery."

Dying of curiosity about this man and his home, she preceded him up the stairs, speaking over her shoulder. "Cathy's family lived here for over thirty years. Don't worry, though. Before you know it, they'll be calling it Doc Stock's, or some other silly thing."

The upstairs walls were also stripped of paper and repainted. "The place seems huge without any carpets or furniture in it."

"Like I said, slowly but surely, I'll fill it." He stopped at the door to the black-and-white bathroom.

Emma had to stand close to see the hideous turquoise tiles were now a delicate grey.

He looked down at her. "What's your opinion about the claw-foot tub? Keep it or junk it?"

"I've always wanted to soak—" She met his eyes. So not the time to even think about bubbles. "Vintage rocks, so definitely keep it. You have enough room in here to install a separate shower." Bubbles running down his back, his chest, over his—

She wandered off down the hall, fanning her face. All the bedrooms except the master stood empty. She hovered at the doorway. As expected, the bed was beautifully made. Not as expected, it was made with gorgeous Irish antique linens, like so many of the tablecloths she saw. "This isn't what I would have predicted from you."

"In what way?" His question came from close behind her.

She turned to face him, easing back a pace. "I thought dark, modern and masculine, not English country house. Your taste constantly surprises me... in a very good way."

"It's family heirlooms from my Grandmother Stockdale's home in Rosedale. I prefer the solid old furniture with some history and heft to it. When she passed away, I brought it up here."

Emma had once wandered through the neighbourhood in Toronto during her brief college life. Asher's two-storey, centre-hall, four-bedroom house was modest in comparison. She lived in the apartment over her china shop. He came from a rich family, was a talented musician, a gifted doctor, handsome beyond compare... and so far out of her league he should be invisible. She was grateful for the lifestyle Gran left her, didn't need to change it.

And yet...

He closed the space between them and raised a hand to stroke her cheek. "You are so lovely."

She placed a hand over his, gazed up at him.

"Hello, Asher!" came a young feminine voice from down below. "Are you home?"

Emma leapt back, grasping the railing for balance.

He tipped his head back and groaned. "My sister has flawless timing." He stroked Emma's arm. "Come down and meet her." He leaned over the stair rail. "We're upstairs, Tenley. Down in a minute."

Emma pushed Asher to lead the way down the steps. To her horror, a whole crowd stood in the hallway, staring at her with assessing eyes.

"Jeez, Ash. If I'd known you had company, I'd have given you a fifteen-minute warning." The young woman flipped her dark hair and gave him a broad laughing wink.

Emma's blushed so hot she feared her freckles would burn off.

"Tenley, that's enough." A perfectly groomed older woman with hazel eyes and hair streaked to perfection slid off her coat. She tucked her purse into her bent elbow in precise imitation of the Queen. "Asher, introduce us."

Two grinning men, one dark-haired and one silver fox, accompanied the women. They shared Asher's dark eyes.

He touched Emma's back and gave her an encouraging smile. "Emma, this is the Stockdale clan. Granddad, Mother, Dad, and Tenley. Everyone, this is Emma Finn."

A chorus of "pleased to meet you" and a round of handshakes followed.

Emma squared her shoulders against his mother's inspection.

A delicate frown briefly creased Mrs. Stockdale's forehead.

His father and grandfather grinned, and Tenley wink secretly; just like Asher. Maybe dinner wouldn't be so bad after all.

"Won't you all come through to the patio? Drinks are ready to serve." Asher herded everyone through the house. He kept Emma at his side, her hand firmly in his big warm grip. She tugged him to a stop in the kitchen.

"Why is it you want me here again?"

He lowered his head to murmur in her ear. "Because I want you."

"Would you pass the horseradish, dear?" Mrs. Stockdale asked from the foot of the table a while later.

Emma checked for the wandering condiment. She groaned inwardly when she found it to the left of her plate. *Oops, forgot about it. My bad.*

"Sorry, Mrs. Stockdale." She passed it to the elder Mr. Stockdale on her right. He passed it to Mrs. Stockdale. Who passed it to her husband, who passed it on until it rounded the table and came back, untouched, to Emma. "No one else wanted any?"

"Of course not, dear. Only Asher takes it. Nonetheless, it needed to be passed."

Was this Wonderland? Emma resisted the urge to roll her eyes. "Would anyone care for mustard?"

"No, thank you, dear." Mrs. Stockdale picked up her knife and fork, allowing the others to begin eating. "Speaking of Dijon, have you ever been to the region?" She raised a portion of roast beef to her mouth.

Emma blinked and swallowed hastily. There was a real mustard place? "No."

"When we visited, we walked for hours in the medieval section of the town. You could almost hear the minstrels. The cathedral has the most charming crypt bearing the relics of Saint Bénigne. The Palace of the Dukes of Burgundy has a vast public square reminding one of the Piazza in Rome. Do you know what I mean?"

"I haven't been to Rome."

"London?"

"No."

"Surely, you've been to New York."

She turned to Asher. *Make her stop,* she begged him with her eyes.

"Sorry," he murmured then raised his voice. "Mother. Not everyone is able to travel."

Not helpful, she telegraphed with a squint.

"You must travel to broaden your mind, my dear."

Oh, joy. She was poor, ignorant, and ill-mannered to boot.

Across the table, Tenley huffed a laugh. "I only broadened my hips with all the luscious French pastry." She rolled her eyes heavenward and licked her lips.

Emma smiled at Tenley, grateful for the break in tension.

"Tenley, don't interrupt," Mrs. Stockdale scolded without taking her eyes off Emma.

Tenley rolled her eyes again with a very different meaning.

"Mother," Asher spoke a little louder than necessary. "Emma's been looking after her grandmother for some time now."

"She should hire a caregiver. They were invaluable when caring for Mother Stockdale. Isn't there a senior's residence in town? That's how you take care of your family. By hiring experts."

At her side, the elder Mr. Stockdale grumbled under his breath. "I only needed someone to cook for me."

"Mother, not everyone can afford private caregivers and nursing homes."

Emma stared at her congealed plate of once-delicious roast beef, horseradish on the side. She wasn't ashamed of her solidly middle-class family. She could have brought Gran to the hospice much sooner. Gran simply didn't want to go until she absolutely had to, and Emma had been happy to care for her.

She raised her chin. "Well, Gran passed away a month ago, while in care, so it doesn't matter anymore."

A stricken silence enveloped the room until the elder Mr. Stockdale patted her hand. "I'm so sorry for your loss." The others echoed his condolences.

Emma fiddled with her napkin, uncomfortable with sentiment from these almost strangers.

"Asher mentioned you own a china shop," the senior continued with a kind smile.

He'd talked to his family about her? Should she be flattered or frightened? She gave Asher another narrow-eyed glance and replied to his handsome grandfather. "Yes, I do."

"And she did an incredible job getting all this service from all over Canada and the States," Asher added.

"You sold my son used china?" Mrs. Stockdale stared down at her plate and dropped her cutlery as if it swarmed with cooties.

Emma's fingers tightened on her fork, sorely tempted to give the old witch a pointy poke. Asher's quick stroke of her hand and his surreptitious wink stilled the notion.

Asher calmly drew her fire again. "Mother, it's all brand new. Came in the factory wrapping or whatever you call it. I chose a discontinued pattern and Emma expertly pulled it all together for me."

"Well, it's gorgeous and it suits Asher perfectly," Tenley rushed in where angels must fear to breathe, never mind tread. "Granddad, what's your latest escapade?"

Emma could have had a lovely time sharing a meal with Asher's family. They were interesting and amusing people, except for the sourpuss at the foot of the table. Her patience worn to a nub, Emma fled to the washroom.

A moment before re-entering the room, the old battle-axe swung one final time. "Asher, I must warn you. The young woman you're so taken with—she'll never do. Wholly inadequate, unsuitable. Too young, barely thirty to your thirty-eight. A small-town girl with a small-town mind. Did she even attend college? You must not get involved."

An hour or so later, Asher dragged in a huge breath to restrain himself. He loved his mom and all that, but she could try the patience of a saint. At long last, he managed to herd his family as far as the driveway. His mother continued to lecture Emma, on the proper management of a household. The flow of words leached out all thought except "leave her alone".

Tenley muttered irreverently in Emma's ear, teasing shocked smiles out of Emma. He'd thank his sister later.

Emma inched her way towards her car. Asher reached out and caught her hand to reel her in. Even though she seemed to get along with everyone but his mother, this had been a mistake. What had he been smoking? He needed to apologize and make it up to her, to set a date for their private dinner.

The screen door on the house across the street slapped shut. "Emma, how are you?" Melody Gossip, er, Grisham, called. Her position as the Hatch, Match, and Dispatch columnist of the *Clarence Bay Beacon* covered for her real job of gossip maven.

Emma waved back. "Hey, Mellie, what are you doing in this neck of the woods?"

Melody crossed the road and smiled at everyone in the group. Her gaze caught on Emma's and Asher's joined hands.

Emma's hand went limp. He refused to take the hint to let go.

"I had an appointment with Meg to take a photo of her new baby for the *Beacon's* Facebook page." Melody lifted her camera as evidence. "Wanna see?"

The women jumped to the universal bait.

This time when Emma tugged, he released her with an intimate stroke of her palm. Her quick intake of breath hooked his hopes for a yes as soon as he could get her alone again.

While the younger women cooed over the photos and his mother lectured about leaving a child to cry to develop self-sufficiency, the three men drew together.

"So, Asher, your friend is nice," Granddad said.

"Yeah, real cute," Dad added.

"Yes, to both of you. Now, anything else you want to know?"

Dad sucked air between his teeth. "I like her. Not so sure about your mother."

Asher huffed his agreement. "Judging by her performance during dinner, I'd say she's undecided." He couldn't help his sarcasm.

His father frowned. "Your mother is trying to protect you. She only wants you to make the right choice."

"Yeah, look where her *right choice* landed me the last time. Smack in divorce court with a side trip to custody hell." He caught the bitterness and regret that occasionally rose up and swallowed it down. "I'll take my chances without her help."

Granddad scowled in his standard response of anger whenever Sondra's name came up.

Dad ignored Granddad. "Despite all the grief with Sondra, you want to give marriage another try with this new girl?"

Asher stuffed his hands in his pockets and rocked back and forth on his feet. "I wouldn't go so far just yet. We're not even dating. I had to sort out the mess of my life first."

Dad slapped him on the back. "Emma's a natural beauty and I wish you the best of luck, son."

"Good things come to those who wait," Granddad said.

"I hope so."

His mother came over, followed by the other women. "Asher, Melody wants to take our photograph for her newspaper's society page."

His excited mother arranged her family to her satisfaction. She then looked doubtfully at Emma. Asher stepped out of line to get her.

Emma waved him back in place and strolled to Melody's side. "No worries, Mrs. Stockdale. This is all about Asher's family visiting him. I'll stand here and watch."

Melody morphed into a professional photographer, adjusting people, telling jokes to coordinate smiles, constantly clicking the shutter.

The Stockdale family were each similar to the others in a way well beyond biology. They held themselves with the confident ease that the world obeyed their commands. They wore expensive clothes; Tenley's shoes had red soles. Between them, they had likely visited every country on the planet, some places twice. They all had higher educations. All three men were doctors. The women had been to university.

Even though Emma had finished high school with honours, her incomplete arts diploma wasn't worth a damn. The china shop earned enough to give Emma a comfortable salary, but it was a drop in a bucket compared to these people.

These people.

Mrs. Stockdale was dead-on right.

Emma was inadequate. She would never belong with these people. She had no problem dealing with them as customers. Any closer? She shuddered. She didn't need the grief.

When Melody clicked her last, Asher's family said goodbye, piled into the high-end SUV and disappeared with an eerie electric purr. Emma sighed with relief, not sorry to see them go. She turned to Asher, hand out for a shake. The movement felt so weird, she clasped her hands and settled for a grateful expression. "Thanks for the dinner, Asher. It was lovely to meet your family. Your place is gorgeous. Empty, but gorgeous."

He gestured towards his house, asking her back inside.

Emma answered his unspoken question. "I'll be on my way. Thanks again. Enjoy your china."

He hesitated, disappointment stamped on his features. "Are you sure?"

"I'm sorry. I'd love to stay, but a ton of paperwork is waiting for me." She moved down the street towards Melody's car and her friend followed. Emma turned one last time to wave to Asher.

She continued to Melody's red mini-SUV, parked several spaces in front of Emma's car.

"Well, what the bebop was *that* all about?" Melody demanded with her arms akimbo. Her black hair, done up in a messy-chic style, danced with her indignation. "That was harsh, the way you blew him off. You never have paperwork piled up. Didn't you want to go in with him?"

Emma picked up a clump of maple keys fallen from the tree overhead to Melody's windshield.

Melody rolled her eyes as she leaned her backside on the door of her car. "Do not play coy with me. I saw you two holding hands and smiling, all cozy and everything."

"Tenley's joking made us smile." Emma split the keys and laid them in a row on the bright red paint.

"A shared sense of humour is important in a relationship."

"I don't have a relationship with Asher other than me being his supplier of fine china." She tore the green keys into their halves and piled them up.

"You're not supplying kisses and other tender morsels of affection?"

"No, I am not," Emma protested a little too loudly—even to her own ears. "And don't you dare tweet about it."

"I only tweet what I know to be true. You had dinner with Asher's family and you held hands in plain sight of them all. Those are the facts are they not?"

Emma grimaced as she arranged the keys in flower patterns. "Facts can be deceiving. I just happened to deliver some china when his family arrived."

"Facts and statistics can tell many interesting stories. Did Asher just happen to invite you to dinner?"

"Yes. Tasty food and compatible company. What more do you want?" Emma refused to mention bubbles, or kisses, or anything about a passionate soul who played his piano so divinely.

Melody stroked Emma's arm. "I want you to start living again after all the time you spent looking after your gran."

"I *am* living." She spread her hands to display her recent effort. "See my pretty art?"

"But are you happy?"

Emma swept the debris from the hood of Melody's car. "I'm content with the way things are. Asher and I are from different worlds. We would only work out in a romance novel titled *The Gajillionaire's Sad Little Shopkeeper*."

Melody frowned at the pathetic joke. "You deserve to be happy, with a home and a family. Asher can give you those if you give him half a chance. I saw it in his eyes whenever he smiled at you. I probably have a picture to prove it."

"No. Every time I get happy, I get slammed. I'll settle for contented solitude." She'd lost her parents and grandparents, her lover, and her dreams. All she had left was her brother and his family. Those people, especially Asher, could not keep her safe. If she stayed alone and unchanged, she was safe.

CHAPTER 2

Pirate on Board

"Hey, George. Are you headed in for lunch?" Asher held open the door to The Pits for the friendly older man.

"Sure thing, Doc. Want some company?" asked George Gossip Grisham who owned the paint and paper store further down the block on James Street.

Asher replied with a nod.

The two men bellied up to the battle-scarred bar, the only empty seats left in the place. Asher's stool wobbled. He found the balance point and scanned the room through the mirror behind an assortment of liquor bottles.

George swiveled around, propped his elbows on the bar, and perused each packed table. He blew a kiss to his wife and continued his sweep of the room.

A person entered from the street.

Emma.

A one-two punch of pleasure and heat rocked his world His seat wobbled. He hopped to the floor before he fell off.

George elbowed him and chuckled. "Nice save, cowboy." A tattooed bruiser of a guy sauntered up to them behind the bar. "Hey, Rocco."

"What'll you have?"

"The usual for me. And a lasso for my buddy here." George chortled at his own joke.

Asher steadied his stool. "Did you know this seat wobbles?"

"Yep. Most everybody does and avoids the seat if they can." Rocco planted his hands on his hips.

"Any plans to fix it?"

"Can't. No parts and no money that Old Man Moureau wants to part with. You ride careful, eh?"

Barstools had parts? Whatever.

Rocco jerked his chin up to prod Asher into stating his choice.

Asher gave the menu a quick read. "Medium steak, side of onion rings and a Brio, please." He had patients scheduled this afternoon at his office on McMurray Street, so no alcohol for lunch.

"Comin' up." Rocco removed a used glass and wiped the bar. He bellowed their order through to the kitchen on his way to deal with patrons at the cash register.

George faced the room again, talking and watching at the same time. "How did the paint finish work out in your dining room?"

Asher turned sideways to do some Emma, er, people watching of his own. "It looks great."

"Shoulda done. The top-quality stuff goes on real smooth with great color density, excellent longevity—"

Rocco served their drinks, interrupting George's post-sale pitch. Good to know a businessman who believed in the products he sold.

"Emma liked it yesterday?"

Asher hesitated over his reply to George then wondered why he bothered trying to hide anything from anyone in this town. "She did. Said it went with all the other stuff." He changed the topic to the latest baseball game.

Emma laughed over something with her friends, appearing totally involved with them. But she kept peeking at him as he stole peeks at her.

Both men turned around when Rocco delivered their meals. Asher crunched into an onion ring and swore he'd gone to heaven.

"So now you got your house all fixed up, you need to fill it with some family. Maybe a dog, too." George paused only to take another mouthful.

A dog. Not a bad idea. He'd had one and loved her with all the passion a kid could muster. Dog, kids, family, home. He wanted those things. Without thought, Asher's gaze went to Emma. Her head tipped back, going for the last sip of beer. His pulse rate went into high gear at the image of her arched in climax beneath him. Making an adorable child looking exactly like her mommy.

They continued to gossip while they ate. At the end of the meal, George nudged Asher's arm. "Emma sure is a pretty girl, eh?"

Asher jerked, and the stool seesawed wildly. He balanced himself and went for a sip of cold Brio.

George guffawed and slapped him on the back.

Asher went for another wild ride. Who'd have thought a guy needed a seatbelt to sit in a restaurant?

"I knew it, boy. When Melody said she saw Emma at your place with your whole family, I knew something was going on. So how many times have you gone out?"

Asher said nothing, only smiled. Zero was way too pathetic to admit, though he still planned to follow through on his promise of dinner.

"C'mon, go and get your girl. Handsome fella like you, she's bound to say yes." George gave him a less-than-subtle push to set Asher's feet on the floor. "You're up now, so off you go."

Groaning at his public display of the situation, Asher stuffed his hands in his pockets and headed towards the table. Only she wasn't there. A frantic search of the room found her leaving the cash desk. Asher strode over to intercept her.

"Emma," he touched her shoulder. She jumped and turned around, Melody and Cathy flanking her like bodyguards.

His mind blanked on contact with her pretty brown eyes. *Mine.* His heart claimed her. *All mine.* "I wanted to thank you again for your shopping efforts on my behalf."

Melody nudged Emma's shoulder.

Emma blinked away her wide-eyed breathless expression. "All part of the service from Finn's."

Melody *tsked* under her breath.

"I also wanted to thank you for sharing the meal with my family and me." He groaned at his stupidity.

"You're welcome. Thank you for inviting me. I like your grandfather."

Her friends hummed approvingly.

"And I also wanted—could we step outside?"

She tilted her head in question, glanced at her friends then pushed through the glass doors.

"Alone if you don't mind," Asher said pointedly to her posse. They exchange glances, shrugged, and followed him anyway. Damn posse.

Fortunately, Emma had walked a few paces and stopped in

front of a boarded-up shop. He flashed a stink eye at Cathy and Melody. This time they stayed put and let him go alone to Emma.

His breath caught at the vision of Emma with the sun picking gold highlights from her chestnut waves. Her eyes held a wary expression. He'd never seen a person whose eyes matched her hair color. With her delicate colouring, she belonged in an Old Master's portrait.

"Hi, Emma."

A small smile pulled her upper lip crooked against her scar. "Hi, Asher."

"Would you care to go out sometime for dinner and a movie? Or whatever else we can find to do."

Her lips flattened, tempting him to soften them with a kiss. Her gaze bounced down the street to her friends and back again She shook her head, gripped the strap of her purse. "No, I don't think so. But thanks for asking."

Well, damn. "Why?" His kiss was welcomed yesterday in the upstairs hall. Now it seemed like she couldn't care less.

She dipped her head to stare at the sidewalk. "I don't think we'd suit each other very well."

"We barely know each other and I want to fix that."

"Don't bother. I'm not looking for a relationship right now. Or ever." She glanced into his eyes, her own shuttered against him. "But thanks, again, for asking."

Asher trudged along the groomed Lookout Point trail on the east side of Killbear Provincial Park, north along the highway from Clarence Bay. In the distance, he heard chain saws, grooming the park for its annual influx of campers starting next week on the

Victoria Day weekend. The sun, veiled in wispy cloud, warmed his head and shoulders wherever the forest canopy parted. Dark earth and green spring scents soothed him. Clumps of old snow lingered in the deep shadows. He was walking to clear his head, to think things through. The rocks and trees didn't say much but they were excellent listeners.

He puzzled over where his tenuous relationship with Emma had gone wrong. They all seemed to be getting along over dinner last Saturday. Well, maybe not with his mother. Emma seemed a little nervous, but okay. She'd withdrawn from him on the front lawn during the family photo. But what exactly happened?

Rustling in the undergrowth ahead caught his attention. He stopped.

"Hello?" he called.

A brown chicken-like bird burst from the thicket behind and beat loud wings in retreat, startling the crap out of him.

He drew a deep breath to settle his nerves.

More disturbance in the bushes.

"Is anybody there?"

He bent over and peered among the thin green shoots of plants emerging from hibernation. A pair of brown eyes in a black-and-white muzzle peered back at him.

"Well, hello there. Who are you?" Asher spoke in soothing tones.

The dog whined a question.

"Yes, I like dogs. Had one as a kid, so I know what to do with you."

The creature crawled forward, tail tucked well between its hind legs.

Asher held out his hand, palm downwards. "Come on, you can

do it. Atta boy, or girl."

The beast crawled out on the road. Matted black fur covered most of it. Grubby white fur splotched one eye, the opposite ear, the tip of its tail, and his right foreleg. Asher squatted in the road and allowed the dog to sniff his hand. "How long have you been on your own, little fella? Must be months, eh?"

The dog whined as if to agree and rose to a stand. The top of his head came to Asher's knees. His tail gave a single low wag His ears rolled forward and pricked up.

Still moving slowly, Asher cupped his hand over the dog's head and gave a gentle rub. After the critter accepted his touch, Asher ran his hand down its back, over ribs lying far too close to the skin. Burrs bunched in the feathers of his rear legs. "Don't tell me you been out here all winter? Poor little dude."

"Would you like to come home with me? Or maybe the vet's first? See if you need more than some TLC?"

The dog's tail unfurled and started a cautious wag. The dog smiled, and Asher smiled back. "I thought you might want to."

The dog's ears swivelled forwards and his nose twitched, sensing something Asher couldn't.

Sounds came from behind Asher, odd growly sorts of sounds. The hair on the back of his neck prickled upright.

Asher rose and turned, then froze.

Two bear cubs tussled about in the middle of the road, vocalizing during their play like a pair of large puppies.

Asher chuckled at their antics.

The dog at his side growled deep in its throat.

Asher found it facing the other way, hackles raised in clear attack mode. Sweat broke out on Asher's back. Every nerve and muscle tightened on high alert. He really, really did not want his suspicions confirmed. He turned.

Another bear lumbered their way.

Not a cub.

A humungous bear with long claws and sharp teeth.

Asher and the dog stood between a mama bear and her babies.

Mama bear roared and galumphed straight at them.

Every bit of backwoods lore he'd ever heard screamed through Asher's mind.

Stand still.

Run like hell.

Play dead.

Flap your arms to appear bigger.

Asher froze, braced for the pain of claws ripping through his flesh. *I never kissed Emma.*

The little dog streaked forward to circle the bear, barking and snarling, just outside the range of long sharp claws.

Rocks. Asher needed rocks. He scrabbled about in the road and hurled every missile in reach. "Get lost!"

A rock smacked it between the eyes.

The bear rose on her hind legs.

"Beat it!"

Direct hit to the chest.

"Scram!"

Bull's-eye to the forepaw.

The dog dashed in and out and around, an intrepid black-and-white blur.

A rock sailed clear over the bear's head and thunked to the path.

He threw rocks, sticks, clods of dirt until his arm burned.

He swore and shouted until his throat ached.

Bawling, the cubs blew past. At the sound of her babies, the mama bear stilled and dropped to all four paws.

The dog backed up, teeth bare, tail stiff.

Standoff.

Mama bear plopped on her haunches and the cubs ran to her. She nuzzled them as if checking for bumps and bruises. Apparently satisfied, she rose and turned her back on the dog.

Asher slumped, hands on knees, in overwhelming relief, his eyes still glued to the bears.

Quicker than could be believed, mama bear turned and swiped at the little animal. The dog screamed and sailed into a thicket of dried bracken.

"No!"

The three bears sauntered away without a backwards glance.

Asher waited agonizing minutes until they were gone, then sprinted to where the little dog had disappeared. A frantic search revealed it cradled on a clump of pine needles. Calling his doctoring skills back to order, Asher slid his hands over the black-and-white body. No broken bones. Blood matted the fur around a jagged cut on the left side running from the ear, over the eye and along the muzzle. Bone gleamed in the open wound. Gently, Asher lifted the furry eyelid. The cornea was scratched, but the eye was whole.

Asher removed his jacket and spread it on the ground beside the dog. With tender care, he laid the little hero on the improvised stretcher, carried him out of the woods, down to the parking lot, and off to the vet's office.

Tense hours later with the dog in peaceful recovery, Asher drove home and flopped on his couch. The children's song *Teddy Bears' Picnic* bounced in his head. He was never going into the woods ever again.

Some days later, Asher played an easy piece from his early years at the Conservatory. After the scene in the forest, he wanted something soothing, without a hint of challenge for either his mind or emotions. He rolled his shoulder, still sore from chucking all those rocks.

Everybody in town had stopped to chat with him about his adventures. Everybody had a piece of advice for the next time; stand still, climb a tree, play dead, wave and shout, wear bear bells, carry an air horn.

Everybody except Emma.

His foot slipped off the pedal. His left hand tripped over his right. Discordant notes crashed among the strings and faded.

Silently he apologized to Miss Pentland. He practiced on a regular schedule in a tacit agreement with the pianist. One day, he would invite her in and ask for her opinion. For now, she honoured him and challenged him with her presence.

He sat in silence until his front door bell rang.

The piano teacher?

No, the vet. Beside Dr. Greg Andrews, the little dog sat quietly on leash. His one visible black eye gleamed with health. He wore a clean lightweight bandage over the other.

"Hey, Greg, come on in. Care for a beer?"

Asher escorted the pair through the kitchen to the sunny backyard, stopping for a couple of beers on the way. The men settled into Muskoka chairs. The dog sat on the flagstones between them, head cocked, his eye alert to further developments.

Asher bent forward and patted the rough coat, careful not to spook the critter into taking off down his unfenced yard and over the stream.

"He's looking well," Asher said. "What about the bear and her cubs?"

"No sign of them. The Parks Department people judge they've moved on to less dangerous ground."

Asher scratched under the small dog's chin, inducing a blissful expression on the black-and-white face. "And this little guy? Have the owners come forward to claim him?"

"We notified the Humane Society and the police, but nothing yet. No identifying microchips or tattoos." Greg gave Asher a sly, knowing grin. "I thought, seeing as he saved your life and all, you might want to consider adopting him." Greg scratched his cheek. "For what it's worth, Emma likes dogs."

The dog had followed the conversation back and forth between the two men as if he knew they were discussing his fate. Now he focused his attention on Asher. He whined, adding his plea to Greg's. Asher's little boy should have had a dog, but his ex-wife Sondra hated them. Emma's liking of dogs only made Asher like her more.

Asher smiled down at the hopeful face. "So, my little hero, would you like to come and live with me?"

The dog placed his spotted paw on Asher's knee.

"I brought along a couple cans of food for him. He hasn't been neutered yet, so I'll do it for free in exchange for you adopting him."

Asher narrowed his eyes at his friend. "This is a setup."

Greg laughed and held out the leash.

Asher glanced down at the dog. The little critter stood and put both paws on Asher's knees and smiled. Asher ruffled his good ear and took the leash. "Welcome to your new home, buddy. Your job, should you choose to accept it, will be to help me get you a mistress."

On Victoria Day weekend, Emma squeezed herself into the hot, crowded premises of the Gray Jay Bookstore. Her friend Nadine signed copies of *Mystery of Depot Harbour*, her recently released historical mystery set in the Clarence Bay area. Summer people jammed the place to the rafters in their pursuit of reading material. She wriggled her way through the noisy lineup, slipped behind the cloth-covered table, and touched Nadine's shoulder to let her know reinforcements had arrived.

Her friend tipped her head in acknowledgement, smiling at a leather-skinned, diamond-studded woman. "Thank you for stopping in, Alicia."

Alicia stroked the signature on the open page of the hardcover book. "I'm looking forward to reading about the Depot Harbour explosion."

Nadine wagged a playful finger. "Remember, it's a fictional account. No villain set explosives. A gust of wind blew flaming debris from V-J Day fireworks into the cordite storage elevator."

Alicia waved a dismissive hand. "My husband and I love the way you mix real events in your stories. He even researches the facts and tells me—" she grimaced archly, "well, bores me, with it all. I prefer your version." She hugged the treasured volume to her chest and stepped out of line.

Emma winked at Nadine. "You gotta love readers like her."

"You know it." They shared a chuckle.

"Can I get you something? Coffee, tea? A new right hand?"

Emma asked her friend.

Nadine flexed her fingers and rotated her wrist. "An ice pack would come in handy." She groaned and shook her head. "Terrible pun. I'd love a black chai tea and a cheddar biscuit, please." She reached under the table for her purse.

Emma stopped her. "My treat. And save a copy for me."

"Will do," Nadine said then smiled up at her next fan.

Emma moved into the crowd that magically parted for her. Ha, the power of connection to the famous. She chatted with a few people on the way and gave a couple of boaters directions to the ghost town.

As she pushed on the doorplate, Asher stepped up and pulled the handle from the other side. She stumbled out and slammed into an impromptu hug.

His deep grunt of surprise filled her ears. His wonderful scent filled her head. Heat filled her blood. Her damn stupid knees wobbled, for crying out loud.

She shoved to her own two feet. "Sorry," she mumbled at his button. She liked this particular shade of pink. Or was it the man under the shirt?

"My pleasure. Anytime." His grin filled his voice.

A nasty clearing of a throat came from behind Emma She jumped and scuttled past Asher to the sidewalk. The throat-clearer grumbled about getting a room and brushed by them. Emma kept moving until something struck her across her thighs and barked.

Barked?

A red leash stretched from Asher's hand down to the red collar on a black-and-white dog.

"Well, hello again you poor thing." She bent and cupped the

dog's head. She ran a tender thumb over a fresh scar along the length of his muzzle. "I heard all about how you saved this big guy here."

"You know this dog before? Where?" Asher asked.

"Yes, we've met before, haven't we?" She continued to talk to his pet. "I tried to get you to come home with me. But no, you didn't want *me*. You wanted somebody you had to rescue before you adopted him. Make him feel properly obliged, eh?"

The dog understood every word and agreed with them all. He hung his head. He apologized for choosing Asher instead of herself.

"So what's your name, fella?"

"We've decided on Pirate."

Giving the animal a final pat, she stood and grinned up at Asher. "We?"

An adorable blush spread across his handsome face. Oh, the cuteness of the man.

"Well, a guy has to like his name you know. We discussed Spot, but it was so obvious it hurt. And he's too modest for Hero."

"So he said *ar* to Pirate?"

He shook his head at her, mock resignation twinkling in his eyes. "You couldn't resist, could you?"

A giggle squeaked out of her as she shook her head back at him. "Nope. Not sorry either."

A grin crimped the corners of his eyes. "Truthfully, he said *arf.*"

She laughed outright for the first time in months. The day suddenly seemed brighter.

"I'm so glad Pirate's found a forever home. Points for you."

Asher gave the dog a puzzling thumbs-up. "Would you like to

go for brunch?"

Her joy fled. "I'm sorry." She gestured through the window at the crowd inside. "I'm getting tea for my friend Nadine. She's signing her new book today and can't get away from the table. She's parched with all the talking."

The twinkle in his eyes dimmed, and his smile faded.

She gently nudged Pirate out of her way.

Asher fell into step with her. "I'll go with you."

"You want to buy tea?"

As they waited for the traffic light to turn green, he took her hand. "Nope. I want your company."

Her fingers clasped his big warm hand against her will. "Why?"

"Because I like you. And so does Pirate." He dipped his head. "Don't you?" Pirate barked his agreement. "Good man."

Her gaze drifted down to Pirate who tipped his head in query. Life with this duo would be so much fun. "No fair bringing your dog into it."

"All's fair—" he said as they crossed the road, still holding hands, and continued down the sidewalk to the coffee shop.

In love and war, Emma finished. "There's nothing between us." No heat, no longing, no love.

"Not yet." He smiled confidently.

She muffled her tiny gasp at how his words meshed with her thoughts. "Not ever."

"Why? We'd be so good together. I can tell." He raised her hand and flattened her palm to his chest. His heartbeat hitched with his breath.

She slid her hand from under Asher's insistent pressure. She reached down, patted the dog's head, and sighed. "I can't see any-

thing working between us. We come from two different worlds."
Angry, she straightened and yanked on the café's door handle.

Asher and Pirate had to jump back or get smacked.

"Don't follow me." She pointed at Pirate. "He's not allowed inside."

CHAPTER 3

A Rescue

"Thank you, Mr. Corbeau. You may sit back now," Asher instructed the older man.

Mr. Corbeau rubbed his eyes and sat back in the examination chair. "So, what's the verdict?"

"Let's go talk with your wife." Asher moved the slit lamp aside and turned on the exam room's overhead light. He rose from his wheeled stool, picked up the patient file, and showed Mr. Corbeau to the consulting office where tweed-suited Professor Corbeau sat reading.

The professor stuck in a bookmark and closed the book. "Sorry," she said, patting the gold-embossed volume. "A fascinating new biography of Boadicea."

Mr. Corbeau grinned proudly at his wife's reading choice.

Asher nodded to his patient. "As you suspected, Mr. Corbeau, you have cataracts. Of the posterior subcapsular type."

"I told you so," Professor Corbeau tapped her husband's wrist.

"No need at all to get flustered. Dr. Stockdale will perform a routine surgery and you'll be back behind the wheel of your school bus. Right, Doctor?"

"Correct. The surgery is routine with a high success rate though, like all surgery, not without its risks. I'll monitor for complications during office visits after the procedure. You'll have eye drops to prevent infection and inflammation, and you'll have to avoid lifting heavy objects and bending forwards. Because these cataracts can develop rather quickly, I'll have to order you to stay off the road, regardless of the vehicle. Even a bicycle could be dangerous."

Mr. Corbeau slapped his palms on the arms of his chair. "You can't take my license away."

Asher gestured for him to calm down. "I'm not reporting it to the Ministry of Transportation. It's temporary until your eyes have healed and your vision has stabilized. However," Asher put his elbows on his desk and hardened his voice, "if I see you driving any vehicle of any kind, I'll have a word with the police."

Mr. Corbeau bristled.

"He won't drive until you give him permission, Dr. Stockdale. I'll see to it." The professor laid a restraining hand on his arm.

"Now, hold on—" Mr. Corbeau began to rise.

His wife pressed his shoulder and gave him a saucy wink. "Think of all the time we'll have together."

He paused, turned fully to his wife.

"So much time, together, at home, just the two of us." She touched his jean-clad thigh.

He grinned at her and placed his hand over hers.

The back of Asher's neck heated. He gazed out his window, giving them privacy. More thin high clouds had moved into the sky.

"Emma will be out this afternoon," Professor Corbeau said.

The name pulled Asher's puzzled gaze back to the loving couple. "Emma Finn?"

"Yes. A storm is coming."

Asher turned back to the window. The feathery clouds didn't look all that ominous. "How can you tell?"

"My husband can sense a storm coming long before it gets here," the professor said.

Poor Pirate would likely spend some quality time under the bed with an old T-shirt he'd claimed as his Linus blanket. "A handy talent. But what's it got to do with Emma Finn?"

"Have *you* seen her storm pictures?" asked Mr. Corbeau.

"Pardon?"

The couple leaned forward. "Emma takes the most incredible pictures of storms—" said the professor.

"At least so we've heard—" added her husband.

"She's very reticent about her pictures—"

"Lots of people have seen her out with a camera—"

"Few of us have actually seen the photos—"

"We thought, as you were close—" his voice drifted into silence.

The couple stared at Asher with matching expressions of open, hopeful expectation.

Should he know that about Emma? No. Their relationship, if you went so far, was still too tenuous for him to even begin to wonder what she did outside her china shop.

They shared a frustrated glance and stared back at Asher.

"She had a real promising photography career at one point. She had a lot of pictures published in the *Beacon*."

"Too bad she gave up school to come back and look after Myra," the professor carried on. "You must ask her to show you her work."

Mr. Corbeau looked to his wife. "Do you think she still has it in her?" Then, for some reason, he turned to Asher.

The professor shrugged. "I hope so. It would be a shame to ignore the huge talent, little though we've seen of it." She turned to Asher as well.

Asher glanced from one to the other, trying to figure them out. When the preposterous idea hit, he pushed back in his chair. "You two want to pique my curiosity so I'll go snooping and then do a tell-all."

They nodded in unison, a fine pair of bobble-heads. And a very curious town.

"No."

Anticipation slid from both their faces, leaving disappointment behind.

Asher barely managed to stifle his laughter. "We'll do one eye at a time, Mr. Corbeau. Pia will call you with the appointment date for your first surgery. You should be ready to go back to school when the kids do."

He escorted the couple to the waiting area and waved them off. As he handed the patient file to his receptionist, he viewed his empty waiting room. Pia, a pretty young Italian, hired fresh out of college, slid the folder into the cabinet. "No more patients, Pia?"

"No, Doctor Stockdale." She stood to put on her coat. "The Corbeaus are a funny pair, aren't they?"

"How so?" Asher untangled Pia's coat sleeve from the belt and set the coat on her shoulders.

"Thanks. Well, a mediaeval women's history professor who loves tweed suits and a bus driver who prefers plaid flannel shirts and jeans? Think of it. Most of us expected their marriage to be over almost before it began. *She* pursued *him*. That was thirty-some years ago and they're the happiest couple in Clarence Bay. *Dio mio,* their conversation is like a tennis match, back and forth and back and forth. Makes me dizzy just listening."

His mouth kicked up at one corner. "I noticed."

"Goes to prove similar backgrounds aren't a guarantee."

He grimaced. He and Sondra had had similar backgrounds—their mothers were best friends—and look at the unholy mess they had made of everything.

Pia slung her purse over her shoulder. At the door, she paused, looking up at the sky. "Guess Emma will be shooting this after-noon."

"Can all the locals sense storms like Mr. Corbeau?"

Pia laughed. "No. He truly does have a sense for the weather. The rest of us use The Weather Network." Out she sauntered, flipping the Open sign to Closed as she went.

Asher headed back to his office where he wasted time trying to settle to routine chores. Sighing loudly, he tossed his pen on his desk to focus on his roiling thoughts. The chain reaction started with remembering his mother's words and ended with Asher smacking his forehead.

"Why didn't I get it? Emma thinks I think she's not good enough for me." He snorted in derision. "As if."

A professor had pursued a bus driver and won.

Asher had pursued, and achieved, a music degree and then a medical degree. Neither of those achievements had been simple or easy. They required persistence and determination. He wanted

Emma, her goodness, her openness and sincerity, her sexiness. He would not give up. He shut down his computer, locked up his files, and hurried to his car.

Once he made the decision, the urge to see Emma grew to blood-pounding proportions. To calm himself down, Asher stopped at home to change into jeans. As he reached for his rain gear, Pirate charged down the stairs with his security t-shirt clamped between his teeth. He pranced around Asher's ankles, asking to go with him.

"You do realize a storm is coming, don't you?"

Pirate cocked his head and glanced from Asher to the door. He laid the t-shirt on the floor, bowed low and wagged his tail.

"All right then. You can be my wing man."

Pirate gave his lets-go whine, picked up his t-shirt, and trotted to the car.

The high pale clouds from earlier had thickened and darkened. The scent of rain weighted the air. A brisk breeze tangled his hair and tugged at his clothes. The two guys headed over to Emma's shop. This time, Asher would see her. Even if it meant following her into the storm.

Asher pushed through the door and Julia Westover, the First Nations singer from the Cedars, looked up from her dusting. "Good afternoon, Dr. Stockdale."

"I'm looking for Emma."

"She's not in. Can I help? She didn't say anything about a package for you."

Despite her assurances, Asher peered through the doorway behind her. He caught a view of the edge of a huge picture frame. Irresistibly drawn, he moved to see the whole. A tree stood on a rocky promontory against a roiling mass of oily black cloud. From the dark mass, lightning reached for the tree with forked fingers.

Asher flinched, expecting a boom of thunder to rattle the windows. A strangled laugh of relief burst from him.

"Fabulous, isn't it?"

"You could say that again."

Julia made as if to speak, grinned at him, and shut her mouth. "Don't worry. I reacted the same way. Emma has a wonderful gift," she said.

He swung his gaze back to the photograph. Incredible. Awe-inspiring.

"You wanted Emma?"

A grin pulled at his mouth; he tucked it away. "Yes. Do you know where she is?"

"Killbear Park. Looking for more pictures like this one.'

Emma was at the park—the scene of the bear incident—by herself. The huge park. Finding her would be impossible. Fear zipped along his nerves.

"She always leaves a note if you want her exact location.' Julia pulled a sticky note off the hidden side of the cash register. "Day use area is where you'll find her."

"Did she go alone?"

Julia shrugged a shoulder. "Yeah. Probably. I never heard of her taking anyone."

He thanked her and rushed out to his car. Pirate whined his deep desire to go back to the house and under the bed. Asher patted his head and tugged his ears. "Don't worry, pal. We're safe in the car. But is my Emma safe out there?"

Asher entered her phone number on his car's Bluetooth device. "Asher?"

Some of the tension drained out of him. He closed his eyes and rested his head back on the seat.

"Asher, are you okay?"

"Yes, I'm fine now." He buckled up, started up, and headed out of town.

"Good. Is there something I can do for you? Another china search? You could have left a message with Julia."

"I'm coming out to see you." How to tell this strong, capable woman that he feared for her?

A short silence greeted his statement. "I don't think that's such a good idea."

"I do."

"Well, I can't stop you."

He grinned in triumph at her grudging agreement. "No, you can't. I'll see you soon. I'm looking forward to it."

She hummed in a non-committal way and disconnected.

Anticipation thrummed through his veins all the way up the 400 to Highway 559. The rising wind scattered leaves like confetti. His grip on the wheel tightened.

Bears and storms. Emma was out in a thunderstorm with bears lurking in the woods. Was she certifiable? What were her friends thinking? What would he do if something happened to her?

The electric tension in the air settled in his neck and shoulders and pulled them tight. Sensing his distress, Pirate whimpered in sympathy.

At the front gate into the provincial park, a ranger strolled out to the car—Mark, Asher's neighbour across the street. Melody had been taking pictures of his and Meg's newborn son that day.

"Mark, you know Emma's out there?" Pirate stepped with care over Asher's lap and peaked out the open window.

"Yep, day use area. You know a storm is coming, eh?" Mark

clamped a hand over the peak of his campaign hat as the wind tried to toss it down the road.

"Yeah, I got that. Did the bear and her cubs ever get caught?"

The puzzlement on the ranger's face cleared and he waved away Asher's concern. "Yep, we trapped them at the garbage dump and took 'em all up to the French River. Emma's safe, and I see you brought protection with you." Mark laughed as he patted Pirate's head.

Asher rolled his eyes at yet another joke at his expense. The locals hadn't yet tired of teasing him about being the big man saved by the little dog. "Directions, please."

Mark reeled them off then bumped his fist to Asher's shoulder. "You listen to Emma and you'll be all right. She'll keep you safe." He waived the standard entry fee and tossed Asher a thumbs-up.

Asher fought his impatience to find Emma and maintained the crawling speed posted on signs along the road. Eons passed before he reached the designated area. The dense forest of pine, maple, birch, and oak stood back from a large grassy area. A shelter hunkered down amidst picnic tables and stone fireplaces. A split-rail fence traced the nearby brink of a wide bay.

He parked close to the shelter, beside Emma's blue mini-SUV. When Asher opened the door, Pirate hesitated, sniffing the air doubtfully. He tipped his head at Asher as if to ask, "Are you sure about this? It's windy as heck out there."

"The storm isn't here yet, so c'mon, let's go to Emma."

Pirate hopped down. Asher spotted Emma by the fence and jogged her way. Passing beneath the solid wooden roof of the shelter, Asher saw a few heavy-duty padded bags covered by a sheet of heavy plastic.

Emma, in an eye-popping turquoise slicker and rain pants,

leaned on the fence. She stared westward, watching the sky. A camera with a long lens had been set up on a tripod—equipment fit for a professional—also covered in plastic sheeting. Far out, whitecaps struck the islands sheltering the bay, spraying water high and wild. Her patterned scarf flapped in the stiff breeze.

She started at Pirate's hello bark. Her gaze met Asher's, a bright welcome on her face. She bent to make a fuss about Pirate, patting him and talking to him. When she rose, she had schooled her face to polite inquiry.

To hide his hopeful tremor, he propped his elbows on the top fence rail, rested a foot on the lower rail. Some ten meters below, at the bottom of a steep slope, green water stroked the sandy shore. A narrow path snaked down between grassy clumps and spindly bushes. On the western edge of the world a ribbon of blue-green sky predicted an end to the storm.

"Hi." He stumbled to a verbal halt. Why did happiness make people stupid? "Julia told me where to find you."

Her lips tried to purse in disapproval. "I'll have to speak to her about that. What did you want?"

"You. And me. Together."

Emotions chased across her features, so quick they were hard to catch. The first revealed joy. The last showed a frustrating doubt.

"We have nothing in common."

"I saw the photograph in your office. You stunned me."

"I'm... glad you liked it." She answered hesitantly.

"What do you think of my piano-playing?"

Her face cleared, and she smiled openly. "Wonderful."

"You said it moved you, made you imagine things."

She nodded.

He stroked his fingertips over her warm cheek. "Don't you see? We're both artists seeking to touch people with our efforts."

She straightened and scanned the slope to the water. Apparently, the concept was new to her.

Lightning flickered to the south. She watched, intensely focused and alert. Now he knew what he looked like when he lived deep in the music.

"You're very talented," he said.

She gave a dismissive wave of her hand. "Pure luck. I happen to be in the right place at the right time and take enough shots to get a good one."

The low-altitude wind ceased, the trees stilled. The high-altitude wind tore ragged holes in the clouds. Long rays of pink and gold sunlight streaked the landscape, intensifying the green of the forest. The clouds refracted the light from a pale yellow to an aching scarlet. His eyes hurt trying to open far enough to absorb the panorama.

Emma's shoulders slumped as she turned to her equipment. "So much for this outing."

"You mean Mr. Corbeau is fallible?" Asher teased.

She tilted her head, considering. "Jacques Corbeau predicted a storm?"

"Yes. In my office, a couple of hours ago. He said you'd be out today."

"Huh. In that case, I'm staying put." She grinned and re-tightened the knob holding the camera to the tripod.

"Mind if I stick around?"

"I won't shoo you away if you want to stay." Her lip twitched as if she tried to hide a smile. The change in her attitude warmed and encouraged him some more.

A tiny, intensely bright light flashed on the sand. Another flashed, and another. In moments, the beach filled with small flickering points of light.

"What is that?" He craned his neck for a better look.

"Lightning bugs," she informed him from behind the lens.

He stood, fascinated by a phenomenon of nature he'd never seen. "How do they do it?"

"Chemicals in their butts, to attract mates," she said, still clicking.

Asher couldn't stop the question. What if his dick could do the same? Would Emma notice? He laughed aloud.

Her head popped up and she laughed with him. "I know, *everybody* wonders what it would be like."

A diffuse spot of light glowed in the clouds. Emma stiffened and stared southwards. A couple more bright spots appeared. "Sheet lightning," she said.

Another natural wonder he hadn't witnessed. How many other incredible things had he missed by living in a large city? His gaze slid to Emma and heat flowed through his blood.

Dipping to the camera again, she fired off more rapid clicks, occasionally changing her angle. When the light faded to a dull smooth grey, Emma straightened. An exultant glow radiated from her, as if she'd absorbed some of nature's light. "We likely won't see the combination sheet lightning and lightning bugs ever again. I hope one of these shots will work."

"How many did you take?"

She folded and shouldered the tripod and headed back to the shelter where she released the camera to view the display. "Three hundred or so."

His brows rose, and she chuckled at him. "Gotta love digital technology."

"And you expect only *one* shot to work?"

"When you're dealing with lightning, count yourself lucky to get one perfect shot. Lots—almost all—of the time, I don't get anything I'm happy with," she replied absently, flipping through the images.

"You must have very high standards."

"I do." A fact, not a brag. The poster in her office proved it.

He pointed at her camera. "May I see?"

She hesitated. "I don't show my work."

The wind picked up, shredding the clouds, drawing streamers of foam across the water.

"Please?"

She inspected the camera in her hand, fiddled with the buttons, cleaned the lens. She sighed from her boots. "Okay " She thrust the camera at him then stood stiff, wide-eyed and tense.

Expecting her to snatch it back at any moment, he took the camera in one hand, sat on the picnic table and held out his empty hand. "Come sit with me?"

As if drawn by an irresistible force, she perched on the edge of the planks. She jammed her hands between her thighs and stared to the west.

Sliding close, he nudged her with an elbow. He held the camera towards her. "Show me?"

She gifted him with a slow, small smile and took the camera back. Together, they settled on the table, shoulders touching. Her scarf drifted against his bicep. Awareness prickled along his arm and over his shoulders. For a few minutes, they concentrated on the tiny slide show. One shot gave him the same cringing response as the scene in her office.

She turned at his movement and their eyes met. Her pupils widened, and her chin rose.

He slid an arm around her shoulders and drew her close.

The sun blinked out, plunged the world into twilight. The waves surged, and the bug lights winked out.

Her gaze dropped to his mouth.

She licked her lips. Her questioning gaze tangled his thoughts.

He bent his head for the kiss he'd wanted since he first met her.

So sweet.

So soft.

So gone.

Asher blinked at her sudden retreat. She'd been right there, kissing him back, and now she ran away. Pirate stood at the fence, barking wildly.

"Asher, do you hear that?" her urgent question pierced his sudden gloom of loss. She ran to the fence, nearly toppled over it in her rush. "Some kids in a canoe. They fell out. They're in the water." She squeezed through the rails and hurtled down the rough cliff path.

Asher followed Emma, slipped on the rocks, landed on his ass with a grunt, slid down into mud. He rose, flinging mud in all directions. Searing pain shot through his ankle. On he ran.

Emma, nimble as a mountain goat and familiar with the terrain, hit the beach ahead of him. She tossed off her coat, scarf, and shoes, and headed straight into the seething waves.

Asher stumbled to the wet sand, dropped his own coat and shoes and followed her into the water. Damn, the cold stung. He strode hip-deep then dove in, struck out in a front crawl. Strong waves challenged his every stroke. He caught up to Emma as she reached the canoe.

Two girls, both wearing bright-orange lifejackets, clung to the overturned boat. One of them screamed and pointed out towards open water.

A third girl, no lifejacket, flailed pink-clad arms.

"Take these two ashore," he shouted at Emma. "I'll go after her."

He battled forward through the waves.

The girl went under and bobbed up. Water slicked her hair flat on her head.

Fear for her strengthened his determination, lengthened his stroke. After a cold hard struggle, he reached Hayley, Ryan's daughter.

She latched onto him, drove them both underwater. Surfacing, he furiously treaded water.

"Hayley, stop panicking." She clamped her arms tighter and wrapped her legs around his waist.

Water closed over their heads. He kicked to the surface.

"Hayley, I need you to let go of me, so I can get us to shore."

Under they went one more time.

Up he thrust with his legs.

He pushed the girl from him. "Hayley. Stop. Remember your safety classes. Don't clutch."

She reached for him, blind panic in her grasp.

"Hayley! Let go!" He shoved her away again. "Hayley!" He shook her once, willing her to calm down.

Teeth chattering behind blue lips, she nodded her understanding and flipped to her back. He grabbed her collar and headed for shore.

The lake lifted and tossed them, thrust them up and dunked

them down like bits of junk. When his feet touched the hard sand of the bottom, he gathered Hayley in and pulled her from the water. She turned and clung to him with her arms and legs, bawling her eyes out. *Like Brendan used to do when he was afraid.*

He patted her back, reassuring her. He strode to the beach, carrying his sobbing burden until he could put her down beside her two friends and Emma.

"Hayley." Emma fell to her knees and engulfed the girl in a huge hug. The other girls joined them in a teary group hug. One of them was Lindsey Chisholm, the daughter of the ranger on duty and cousin to Hayley. Asher had never met the third girl.

Bent over, hands on his thighs, water streaming from his body into the sand, Asher's lungs heaved in and out. He shook from the cold.

Pirate danced around him, alternately barking and nuzzling, confirming his master had survived.

Asher reached out and rubbed his head. "I'm still here, buddy boy. It takes more than a little cold water to do me in."

He straightened as Emma jumped up, grinning like never before. "Asher, thank God you saved her!" Without warning, she plastered herself against him, wrapped her arms around his neck and laid a kiss on him, heating his body from the inside out. He put his arms around her waist and drew her tighter. Cold? What cold?

If not for the giggling of three young girls, Emma would never have released Asher from her life-celebrating grip. She shivered hard and deep at the loss of his warm mouth and strong body.

No, you do not miss his hot body against yours.

Really.

It's just too early in the year for a swim.

The lake tossed the canoe ashore, without paddles.

"C'mon girls. Let's f-fetch the canoe and s-stash it behind the outhouse. Then I'll d-drive you home." Her teeth chattered as she continued to shiver.

"I'll do it." Asher limped a couple of steps across the sand.

Emma gripped his forearm. "Asher, you're bleeding." She pulled him closer to inspect the nasty gash on his head where he usually parted his hair. Blood, mixed with rain and lake water, streamed down his features and dribbled off his jaw.

Asher swiped his hand down his face then stared at his bloody palm. "An oar hit me on the way out. I'll be okay. I don't even feel it. Let's get the girls home."

Overwhelmed with the might-have-been, Emma turned and scooped Hayley, Lindsey, and Sarah into another tight grateful hug.

Over the girls' heads, her gaze connected with Asher's. Sodden and sandy, barefoot and battered, he had never looked more handsome. Her chin wobbled, and tears slid down her cheeks, mingling with the rain.

"Thank you," she choked out.

"You're welcome," he said. His dark-eyed gaze warmed her. He headed towards the canoe, moving like the Tin Man in need of a good oiling.

"You're limping, aren't you?"

"Yeah, I tripped on the path. Stupid, but it happens." He staggered on, pain visible in every step.

Stoic fool. "We'll do it." Between the five of them, they dragged the canoe from the water and stored it by the change cabin.

They were all quaking from the cold, now. Climbing the cliff path got their blood flowing, but the wind sucked away any heat gained from exertion.

Emma tried to help Asher walk with his twisted ankle, but the narrow rough path wouldn't allow it. Asher lagged farther behind.

When they reached the top, Emma herded the trio to her car, scooped up her abandoned camera equipment on the way. She turned the car's heater on full blast, got the girls to strip off their soaked clothes and slip into the dry things she carried during her storm shoots.

There weren't quite enough clothes for everyone but she managed to dress them decently at least. She covered them with a blanket as they huddled together in the back seat.

Too bad she'd finished her tea at lunch. Something hot would have been useful to warm them.

By this time, Asher and Pirate had crested the cliff. She ran over and tucked herself under his arm to bear some of his weight when he stepped on his bad ankle. She directed him towards her car. He headed towards his.

"C'mon Asher, I'll take you to Emergency." She tried again to move the stubborn mass of man.

"You have to take the girls home. Lindsey's dad is at the front gate. He'll take care of her. You'll still have two more to take home. I'll be okay."

Compelled by his greater weight, she helped him hobble to his car.

He grunted hard when his butt hit the driver's seat. She opened the back door for Pirate. The dog hopped over the console to the passenger seat and licked Asher's ear in a sympathetic way.

She bent into the car's interior. "I hate to leave you here."

A shiver rattled through him. "I hurt my left foot. I can drive myself home."

"You have to go to Emergency. Your ankle might be broken, and you might need stitches."

He flipped down his visor and examined his forehead in the little lighted mirror. "Butterfly bandages will be enough. My ankle is only sprained, not broken. No big deal."

"You should go to Emergency."

"I *am* a doctor. I can take care of it."

She popped her hands on her hips. "Asher—"

"Emma. Your hands are full. You don't need me in them as well." He grinned. "At least, not like that." He wiggled his eyebrows then winced. More blood oozed down his forehead. "Emma love, your caring is wonderful, but you have to go." He shivered violently, his complexion grey under his tan. He turned in his seat with agonizing slowness.

"Okay, I'll let you go though I wish I could clone myself. But I *will* check up on you." On impulse, she planted a swift kiss on his mouth, smiled into his startled eyes. "You're a hero."

At the park's front gate, Emma left Lindsey with her dad, stopped only long enough to explain what had happened and where the canoe was stowed. She asked Mark to call ahead to the families. She dropped Sarah off first, with more hasty explanations. Then she drove on to the house where Cathy and her family stayed with her father-in-law while their home was under renovation.

A terrified Cathy greeted them when Emma knocked on the front door. Cathy fell to her knees and wrapped her daughter in a fierce hug. Ryan joined them moments later, put his arms around both.

Emma left the reunion and walked to the kitchen. Asher had called her *Emma love*. He called her an artist. No one had called her either in a long time.

While the Chisholms gave thanks for being with each other, tears brimmed in her eyes for other reasons. What would life be like with Asher's understanding support? Heaven, absolute heaven. She mopped up the few fallen tears and blinked back the rest. She and Asher might have artistic souls in common, but they still lived in different worlds.

She started a fresh pot of coffee and a cup of hot chocolate, found some cookies and set them out on the table.

Cathy's infant son Daniel babbled from the porta-crib in the corner. Smiling, Emma leaned over the crib rail. The baby was the image of his dad, with his mom's dark eyes. He smiled at her, showing his gums. "How's my little man today?" She tickled him under his chin. He chortled and waved his hands. "You're an adorable infant, aren't you? I bet you give your mom and dad plenty of trouble just because you can." He pumped his chubby legs. "Come up here and visit with your godmommy."

As Emma hefted him, he flapped his arms and legs. "You think you can fly, eh?" Emma laughed, and all her troubles receded. If only she could bottle this wonderful light feeling for later consumption. She lowered him to her hip. The unique scent of baby wound its way around her heart and filled her with a deep yearning for a child of her own. A child with Asher's brown eyes.

"Daddy makes Daniel fly," Hayley came into the room and kissed Daniel's round cheek. "He zooms him around on his arm." She glowed with her love for her brother.

"A baby looks good on you, Emma." Cathy and Ryan entered the kitchen. Daniel lunged for his mother as she approached. She swept her child into a fierce hug.

"Emma, we're in your debt for rescuing our Hayley," Ryan said in a hoarse voice.

"She didn't rescue me—" Hayley began.

"Asher did," Emma said at the same time.

"Dr. Stockdale did. He's very big and strong. Emma kissed him, and he kissed her back. Big time." Hayley's eyes twinkled with the glee only a young teen girl could manage.

Emma's face flamed. She tugged one of Hayley's springy curls. "Hayley, why were you out in the canoe in the first place? And where was your lifejacket?"

Hayley rolled her eyes. "Can you believe it? Sarah can't swim. So, I gave her mine."

Cathy's hand flew to her mouth. A grim-faced Ryan cupped his daughter's shoulders and bent down to her height. "It's good to share, but you risked your life unnecessarily. You know the rules, a lifejacket for everyone, and everyone *in* their lifejacket. No exceptions *ever*."

She popped a fist on her slender hip. "Lindsey's grandma said it was okay to go out."

Ryan frowned. "What did I say?"

Hayley shuffled her feet and looked everywhere except at her father.

"Hayley," he prompted.

"A lifejacket for everyone, and everyone in their lifejacket," she muttered as she wrapped the other arm over her waist.

Ryan crossed his arms.

"No exceptions ever. No matter what anybody says," Hayley mumbled.

Ryan tipped his head towards the door to the hallway. "Now

go on upstairs and change into your own clothes so Emma can get hers back."

"Okay, Daddy." Shoulders slumping dramatically, she shuffled away.

"And one final thing, Hayley," her dad called to her retreating back.

She peered over her shoulder, apprehension in her eyes. "Yeah?"

"We love you and we're very very glad you're safe and sound."

"But you're still mad at me."

"No," Cathy said. "No, we're not." She held her free arm open and Hayley ran to her mother.

Ryan enclosed his family in another strong hug. "I think you learned your lesson the hard way," he said. "Now hurry up and change so you can have the hot chocolate Emma made for you."

"Okay." Off she scampered, safe and loved.

Ryan scooped the baby from Cathy and gave him the sniff test. His puckered features revealed the results. "You, young sir, are a stinker." Daniel crowed with delight as his dad lifted him overhead. "Off to the change room we go." Ryan zoomed his son out of the kitchen, Daniel laughing all the way.

On the brink of tears again at the love this family shared, Emma focused on getting mugs down and pouring coffee for her emotionally wrung-out friends. Hayley was a lucky girl to have such incredible parents.

Emma's own parents had been the same, unconditionally loving each other and their two children. She'd lost them when she was a year younger than Hayley. Myra had been stricter, but still caring. She rubbed at her chest to soothe the ache of loss.

Cathy sagged into a chair. "Were we ever that stupid?" she

asked of no one in particular.

Emma's mind hollowed out. The memory of a camera flash followed by the screech of tires on pavement, the incredible pain of impact, the blessed darkness overtaking her. Her nerveless fingers lost their grip and the coffee mug crashed into the stainless-steel sink. The breakage clanged into the astonished silence.

Emma drew a steadying breath and reached for the dishcloth, hoping Cathy didn't notice her tremors.

Cathy slapped a hand over her mouth. "I'm so sorry, Emma. I totally forgot about the car crash."

"Oh, that." Emma brushed it off. "I forgot as well. No, I remembered Asher swimming for Hayley, bringing her in, they went under so many times. What if we hadn't been there—" Emma's voice broke. "All three of them could have—"

Cathy hugged her. "Shh, you were there. Let's not dwell on what-ifs and maybes. You were there, and you saved her."

"Asher saved her. I simply took Sarah and Lindsey ashore in their lifejackets. He went after Hayley. He brought her in. He saved her." Her mind filled with the image of Asher staggering, sodden and spent, with the effort to bring Hayley to safety. Emma focussed on cleaning up her mess. She took another mug from the stand on the counter and filled it with coffee. "Asher's a hero."

Cathy grinned at her and waggled her eyebrows.

"No, don't go there." She raised her hands in protest. "Just because I acknowledge his bravery does not mean I'm falling for the guy. No way. Nope. Not happening."

CHAPTER 4

A New Arrival

"We're here, Granddad." Horace Stockdale's only grandson Asher stated the obvious as he parked by the front doors. The Cedars Retirement Community, a sprawling two-storey brick-and-stone structure, perched on a high eastern cliff overlooking an expanse of sparkling blue water and dense green forest.

"Banished to the back of beyond," Horace grumbled from the passenger seat.

"You chose this, Granddad."

"Don't remind me. Decide in haste, repent at leisure. I made a colossal mistake two years ago when I sold the house after your grandmother passed." He'd just wanted to escape the memories. He should have known it wouldn't work. "And here I am, ready to try another prison."

"You don't have to do what Mother and Dad say. You could still change your mind and move in with me. I'd love to have you, and I have plenty of room."

Horace snorted under his breath. "And get in the way of you

starting your new life? Not a chance." He slid out of his grandson's car. His old bones were grateful Asher had an SUV instead of the hot little sportster owned by his only granddaughter Tenley. He opened the rear passenger door and took out his overnight bag.

Pirate stood at the edge of the back seat and whined a question.

Horace scrubbed Pirate's head, making his ears flap. "Of course, you can come in. Your manners are so good, I know you'll behave yourself."

Pirate yipped and jumped down to sit at Horace's heel. After he clipped on the leash, Horace stared at his new home. The brochure said there were shuffleboard courts and a barbeque pit out back. Benches lined a small lawn looking west out over water and islands. There'd be some beautiful sunsets. Could be worse.

"Let's hope they're livelier here than at the place in Toronto your mother chose for me. Two years almost put me in my grave." Horace continue to grumble.

"I'm sure you'll fix that, like you did at Northfield."

"The folks running Northfield were older in their heads than all the residents added together. Feeding us supper at five o'clock, sending us to bed at nine. Tying themselves in knots because I had friends in to play bridge and have a few drinks." He curled his lip in disgust. "We're adults. Not a bunch of delinquents." Like himself, his widowed friends had been looking for some company to while away the time and ease the loneliness. He didn't hold out much hope for this new place.

Asher came to stand beside him, a huge suitcase in each hand. His grandson was a real looker for sure. Just like Horace at his age. Now, Horace's hair was more salt than pepper. Still had plenty of it though. Horace smoothed a fingertip over his moustache, pulled his shirt cuffs the requisite half-inch below the sleeves of his navy blazer, and squared his shoulders. "Let's get this done." Day lilies nodded a welcome as they walked the smooth concrete path to the front door.

Horace punched the handicapped button and they entered the building. The splash of an indoor waterfall greeted them. People chatted as they settled in rows of chairs in a large room behind the fountain. A casually dressed young man warmed up at the baby grand piano in front of the windows on the far side. A pretty young First Nations girl wrote requests from the audience on a scrap of paper. A performance was about to begin. Probably songs from World War I. Why didn't these places do their math and realize his generation had been too young to serve in even World War II? Tipperary indeed. Gimme some *Blue Suede Shoes*. Seriously, how old did they think he was?

"Hello, Doctors Stockdale," the receptionist, aka guard, recalled Horace's attention to the business at hand.

Horace stepped up to the desk and dropped his briefcase. "Horace Stockdale checking in."

Asher followed and stood the suitcases behind Horace. "Hi, Wendy. Granddad this is Wendy Hadley. Wendy, Horace Stockdale, my grandfather."

The receptionist gave Asher an open smile of greeting and turned back to Horace. "Hi, Horace. The director told me you were arriving today. Did you have a good trip up from the city?"

"Don't know. Didn't pay attention."

"Granddad," Asher said.

Horace ignored the scolding. At least Asher didn't hiss and carry on, as his daughter-in-law would have done. Barbara had her uses, but she treated her father-in-law like a troublesome brat.

"I slept for most of it," Horace told a little white lie.

Wendy nodded. "Excellent, then you'll be up for a round of bridge. Do you play?"

"I do." Probably be playing in the morning to suit the guards' timetable.

"Excellent. We've been looking for a fourth for a new table this evening in the lounge at eight PM, sharp." She handed him a folder and key. "You're in suite thirty-nine on the ground floor, east wing." She came around the desk, stopped and looked down. "Well, hello there. I've heard all about you."

Pirate lifted a forepaw. Wendy grinned and bent to shake hands. "Looks like our town's littlest hero is all better and has found a home, too. Well done, you. You can visit any time as long as you behave yourself."

Horace and Asher grabbed the luggage and followed her across the front hall.

The songstress opened her show with a catchy Shania Twain tune. Horace stumbled in surprise.

The receptionist reached for his elbow. "Are you okay, Dr. Stockdale?"

Horace moved his arm out of her reach. "Fine. The young girl has quite a voice."

"That's Julia Westover. We seldom have singers of her calibre volunteering to entertain us. You can meet her after the performance." Arrived at his cell, she unlocked the door. "We've set your furniture up as we thought best. If you don't like it, tell Reception, and we'll move it around to suit you if we can."

In a bright suite of adequate size, his few remaining bits of living-room furniture were placed with some thought and imagination.

Humph. He tossed the folder on the coffee table and stuck his head into the bedroom. His familiar furniture crowded the room. "It'll do for now."

"Shall I have housekeeping come and unpack your cases for you?"

"I'm not dead yet," he snapped.

"Granddad," Asher warned again.

Horace rolled his eyes. "No, thank you, no need to fuss. I like to order my things my own way."

Wendy nodded. "We prefer you to. When some residents move in, they don't bring much in the way of independent spirit, and we do whatever we can to give it back to them."

Humph. Horace wandered over to the window and stared out at a bird feeder. A goldfinch zoomed in and started pecking at the food. His mate joined him, and they cracked seeds together in peace for a while.

Behind him, Wendy rattled off a long string of instructions and directives. He didn't bother listening. It would all be in the rules document in the folder.

The birds flew into the trees. A piercing loneliness struck him, and his eyes stung. Over the four years since his dear Erica had passed, the grief had abated to a faint persistent ache. At times like this, it rose up and cut like a surgeon's blade.

"Granddad?" Asher's hand settled on his back, spreading comfort.

Horace squared his shoulders and forced a smile.

Wendy's voice interrupted. "If you want to unpack later, you can enjoy Julia's performance and meet your fellow residents at lunch. Asher, you're welcome to stay though you'll have to pay for your meal."

Horace muttered his agreement and they caught the final song announced as a birthday request from a woman who had to be over a hundred years old. Horace laughed aloud at the opening notes of *Long Way to Tipperary*.

Everyone clapped for Julia and her accompanist. As the audience rose and shuffled about, chatting and laughing, Asher stiffened at Horace's side, and so did Pirate. Man and beast stood with gazes riveted. With a happy bark, the beast took off, weaving through the crowd. He stopped before a pair of women. The younger bent to greet Pirate.

Ah, he remembered Emma from the dinner at Asher's place, when Asher's mother behaved so poorly. He'd wanted to strangle the silly snob. Didn't she realize her stuck-up nose stuck in people's throats?

Emma scanned the thinning crowd and zeroed in on Asher. A funny little strangled noise erupted from his grandson. He had a struck-by-lightning look about him.

Horace couldn't stop his grin. Well, well, well. Now he had proof—Asher had gotten over Sondra and her cheating ways. About time, too. Horace elbowed Asher in the ribs; he jumped about a mile. "Seems like the pretty Emma is more to you than your china dealer."

"We're friends," Asher's gaze followed Emma as she approached through the tangle of chairs and people.

Horace nodded and said nothing more, just kept grinning. His gaze wandered to the woman walking behind Emma.

Chin-length sandy grey hair framed large grey eyes in a sweet face. Her trim, upright figure denied her age.

Holy jumping. He drilled through his memory of the meal. Hadn't Emma said her grandmother had passed? Was this lovely lady her other grandmother? He smoothed a quick hand over his moustache.

"Hi, Asher," the woman helped herself to a kiss on his grandson's cheek. His grandson was too damn good-looking. She offered Horace a handshake and a neutral smile. "You must be Horace, Asher's grandfather and our newest resident."

Horace took her outstretched hand. Energy surged through him, snatched his breath.

"Granddad? You okay?" Asher asked.

He let out his air on a great grinning gust. "Yes, fine," he tossed to his grandson. "And yes, I'm Horace Stockdale. And you are...?"

"Jean Chisholm. Welcome to the Cedars," she dropped his hand, and her smile faded. She drifted off in the direction the others had gone—presumably the dining room.

Horace's cheery mood faltered at her blasé response to him. "Emma, who was—?"

Emma stared at Asher and he stared back.

Great, a man needed information and all he got was old news. Those two youngsters were stuck on each other.

Pirate issued a polite bark. Asher and Emma startled, and Horace laughed at their guilty faces. Emma bent to pat the dog, talking rapid nonsense to the critter.

Wendy the receptionist approached. "Emma, Jean's at the table. Horace, I'll introduce you to your tablemates. Asher, will you be joining us today?"

Horace looked away from the forlorn expression in Asher's

eyes as he watched Emma hustle after Jean.

"Yes, please. But I'm not sure about Pirate."

"He's welcome to keep me company at Reception." Wendy whistled the dog to her side and off they went.

After sitting down with two other residents and his grandson, introductions were made. During the soup course, Asher's gaze focused over Horace's shoulder. A discreet scan revealed Emma and Jean dining with two other women at a table behind him. He lingered over the sight of Jean, her face wan and sad. He wanted to go tease the sadness from her. Bet she was even more beautiful when she smiled. Horace's mouth twisted in self-mockery. Asher wasn't the only man at their table who had it bad.

"Asher?" Horace tried twice more before Asher managed to drag his gaze off Emma. Horace tilted his head back towards the ladies' table. "Now you have a new house and a new dog, you should ask Pirate to steal Emma's heart, so you can start a new family."

Asher scowled at him. "If a heart needs to be stolen, I don't want it. A heart has to be given freely, honestly, without secrets." On a wistful sigh, Asher murmured under his breath, "The way I'd give her mine if given half a chance."

Jean sank into her flowered recliner by the window of her suite. Her afternoon coffee sat on the side table, and Nadine's latest book lay in her lap. Her exercise quota was done for the day. She wanted some quiet time, alone with her book and the birds twittering out at the feeder.

Someone knocked on her door.

"Go away," she muttered.

A second knock.

Jean groaned. Didn't people understand she needed to mourn the death of her life-long friend Myra for longer than thirty seconds? They'd been through thick and thin together, graduations, marriages, deaths of husbands and children. For now, she avoided social activities, unwilling to face the fake cheerfulness.

A third knock.

"What kind of stubborn idiot are you?"

Jean pushed up out of her chair and yanked open the door.

"Afternoon, Jean," Horace said. "Would you care to go for a walk?"

Her heart thumped at the sight of the new resident. It had done the same strange thing when they met after he moved in. Must be indigestion. "It's raining."

"It stopped an hour ago. It's a lovely summer day." He held out his hand. "Won't you come out and enjoy it with me?"

Jean stared at his broad palm and long fingers. Gossip said he'd been a surgeon. She could imagine his hands at the delicate task of healing people with kind cuts and stitches. She took in his broad un-stooped shoulders, thick wavy white hair, and dark eyes.

Unbidden, her shoulders drew back, and her chin rose.

He'd been at the residence for a mere three days and had already created a stir among the unattached women. When Asher and Horace had stood together, not a single woman had missed the pair of outrageously handsome men. Young and old alike, women were fools.

"No. Thank you for asking." She started to close the door.

"I'll go with you, Horace," Lillian said from beside him in the hall. The brassy redhead was one of the old hens clucking over the new rooster.

Jean sucked in a surprised breath at the pinch in her heart. She patted her chest. What *had* she eaten for lunch?

Horace tilted his head at her gesture.

She stepped behind the door, half-hiding herself from the curious doctor. "I'm fine. Nothing some antacid tablets won't fix. Enjoy your walk you two," she said with false cheer. Ignoring the disappointment in Horace's face and the triumph in Lillian's, she closed the door all the way.

She sat in her recliner and picked up her book. Some minutes later, she heard laughter from the path meandering through the trees and lawns of the property.

"Piffle." Grumbling some more, she slammed the window shut. She snatched a pillow off the couch and hurled it at the precise moment the door opened.

The puffy projectile hit her grandson square in the chest. He shouted loud enough to wake every napping resident along the hall.

Jean clapped her hands to her hot face. "Ryan! I'm so sorry." This is what happened when a sensible older woman allowed her inner teenybopper loose.

Thirteen-year-old Hayley peered from behind her father, brown eyes lit with incredulous glee. "Nana Jean, did you just throw a pillow at my dad?"

"No. Of course not." Jean drew a steadying breath and sat down.

Hayley slipped by her dad, picked up the cushion and waggled it. "Riiiight."

"I'm so sorry, Ryan. You just got in the pillow's way."

Ryan took the pillow from his daughter and placed it on the

couch. "Why did you feel the need to throw stuff around?" He touched Jean's shoulder in reassurance.

She shrugged, unwilling to reveal her foolishness.

"Were you angry at somebody?" He slid off his coat and draped it over a cherry-wood dining chair then ruffled Hayley's curly hair.

"Daaad." She dodged his ministrations.

Ryan sat down and twisted to face her. "Well, Nana?"

Piffle. "No. I... um... I wanted to go for a walk but it was raining too hard."

Her grandson's sandy brows arched in disbelief.

Jean shot a pointed look at Hayley. "We'll talk later." Jean went to her bookshelf, pulled out the dice box and scorecards, and set them on the table. "Right now, we're going to play Yahtzee."

Jean expected Emma to arrive at any minute to watch the show with the brainy forensic anthropologist and the brawny FBI agent. She didn't care for the blood and guts; she watched for the romance that always made her smile.

Jean scooped grounds into the basket of her coffee maker. Ah, nothing beat the smell of fresh grounds. She glanced at the kitchen clock. Knock, knock. Jean hurried over and flung open the door.

"Emma, why didn't you—"

"Evening, Jean," Horace said. "Would you care to go to the movie in the lounge with me tonight?"

His white teeth gleamed under his white moustache, contrasting with his tanned face. Jean caught her breath. "No, but thank you for asking."

He peeked around her to the TV. "Why don't you record your show for later? They're showing *The Artist*."

"I'll go with you, Horace," Lillian tucked her hand in his elbow and tried to draw him down the hall. He pulled the other way with a slight look of distaste. My, he looked awkward with his arm cocked that way.

"Hi, Nana Jean. Hi, Horace, Lillian." Emma squeezed past the duo and plopped a white string-tied box on the coffee table. "I brought cupcakes to go with the beefcake." She grinned broadly at her own joke.

Horace's smile faded. "I'll leave you to your company. See you at breakfast." He let Lillian lead him away.

A faint regret nudged at Jean. She huffed at herself. Silly old woman.

Jean faced Emma, desperately trying to curb the blush creeping up her neck. Emma's teasing smile made the heat race to her hairline. Piffle.

"Is Horace crushing on you?"

Jean flipped the switch on the coffeemaker before answering. "What is this? High school?"

"No. Real life."

Tears filled Jean's eyes and she turned her back in horror. Emma immediately embraced her. A couple of hard sobs for her dear friend Myra racked her body. She pressed her hands over her eyes, drew a deep breath and held it. Her tears dried, and her sobs receded. She let the air seep out of her.

"Sorry about that." Jean sat on the couch and allowed Emma to cosset her a bit.

"Did you want to go with Horace?"

Jean pretended to think about it. She patted Emma's hand.

"You came all the way over here and I want to spend time with you."

Emma smiled. "Clever dodge, that."

Jean grabbed the remote control and aimed it at the TV. "I thought so." She was too old to make eyes at a man. No matter how appealing.

"Do you miss a man in your life?"

The unexpected question startled Jean into truth. "Yes, I do. I miss the intimacy." She chuckled at the expression on Emma's face. "You can stop grimacing, young lady. Just because we're old doesn't mean we're sexless. I meant the intimacy of chatting over wine at the end of a meal, tea in the afternoon, a pat on the bum, kisses in the kitchen, countless other things that happen between two people who love each other."

Emma's heavy sigh drew Jean's attention to her young friend.

"Have you never been involved—beyond a few dates—with any man since Nico when you were all of nineteen? Are you still in love with him after all these years?"

Emma stared into space for a bit. The opening music for the show began. "I haven't met anyone as exciting as Nico. Nobody who's swept me off my feet." She hung air quotes around the last phrase. "I've been so focused on Gran and her shop since Gran's first stroke that if anybody appeared, I didn't see him. And these last few years, forget about dating."

"What about Asher? I've heard things about you two."

Though Emma's eyes filled with turbulence, she said nothing.

As the brawny FBI agent came on the screen, Jean guessed she wasn't alone in thinking of dark-eyed men named Dr. Stockdale.

Jean concentrated on knitting the left sleeve of a sweater for Hayley. Jean's great-granddaughter had asked for a larger version of the flower-power cardigan her grandmother Yola had made, and Jean delighted in the purpose. Jean wanted to get the project off to a good start, so she had something in hand for the Stitch & Bitch meeting tonight. A knock sounded at her door. Jean blew an annoyed breath then slapped-on a sort-of welcoming smile before she answered.

For the third day in a row, Horace stood on the other side. "Hello, Jean," he said. "Will you help me?"

She arrested the automatic no on the tip of her tongue. She couldn't arrest the sweet thud of excitement in her heart. "With what?" Dear lord, he was so handsome and always so nicely dressed. Not like some of the old fuddy-duddies with their droopy sweats and over-long hair.

Horace grinned. "Well, it's private."

"The doctor visits every Monday, Wednesday, and Friday. You'll have to make an appointment with him." A little grin tugged at the corner of her mouth. She stepped back in invitation.

An answering grin appeared on Horace's face. He stepped forward. "It's not that kind of a problem."

"I'll help you, Horace," Lillian's voice drifted from behind Horace.

Seriously? Did the woman live in the hall? She ought to be in her apartment instead of harassing handsome men.

"Sorry, Lillian, only Jean can help me."

Lillian grabbed Horace's arm, leered up at him through her lashes. "Anything she can do, I can do better."

Jean gasped at the woman's shameless behavior. She was

plenty old enough to know better.

Horace's mouth straight-lined as he released himself from her grip and stepped into Jean's room. "No, you can't. This concerns Emma." He shut the door on Lillian's astonished face.

Jean dogged his footsteps to the couch and plopped down beside him. "What's happened to Emma? And why have I not been told?"

Astonishment opened Horace's features. "I thought you weren't related."

"We're not. Her grandmother and I were best friends." A sticky lump of sorrow blocked further words. She sagged down beside him, her hand clamped over her mouth, vainly trying to stop the tears. A sob clawed at her throat. She wrapped her arms around her waist and hunched over, rocking back and forth.

Horace's arm circled her back, and he rocked along with her, murmuring soothing noises. As the storm in her heart abated, she reached for the box of tissues on the side table. What a fright she must look.

"I haven't cried like that since the funeral."

"You miss your friend. No shame in that. How long ago did she pass?"

"Seven weeks and five days." Tears welled again, and Jean dabbed a tissue to catch them. "We were so close. You have her room. I miss her so much."

"It's only natural to miss her and to feel her loss some times more than others. You learn to live with it."

"You do." Pangs for her husband and daughter trebled the pain of losing her dearest friend. She drew a shuddering breath. "Myra and I have known—knew—each other since we were babies. Emma calls me Nana Jean like my grandkids do."

"I heard Emma's shop belonged to Myra."

Jean mopped up a final tear. "Myra's great-grandmother opened it back in the early 1900s. She swore to bring culture to what was little more than a logging town at the time. It's been passed down the female line ever since."

"A venerable institution in this town," he said.

"And a real lesson in generations of independent women," she said. "Which brings us full circle. What's wrong with Emma?"

He dipped his head and stared at his clasped hands. "Hmm, now I don't know if...."

"Tell me," she ordered.

The spark in his eyes belied his solemnity. "It's more about what's wrong with Emma and Asher together, and what we can do to help both of them."

CHAPTER 5

Moving House

Emma clicked back to the previous photo on her desktop computer. Yes, this one. Of the hundreds of storm shots taken last week, this was the one. Grey-blue clouds, shimmering with sheet lightning, loomed over a beach lit with hoards of lightning bugs. An errant slice of sunlight poured golden light over the landscape and intensified the greens until it almost hurt her eyes. She embedded her signature in the image and titled it *Lightning Bugs*.

Too bad she'd been too busy to take shots of the dramatic rescue of Hayley and her two girlfriends. Melody would have loved them to go with her front-page story. Well, who could think under those conditions?

The water had been so rough and cold. Asher's kiss had been so gentle and hot. Emma shivered with the memories.

The shop bell announced the arrival of customers. Grateful for the interruption, she left her office to greet them. "Hey, Cathy, Hayley, Daniel. What's up?"

Emma returned Hayley's affectionate hug. The baby slept in a high-end stroller; Emma's yearning swelled again within her. She stroked his curls and moved away before the want swamped her.

"Wow, sparkly clean," Cathy said, her gaze roaming as she sauntered through the newly re-arranged tables. Hayley tagged along for a few steps then veered off to a cabinet full of Blue Mountain animal figurines. They never failed to attract young teen girls. "I would never have guessed grey walls could be bright."

Emma nodded, satisfied again with the results of her china shop's makeover. "Thanks, I gave the place the cleaning it so badly needed. George Grisham suggested the neutral shade to complement so many other colors. The guy's got an incredible eye."

"The whole town is buzzing with the news about you and Asher rescuing the girls. And this time, I'm contributing—bragging on you to everyone."

Emma picked up a plate and turned it over to read the blue under-glaze mark identifying the maker and the date of manufacture. Not that she didn't have it memorized. She needed to be looking at something other than the gratitude and admiration in Cathy's eyes. "Thanks. But Asher did all the real work." She shuffled her feet, uncomfortable with all the attention.

"The poor guy has limped around all week. Everybody wants to show their appreciation, buying him drinks, taking him home-cooked meals. The little-dog rescue jokes have ended. The sporting goods store gave him a ball cap with HERO stitched on the front. The women are all over him. Nothing new, but now—" Cathy rolled her eyes. Then she scoped the shop again, her brow creased. "Where are all the flowers people sent you? I expected your place to be overflowing."

"I kept a few favourites upstairs. The others I shared with the Family Shelter and the Cedars."

Cathy's face softened. "That's so sweet of you."

Emma smiled her thanks. "So, did you want something for Wendy's grandbaby's shower?"

Cathy sighed, nodded her head and stroked Emma's arm. "Okay. I get it. You don't like the attention. Ryan and I will forever be grateful to both of you. Anytime you need a favour, call me. Now, before my munchkin wakes up, do you have a supply of those *Bunnykins* dishes? Has anyone else bought one for her new grandbaby?"

Her friend's understanding eased the tension gripping Emma's upper back. "Yes, I have a supply and no, nobody's bought one yet. Wonder why?"

Cathy shrugged. "Because everyone thinks it's so easy and someone else has already got it?"

Emma walked to a table by the front window. "Probably. The *Bunnykins* collection is on this table and more in the window."

Cathy picked up a double-handled mug decorated with charming picnicking bunnies. "I had one like this when I was a kid. Don't remember it, of course. I found it when we packed up Yola's things." She put the mug back in its place. "Such a lovely tradition to mark a baby's birth."

"The price depends on the vintage. The artist bunny bowl is my oldest piece, from 1936. My newest is this year's release." Emma indicated a shelf. "I have *Bunnykins* figurines as well. Everything's collectible and surprisingly reasonable."

Cathy bent to examine the contents of a small display case. "Huh, figurines and jewellery, too. Who knew?"

"Yep, amazing isn't it? It sells so fast, I can't keep it in stock during the summer."

"You have a solid reputation in the region's china trade, don't you?"

Emma grinned and stood tall. "I like to think so."

"Atta girl. Own your brand," Cathy nudged her with a gentle elbow. "Asher's been telling everyone what a great job you did for him."

Emma bowed from the waist. "All part of fabulous of the service at Finn's Fine China and Gift Shoppe." Emma waved a hand over the display. "And what is your choice today, my lady?"

Cathy grinned at Emma. "You're proud of what you've done here, aren't you?"

Surprised, Emma stilled. She stared at the old-fashioned logo inlaid into the floor by the entry. If not for her mother's death, Emma would be the fifth, rather than the fourth, generation of Finn women to own the shop. Own. Emma owned Finn's. More than her surname was on the sign spanning the building. Her heart, her imagination, her devotion hung there. Owning a business was different than managing it. The pride went deeper, more personal.

Emma stared at her waiting friend. On impulse, she swept her into a grateful hug. "Thank you for making me understand. Consider your favour called and cleared." She released a teary Cathy. "So, decide already, will ya?"

Cathy shouted with laughter and dutifully examined a rimmed dish. "Rocket ship bunnies?"

"Way cool, Mom." Hayley had drifted over and peered at her mom's selection. "My little brother will like it."

Cathy nodded and reached for another bowl. "You're right. We'll buy the artist for the grandbaby shower and the astronaut for your baby brother."

Emma escorted Cathy to the cash desk, Hayley wandering behind.

Cathy handed over her debit card. "I have a huge favour to ask of you. Feel free to say no if you want. It's kind of a huge deal but it sure would help us out. We'll totally understand if you say no."

Cathy's uncharacteristic babbling piqued Emma's curiosity. "Do what?"

"Umm, well you see—forget it. We're asking too much."

Emma frowned at her dithering friend. "Hayley, do you know what your mom is going on about?"

"We want you to let Nana Jean move in with you."

Emma stared from Hayley to Cathy. "Jean move in with me?"

"Not forever. Good grief. Only for a month or so, maybe six weeks," Cathy added.

"What's wrong with her room at the Cedars? Isn't she happy there?"

"Oh, she's happy enough—"

"Ants are eating her house. Gross, eh?" Hayley scrunched her shoulders in gleeful horror. "Can you imagine ants living in the walls and the ceilings and the floors, and chewing, chewing, chewing?" She made avid munching, crunching noises.

Emma chuckled, finished processing Cathy's purchase and handed her the card reader. "Ants?"

"An infestation of carpenter ants at the residence caused major structural damage and some rooms need to be vacated. We'd take Nana Jean, but our place is renovation hell and Bucky simply doesn't have the room. Mark and Meg can't take her. Their house is full to bursting with the new baby. And being summertime, there isn't a single room for rent. Horace is moving to Asher's for the duration."

Emma froze briefly at Asher's name. Drawing a quick, thawing breath, she turned to the wrapping paper hung in large rolls beside the register. "Which paper?"

A small shriek issued from Emma's office. "Mom, look at this," Hayley called.

Before Emma could protest, Cathy hustled around the counter and through the door. She gasped. Emma pushed past them both and minimized her photo-editing software.

Cathy slapped her mouse hand. "Emma! Why did you hide such an incredible picture? Why haven't I seen your photographs before?"

"I don't like showing them."

"Why ever not? Look at the one hanging right there." She pointed at the framed poster. "They're wonderful!"

"No, they're not. I'm a rank amateur." Her college teacher had condemned her work, calling it trite, trivial, *calendar*.

"A highly talented amateur. I know gallery owners who would sell their souls to give you a show."

"No."

"But the opportunity—"

"I said no. And that's that. Which paper do you want your gift wrapped in?"

"Will you take my picture?" Hayley asked. "Please, please, pretty please. I want a glam shot for my Snapchat."

Fear-frozen memories of the moments before her crash streamed through Emma. "No!"

Hayley flinched at the sharp reply.

Immediately contrite, Emma softened her voice. "I'm sorry, Hayley. I don't take pictures of people."

Cathy's brows drew together in puzzlement. "You used to be mad for people shots. They're all you ever took. 'Rocks are boring' you used to say. You were so good at it. Remember the pictures you took of—"

Emma sliced her hand through the air to cut off further questions. "Not anymore."

Her friend opened her mouth again.

"Cathy. Leave it alone. Okay?"

Cathy shut up, though her eyes shone with determination to get to the bottom of the puzzle.

Emma's determination equalled Cathy's. It was nobody's damn business why she no longer photographed people. None of her photographs were anybody's damn business.

Jean set her coffee cup on the dining table in Emma's place and flipped to the next page of the *Clarence Bay Beacon*. After moving in two days, she was settling in. Funny how the shop below felt small and the living space above it felt big. "What should I make for supper tonight, Emma?" Jean asked her young friend as she strolled from her bedroom.

"You don't have to cook for me," Emma said, slipping her left earring into place.

"Yes, I do. You won't let me pay even a token rent, so I'm cooking. The grocery store has chicken breasts on sale, so chicken on the menu."

Emma popped her hands on her hips and opened her mouth. Nothing came out.

Jean grinned at her. "Say thank you, Emma."

"Thank you, Emma," Emma chanted before she crossed the

room and gave Jean a hug as reward for her stubbornness. Now that ought to happen more often. Folk seldom appreciated a good stubborn moment.

"Thank you, Nana Jean. I'm looking forward to a meal I don't have to cook. Especially since Saturdays are always crazy busy with the summer people."

Emma strode towards the inside stairs leading down to the shop, waved and disappeared.

Jean checked her comfy temporary home to see what else she could do to make life easier for Emma. Vacuuming and dusting needed doing. She couldn't find the vacuum cleaner in the kitchen or hall cupboard, so she headed into Emma's bedroom at the back of the apartment. The room was tidy, done up in crisp new bedding and draperies. Nothing flowery or over-the-top, yet unmistakably feminine. Just like Emma.

Hidden behind the open door stood a tall maple dresser. She frowned at the things arranged on top. If she didn't know any better, it was a shrine. A portrait of a handsome young man was surrounded by odds and ends, a sparkly stone, a green ribbon, a yellowed letter, a snapshot of four teenagers. Nico Rassenti. Emma had loved her high school beau with all the passion of her young heart. There'd even been talk of a wedding—until the car crash that took his life and the lives of two other teens—the ones in the smaller frame. The same crash left Emma in a coma for a couple of weeks. Everyone had expected her to die. She still bore faint scars on her face from the crash. Try as she might, Jean couldn't recall the details from—when was it—summertime, ten or more years ago?

Did Emma still grieve for Nico?

Jean picked up the larger frame and dusted it with a soft cloth.

Grief lost its sting and could be forgotten for weeks at a time. Grief also lunged out of nowhere to remind you of your losses.

Jean started at the sound of steps running up the stairs. She scooted out to the living room, glad to leave her maudlin thoughts behind. Her great-granddaughter Hayley bounded in with amazing energy.

"Hi, Nana Jean." The girl put a paper bag on the table and then bounced over for a loving hug. Jean planted a smacking kiss on her cheek. Hayley was the image of Francie, Jean's own deceased daughter. Funny how features could skip a generation and come back to bless, or curse, innocent children. Wild sandy curls were the Chisholm curse for Hayley. Francie's gamine face was the blessing.

"What's in the bag?"

"Dad and I went out to Bateau Island and picked wild blueberries yesterday. These are for you and Emma."

"Thank you and tell your dad thanks as well."

"Okay." Hayley wandered over to the window and stared at the cloudy sky. "Won't be much fun to go out today." A damp breeze blew in the scent of hot bread from the Bayview Restaurant next door. Hayley drew in a deep breath and turned around, her face bright with curiosity. "Will you show me how to cook?"

"I guess it would be fine. Anything in particular?"

"What's Daddy's favourite dessert?"

"Raisin butter tarts."

"All right! What do we do first?"

Did anything to beat the enthusiasm of a young girl? "Great idea. First, we need a recipe. Be right back." Jean smiled as she went to the smaller guest bedroom and dug out her box of treasured recipes from the cardboard carton of her assorted things.

"Perhaps we'll find something less complicated for you to begin with," she said as she came back into the main part of the apartment.

"Can I see the cards, Nana Jean?"

"Of course, you *may*."

Hayley rolled her eyes but corrected herself. Then she dug into the small wooden box. "Chocolate pear pie," she read the title of the first card.

"Francie's favourite dessert."

"She's the girl in the picture I found at Lindsey's place. My dad has the same picture."

"Yes. Francie was your dad's and your uncle's mother, your grandmother. My daughter."

"I love having a family tree." Hayley tugged out another card. "Chicken with three onions and a pepper."

"Your grandpa Bucky's favourite. You may copy the recipe for your mother for when her kitchen is finished."

"Can't we take a photocopy or scan it?"

Jean handed her a blank card from the back of her box. "We could if I had the machine for it. You may practice your penmanship while you write it out." Jean almost rolled her eyes at herself. You can take the teacher out of the classroom, but the classroom lives on in the teacher forever.

Hayley looked up from her writing. "What's *dredge* mean?"

"It means you put some flour and spices on a plate and then roll some food around in it to make a nice thin crispy coating when you sauté the food." Talking about it brought back the remembered the scent of the herbs hitting the hot oil.

Suddenly, she anticipated her task this evening. Gosh, what a long time since she'd done any cooking at all. The catered meals at the Cedars, though reasonably tasty, had cost her one of her significant joys. She hadn't realized how much she missed working in the kitchen. Between the loss of her dearest friend and her dearest pleasure, it was no small wonder she was in the dumps. She wanted cooking back in her life.

"Sour cream and blueberry muffins," Hayley read out from the next card. "We can use the berries I brought over."

Jean tapped Hayley's nose. "Use the best and freshest ingredients. Exactly what a good cook does. Why don't you check to see if we have all the other ingredients? Make a list of what's missing."

Hayley took the spotted card to Emma's little kitchen and combed through the cupboards, noting items on a pad of paper. Proudly, she handed her list to Jean.

Jean reviewed Hayley's list. "Well done, Hayley. It looks like we've got some shopping to do."

When Jean went to the guest bedroom for her jacket, she paused by the dresser and touched her photograph of Francie. Grief aside, there was still a whole lot of living to do.

"Are you iDoc?" Granddad asked from the archway between the front and back parlours.

In the middle of his Saturday morning practice session, Asher looked up from the piano keys to his grandfather. "Excuse me?" His fingers carried on with the warm-up exercises without Asher's full attention.

Granddad stepped into the room and showed his phone to Asher. "I asked if you were iDoc." Pirate came out from under the piano and stood at Granddad's knee. He bent to tug on the dog's ears, putting the critter in a happy stupor.

"I still have no idea what you're talking about."

"On Twitter. Melody Grisham tweeted when I moved to iDoc's. She spells it I-D-O-C. Clever. Didn't you know she had a Twitter feed?"

"Yeah, I knew. I don't read it, though I know plenty of people who won't miss a word." He switched from Hanon exercises to scales.

"She's kinda gossipy, isn't she?"

Asher smiled at the understatement. "Her family's the Clarence Bay clearing house for gossip. If *they* don't know it, it isn't worth knowing."

"Does she have a thing for you?"

Asher's fourth finger slipped off the black F-sharp key, down to the white G key, into dissonance. He carried on with the G-major scale as if nothing had happened like the well-trained pianist he was. "What makes you say so?"

"Because she's constantly tweeting about you."

"She's a gossip columnist. The *Clarence Bay Beacon* pays her to tweet about everyone and everything in town. Aren't there tweets about you? Look for a newguy label. Apparently, I hit the list when I moved here."

"It's not a label, it's a hashtag." Granddad thumbed through the messages. "There are tons of messages about iDocHero. This place is nuts about you—with excellent reason. I'm real proud of you, Asher."

He stopped playing. His chest tight with pleasure, he smiled up at Granddad.

"You did a brave and good thing and deserve the recognition."

"I did what anyone would have done." He shifted on the hard

piano stool, wishing for a cushion for his bruised tailbone.

"True. But you're the one who did it. You're a good and honourable man, Asher."

Asher's cheeks heated, and his smile wobbled. "Thanks, Granddad."

Granddad winked and went back to his phone.

Asher carried on with his practice, his heart full and light at the same time.

Granddad straightened and puffed out. "Check this out. Melody tweeted when I moved into the Cedars. You were iDoc even back then."

"Whatever the label thing is called, you get used to her knowing everything about you after a while. And I admire her restraint in sticking to positive things. She's never nasty."

Granddad peered across the piano at the scribbled score sheets. "You're composing again." Horace clapped Asher on the back. "I thought you'd never get back to it. Are you doing a recital?"

Asher hunched a shoulder. "Eventually. Maybe. I dunno."

Horace laughed. "At least you're definite about it."

"Is there anything else you wanted?"

"Lunch."

Asher tipped his head towards the kitchen. "Help yourself. We have plenty of stuff for making sandwiches."

Granddad gaped at him.

"You do remember how to make a sandwich don't you?"

"Of course. You mean I have to make them?"

Concentration, even for something so deeply embedded in muscle memory as scales, was out of the question when challenged by laughter. Asher dropped his hands in his lap. "Yep. I don't have any staff. You live here. You're not a guest."

"How do you feed yourself?"

"Eat out, order in."

Grumbling under his breath, Horace stalked out of the room. Pirate barked, peered over his shoulder to check with Asher. "Of course, you can go with Granddad." Pirate followed the older man.

"Will you let Pirate out?" Horace caught his grandson's request as he crossed the hall. Music, a happy Mozart piece, filled the house once more as Horace let the screen door slap closed behind Pirate. The dog scampered down the long yard, leapt the shallow rocky creek, and disappeared into the forest at the back of Asher's property. "Ha. Serve him right when his mutt comes back filthy and in need of a bath."

Horace opened the fridge and rooted about for fixings; plenty of things to make some ace sandwiches. Better than the white bread at the residence; junk stuck to the roof of a man's mouth. Blech.

Horace built himself an awesome sandwich, grabbed a bottle of micro-brew, tucked a book under his arm, and sauntered outside to the patio. The plate grated against the grit on the broad arm of the Muskoka chair. Horace groaned and went back for a cloth to wipe it clean. Someone's cleaning lady needed a reminder. At last, he lowered himself into the comfy seat and chowed down, listening to the music of his grandson's making.

Asher should have hit the world stage with his piano, not been stuck in a doctor's office in some one-horse town in cottage country. Clarence Bay was fine, perfect even, if you were retired. Ah well, it was fine to be here.

Pirate, the muddy little wretch, peered out of the trees every once in a while to assure himself one of his humans was still in sight. Then off he went again in search of chipmunks to harass into a game of chase. Horace was pretty sure he always let them win. Exhausted at last, Pirate made his way to the patio and flopped beside the chair of his older human.

Horace tossed the last bite of chicken to Pirate and picked up *Mystery of Depot Harbour*, the latest from a local writer. A couple of chapters later, Asher limped about in the kitchen and eventually joined him outside with a plateful of sandwiches and a beer.

"Did you get enough to eat?" Asher asked.

"Yep. Good stuff, too."

His grandson nodded and took a huge bite. "Thought you might like it."

Horace rubbed his shoe along the back of the sleeping dog. "What's for supper?"

"You just ate and you're asking after your next meal?"

"There's nothing else to do here. No activities or outings or lectures. How do you fill your time?" Who would have thought he might actually miss Cedars? Well, not the waiting-for-death attitude of some of the residents. But he sure did miss the few happy times he'd spent with Jean.

"I work."

"Yeah, I remember doing that." Horace chuckled and winked at his grandson. "So, what's for supper?"

Asher shrugged. "Pizza?"

"For the third time this week? Why don't you cook something?"

"We're having roast beef tomorrow. Do you want scrambled eggs and bacon?"

"Breakfast for supper? No thanks. Let's go to The Pits."

"It'll be jammed on a Saturday night."

"The food's worth it."

"I went there for lunch yesterday. You wanna order in Chinese? Or we could bake Jean's excellent lasagne."

"Geez, kid, you need a wife."

Asher sighed and picked at his sandwich. "I would if I could." The slight bitterness in his grandson's voice bothered Horace.

"Emma seems like a caring, considerate young lady."

Asher slumped in his chair and swigged down the rest of his beer. "Possibly. But she keeps declining my invitations. She phones to see if I'm okay, if my cut healed, if I'm still limping. Say yes to dinner? I may as well talk to that tree." He gave the tree a look that should have blasted it to splinters. "What more can I do?"

Horace hid his grin behind his bottle. He needed some decent food, and Asher needed some decent loving. His and Jean's moves to temporary homes had required significant revisions to their plan to get the kids together. Time to put said plan into action.

CHAPTER 6

Scheme and Make Merry

"Lindsey!" Hayley's squeal pierced Jean's eardrums as they hit the town beach after the grocery store and lunch with Emma. The rain clouds had flown, leaving a steamy day in their wake. "Can I go see her, Nana Jean?"

"Of course. I'll call you when I head home." Jean handed over the apple fritter and milk before Hayley scampered off to join her cousins and her aunt. She heaved a sigh as Hayley and Lindsey hugged each other. Tired and grateful to be alone, Jean sagged down on the picnic table's seat. She'd forgotten how much hard work it was to go shopping with a curious kid in tow. The questions her granddaughter came up with beggared the imagination. But it sure had been fun.

As Jean took her tea from Timmy's out of the paper bag and enjoyed her first sip, a masculine voice interrupted her reverie.

"Hi, Jean," Horace said. "How goes it at Emma's?"

Jean's weariness eased at the sight of his handsome face. It had been ages, or so it seemed, since she last saw him. "Fine. Hayley wants to make muffins later, so we've been shopping. How are you doing at Asher's?"

Horace also had a bag from the doughnut shop. He seated himself at her invitation. Not too close, she was pleased and disappointed to note.

"I'm doing well enough. Asher on the other hand...." His voice trailed away. When he offered to share his doughnut, Jean shook her head and waited for him to speak. He doctored his coffee, nibbled his goodie, and wiped his moustache.

Done with his fussing, he met her gaze, a wry twist on his mouth. "Our plan didn't work. Emma called Asher to double-check and I had to cook up an instant lie that I wanted to surprise him with more china. I had to call myself a forgetful old man for him to swallow the story. It was awful. And now I have to commission Emma to find something for him." He crumpled the paper bag and tossed it in the nearby trash.

Jean tucked in her lips to stop the laughter. Which made him madder; his plan gone awry, or calling himself an old man? "I did warn you they'd see through it. Why are you still worrying about this? Didn't you learn from your first attempt? Asher's a grown man. Can't he ask Emma for a date himself?"

"He's tried many times with no luck. Sad to say, I think he's about to give up."

"Funny, Emma never said anything about his asking." Jean recalled the little shrine in Emma's bedroom. "She *might* be stuck on an old boyfriend who died when they were very young," but there was a neglected layer of dust on Nico's picture..., "I believe her attachment is more habit than anything else. It's obvious how attracted she is to Asher."

He peeked over both shoulders checking for nosey parkers and leaned closer to her.

Instinctively, she leaned in as well. The scent of his citrusy woodsy aftershave filled her head. The look in his beautiful dark eyes gave her naughty ideas. Could she get more than the joy of cooking back in her stale life? She blinked at him, having forgotten the topic of conversation.

He winked.

A scalding blush stung her cheeks. Silly old woman. She straightened, gulped her tea and scalded her tongue. Silly and stupid old woman. "You were saying?"

"You're a beautiful woman."

"Piffle." She pulled in her smile. "You were talking about Asher."

A soccer ball rolled at speed up, hit the table leg and ricocheted against Jean's shin. "Ouch!" Jean grabbed the black-and-white missile.

One of Jean's great-grandsons, a four-year-old dark-haired moppet, ran up to retrieve the ball. "I'm sorry, Nana Jean. Randy did it." His twin followed close behind.

"Hi, Charlie," Jean said. "Then Randy should say sorry."

"Charlie did it," Randy said.

"How's your baby brother doing?" Jean asked, bypassing the tangle of who did what.

"He eats and poops and cries," said Charlie.

"Except when you change his diaper," said Randy.

"Then he pees on daddy's shirt," the kids crowed in unison. Shocked, they exchanged snorts, and burst into raucous laughter.

Jean laughed along with them. "You go on back to your mother and tell her I said hi." She watched them until their mother Meg spotted her and waved. "Little boys and their pee jokes." Shaking her head, she turned to Horace. And gasped at the transformation of the man.

His entire body was rigid, yet he trembled. His hands fisted so hard his fingers were white. His eyes blazed with longing as he tracked the little boys kicking their ball back and forth.

"Horace, what's wrong?"

He continued to watch the boys.

Jean reached out to cover one agitated fist, hesitated, then cautiously placed her hand over his.

He jumped and dropped his gaze to stare at their hands. Convulsively, his hand opened and took hers in a hard grip. He stared at their joined hands, his throat working against his emotions.

Jean wrapped her free arm around his waist and leaned against him, offering whatever comfort he needed. Compassionate tears filled her eyes.

The tension seeped from his spine. His head dropped forward as if it weighed far too much. More time passed before he freed her numb fingers. He rubbed sensation back into them.

"I'm sorry." His voice was rough and raw.

"They'll survive." She waggled her fingers.

A tiny tight smile tugged up one side of his mouth.

"What happened?"

He glanced sideways at her where she rested against his arm. His eyes were black with residual pain. He suddenly showed all his years and more. "We don't talk about it."

Jean struggled with the embargo. This dear man needed to unburden the grief she saw in his eyes.

"Asher—" Horace began and broke off. He shook his head as if arguing with himself.

She badly wanted to hear what Horace had to say. How would

this affect Emma?

He tapped his hand on the planks. Decision made. "Jean, I can't stay silent anymore. It tears up my guts to keep it inside."

"I'm listening."

"Asher is so humiliated and hurt by it all. He won't talk about it. I'm sure he even tries not to think about it. If Emma ever needs to know, she has to ask Asher. Okay?"

She met his gaze. "You have my word."

He nodded, yet was silent for so long, Jean suspected he changed his mind.

"Asher and his wife got married the summer after he graduated med school. She travels all over the world working on behalf of children. She excels at it and is in high demand. Asher was alone a lot of the time. After their son was born, she went back on the road. Instead of leaving the baby with a nanny, Asher gave up a promising surgical career and took an administrative job at a hospital, so he could be home with Brendan." He pounded the table with his fist. "Then, out of the blue, she announced she's divorcing Asher and taking his son."

"Dreadful. How could she be so cruel?"

"During a custody meeting, Asher found out Brendan isn't his. His wife cheated on him, lied about the paternity of the child he loved—" his voice cracked. He shut his eyes tight and turned his head.

Her eyes watered in sympathy with his struggles.

"After a DNA test proved his son wasn't his, Asher didn't fight for custody. Damn near killed him not to. He said it's better for the boy to have a relationship with his real dad, said it's the right thing to do. I sure as hell don't see it. He loves that boy. We all do. I understand Asher's decision though I can't agree with it."

He drew a harsh breath and blew it out. "I try not to let my anger get the better of me. We haven't seen our little boy for months. Brendan is the same age as your two great-grandsons."

"Poor Asher. He moved up here to escape a painful situation and start a new life?"

He took her hand again.

"Did you move up here to keep Asher company?"

Watching Meg and her children, Horace jerked a nod.

The silly man could admit to anger but not love. "Or are the rumours true, and your old retirement home wasn't big enough for you?" Jean held her breath against his reaction. She hoped to tease his mood to a brighter tone.

He huffed and harrumphed. "It wasn't the space at fault. It was the stultifying rules. Just because we arranged our own entertainment. Drinks and cards in our rooms, not strippers, for crying out loud, and—" He stopped when he noticed her smile. He kissed her hand.

Tingles tiptoed along her spine.

His beautiful smile flashed across his face. "Thank you for distracting me."

"Some things are best left alone." His hand tightened once more. "As painful as it is to you, you have to honour your grandson's decision."

"But, he's making a gigantic mistake!"

She stroked her thumb over his hand to hush him. "When my daughter Francie was young, she fell in love with Bucky, Ryan's father and he fell in love right back. Except, he was engaged to another woman. My husband and I talked to her again and again. Nothing would change her mind or Bucky's. They were determined. He broke off his engagement, and they got married. I was never thrilled with Bucky as a son-in-law. But he stayed faithful to Francie; still is as far as I know. I love my grandsons and their children. As hard as it was at the time, it turned out to be the right decision in the long run. Which is why I feel so strongly that you should leave Asher be."

"What happened to the fiancée?"

"Bucky broke Virginia's heart. She married Evan Grant on the rebound and appears to have it all. Though, to this day, I think she carries a grudge, and a torch, for Bucky."

Horace blustered a bit.

She tipped her head. "Would you have appreciated the interference when you were his age?"

His mouth thinned, hiding his upper lip beneath his moustache.

"Your grandson's here to start a new life. Help him move forward instead of looking back at what can't be changed. Your anger gets in his way, and yours. I know how tough it is, but you have to let the past go."

He gazed into her eyes and his face relaxed. "You're not only a beautiful woman, Jean, you're a wise one as well. I'll try to do what you say."

"Thank you." Jean checked on Hayley and Lindsey walking along the sand, heads close together, chattering. When she turned back, Horace had come closer.

Close enough for Jean to see the golden flecks in the dark brown of his eyes.

Close enough to take her breath.

Close enough to kiss.

Hayley raced up to the table. "Nana Jean, can I go to Lindsey's place?"

Piffle. Jean snatched her hand from Horace's and put it around her cup. "What about those muffins we're going to make?"

Hayley's face fell then brightened. She placed her hands on Jean's forearm. "Please can we do it tomorrow instead?"

"Please *may* we do it tomorrow?"

"That's what I said. Please?"

Jean shook her head, wondering if Hayley had out-smarted her. "Okay. Ask if Lindsey may join us."

"Yes! Thank you, Nana Jean." Hayley gave her a quick hug and flew off to join her cousin.

Horace drew a flyer from his trouser pocket and handed it to her. "Since you support a new life for Asher and Emma has definitely caught his eye, I want to do everything possible to help him with his new start. We need to think of another way to get them together and keep them together."

The flyer announced the seasonal schedule of the *MV Chippewa III*, a sixty-foot excursion vessel offering sunset dinner cruises.

She tossed a questioning glance at him. "You want to go on a cruise?"

An irresistible smile pulled at his mouth. "Yes, I want."

Her pulse quickened at his renewed intention. Irresistibly drawn, she met him halfway. His lips were soft and warm, and she kissed him back. *So long since I've been so thrilled.* His moustache tickled the skin above her lip. Giggles bubbled up from her chest and shattered the mood.

He stroked his fingertips across her upper lip, soothing the itch. "Don't worry, you'll get used to it."

"Does that mean more kisses?"

He grinned and winked. "Only if you want them."

She tipped her head and rolled her eyes to the sky, pretending to think. "We'll see." She patted his hand. "Enough of this silliness. Tell me more about your newest scheme to bring our grandkids together."

"When is your new Cadillac supposed to be fixed?" Asher asked Granddad as he came down the stairs to join him in the front hall of his house. "What are the symptoms?"

Granddad fussed with his tie in the mirror. "The check engine light is on and the car doesn't feel right. Sluggish to accelerate, slow to respond to braking. It doesn't feel safe."

No arguing with safety. Blowing out a resigned sigh, Asher picked up his keys and wallet.

"Do you think maybe you could put some nicer clothes on?" This from a man dressed to impress in a navy blazer, grey slacks, blazing white shirt and patterned tie.

Asher spread his arms and looked down at himself—jeans and a short-sleeved plaid shirt. He arched a brow, questioning Granddad's judgment. "I'm the chauffeur. What more do you want?"

Granddad pulled himself up and dug a thumb into his chest. "We Stockdale men have a reputation to uphold."

Asher opened his mouth to protest but gave in without saying another word. He trudged upstairs to his room and put on charcoal trousers and a white button-down shirt. He refused to put on a tie.

Back down in the front hall, he spun a mocking circle before Granddad. "Will this do?"

"Get a sports jacket."

Asher stared at the older man. "July is too hot for a jacket."

Granddad tugged on the lapels of his own jacket and gave Asher the look.

"People are more casual up here."

Granddad frowned at him and pointed an imperious finger up the stairs.

Asher slouched to his bedroom and got a light grey tweed jacket.

"Better." Granddad headed towards the garage. "C'mon, get the lead out. The boat sails at six thirty and I don't want to miss the cruise."

Asher was still laughing at Granddad's high anxiety as they climbed into the SUV.

"Believe me, I'm as sorry as you are to pull you into my social life on my first date with Jean. There is no way I'm driving this monster of yours. I'm an old man and can't adapt so easily."

Asher cut a suspicious glance across the gearshift. Granddad only used the old-man line when he was up to mischief. He'd used it twice in as many days. And Granddad's Caddie was no small vehicle.

Asher turned right onto Bay Street. Further up the near-empty street, Emma and Jean, both in pretty summer dresses, stood on the sidewalk in front of the closed china shop. His heart did a little happy dance of surprise. "You didn't say Emma was coming."

"I didn't know. Honestly."

Asher shot Granddad a look, which the *old man* failed to meet. Yep, way too much protesting going on.

"Well, we're here now. So let's not fuss about it." Granddad carried on as if no question hung in the air.

Asher pulled up and Granddad jumped out of the car. He

kissed both women on the cheek and very deliberately escorted Emma to the front seat. He helped Jean into the back and climbed in beside her.

Asher glanced in the rear-view mirror. The two seniors grinned, oh so innocently, back at him. Yep, Jean was in on it. Asher turned to Emma. She sat primly buckled in, hands folded, eyes forward, a little pale, a lot tense. A sudden grin swept across his face. Nope, Emma wasn't in on it. That made his day.

He put the car in gear and completed the trip to the marina where the crew of the family-run *MV Chippewa III* waited for passengers to board for the sunset dinner cruise.

They strolled to the foredeck to watch the small green-and-white vessel manoeuver past the swing bridge and through the first channel. At 6:30 in the evening in early July, sunset was a few hours away. Coolness rose from the atypically smooth water and balanced the heat from the sun-soaked deck. Gulls followed in their wake, squawking for handouts. As they passed one cottage on the port side, a teenager ran out, bounced off a trampoline and executed a perfect swan dive into deep water. The folks on board cheered and clapped. The show-off hoisted himself out of the water, took a bow, and waved them on their way.

Asher propped himself on the railing close to Emma. She stiffened but didn't move.

He aimed for impersonal conversation, pointing out various features and creatures on the shore as they cruised by, a deer, an otter, a windswept pine. She relaxed by slow degrees until she laughed at his lame puns.

"I'm sorry—" she began.

"I apologize—" he started.

"After you—"

"Ladies first." Gesturing with an open hand and a slight bow, he invited her to speak.

She nodded and turned her head, a faint glow in her cheeks. "I'm sorry Jean and Horace put you on the spot with their tricks. I didn't ask Jean to do this."

"I didn't think you had. I apologize for the same thing. I admit I'm a bit embarrassed." He tapped her shoulder to draw her gaze back to his. "I also have to admit I'm glad they did."

She tipped her head. "You are?"

"Yes, very glad."

She stared up at him, prodding his intentions. He held onto his smile and braced himself for anything from a slap in the face to a full-on kiss. Hesitantly, she raised her hand to hover at his temple.

His breath stalled, waiting for the delicate stroke of a fingertip over the scar from the paddle. "Your cut's healed." Then, as if she couldn't resist, she slid a light caress down his cheek.

He cupped her hand laying on the ship's rail, squeezed lightly, and released her. He longed to take her somewhere private and kiss away her resistance. Or at least get her to talk.

A light breeze wafted by, bringing the deeper chill of open water. She reached for the fluffy white shawl hanging over her arm. The fabric twisted as she wrapped it around herself.

"Here, let me do it for you." He took the shawl, untwisted it, and held it open.

With a flickering smile of thanks, she turned her back. Her shoulders, exposed by the straps of her yellow dress, bore a sprinkling of freckles. He tucked his lips between his teeth to control his need to kiss each one.

She shivered again though the breeze had dropped as the ship manoeuvred between the high granite cliffs of the Hole in the

Wall channel. He drew the soft fabric around her, hiding the smooth temptation and let his hands rest on her upper arms. She tipped her head and rubbed her cheek on his wrist. Her skin was softer and warmer than her shawl.

His chest swelled at the tender gesture of gratitude. Lowering his head, he planted a brief kiss on her temple. She stepped forward, leaving a small gap between them. Cautiously, ready to withdraw at the least resistance from her, he placed his hands on the railing to shelter her within his arms.

She smiled at him then snuggled into her shawl.

A strong sense of unfamiliar rightness settled in him.

Strands of her chestnut hair drifted against his mouth, tickling his lips. He moved his head to free the strands. No sooner had he resumed position; he got entangled again. Images rose of her curls lying across his bare arm, her head snuggled on his bare shoulder.

She pivoted to look behind the vessel at the raucous gulls. Her hip brushed the front of his slacks. He stifled his groan. The ship's bell rang, calling the diners to their meals. Asher breathed a sigh of longing and relief as Emma slipped away.

Jean led the way past four tables in the tiny central cabin and out to the open-air aft deck. Five more tables were arranged two-by-two against the steel sides of the boat. Brightly coloured plaid tablecloths fluttered beneath the dark-green canopy. Matching cushions in white wicker chairs invited guests to be comfortable. Grey carpet muffled their steps on the steel deck.

Jean and Horace took places on one side of the table in the curve of the stern, ensuring Asher and Emma sat beside each other. The waiter came by to pour water and ask for their drink selections to go with the pre-set menu.

Jean tucked her hand into Horace's elbow and tipped her head towards the others. So far, so good.

Horace winked his agreement.

Even from across the table, Jean got a little warm watching Emma and Asher. They suited each other. Sure, they had issues with previous relationships. Who didn't these days? Unlike herself, who'd married the first man she kissed, spent decades with him, raised two children with him, and buried him. She and Terrence had always— Blinking madly at the sudden gush of sentimental tears, she quickly withdrew her hand.

Drawn by her hasty movement, Horace frowned. Without speaking, he passed her his handkerchief under the table. Staring out over the water to the islands beyond, she wiped her eyes.

Emma and Asher broke off their conversation.

Piffle. "Dust in my eyes," Jean replied to their curious gazes.

They nodded and re-focused on each other.

She handed his handkerchief back to Horace and lowered her voice. "Thank you. My husband and I always celebrated special events on this cruise. He's been gone so many years now, I feel silly for choking up."

He covered her hand with his large warm palm, comforting her. "Don't. I know exactly what you mean. I sold a great house because I couldn't bear to be in it without my Erica. I thought a senior's residence would ease the loneliness." Horace had lowered his voice as well.

The boat thrummed beneath her feet, as she searched for the words she needed. "Do you feel... homeless... sometimes?"

A small crease appeared between his eyebrows. "Because you're at Emma's?"

"No, she's wonderful, like visiting family. It's so hard to explain... living at the Cedars is lovely, but...." She huffed, frustrated by her inability to express herself.

He stroked his moustache as he pondered. "I think I understand. Is it because it's not a real home? More like a dormitory. It feels temporary even when you know it's not."

She jumped in her seat. "Yes. Exactly. Home, yet not home."

His smile faded. "I miss having my own front door."

"I miss having my own kitchen."

"I miss having two bathrooms."

"I *don't* miss *cleaning* three bathrooms."

Horace's gust of laughter at her little joke reminded Jean that she also missed sharing laughter with a man.

"Have you ever thought of moving back into a house of your own?"

Jean pursed her lips. "Not really. I went into the Cedars three years ago because my family worried about my safety. Even though living in a retirement community has its problems, I don't want to upset them again."

Though try as she might, the tantalizing thought of independence stayed in her mind for the rest of the evening.

Hours later, back at the dock, Emma waited while Asher chatted with the *Chippewa's* captain about using his older teen children as waiters. Jean and Horace had disembarked and now strolled hand-in-hand across the parking lot towards the car. Streetlights buzzed to life. Lights popped on in the houses strung along the forested slopes opposite the marina. Rising behind the trees, the moon laid a glittering path on the water. Timeless and unchanging, the rhythm of the town had slowed and quieted.

She started when Asher placed a hand at her lower back to nudge her down the gangway.

"Something wrong?" His gaze followed hers. "Are you nervous about Granddad and Jean getting together?" His deep voice held a note of impending censure.

"Yes. No. A little." She sighed.

"That was decisive." His smile softened his teasing tone. "I doubt there's anything to worry about. They're not clueless kids." On solid land, he entwined their fingers as they followed the older couple into the long grey twilight.

Emma savoured the pricking awareness under her skin caused by Asher's touch. "True. It just seems so fast, impetuous."

"They'll be fine."

"Why would a person want such a drastic change at their time of life?"

"Because they like each other and it feels good to find someone to not be lonely with?"

She conceded with a lopsided shrug. In her head, the argument continued. Change is bad. Change is scary. Change hurts every time; Mom and Dad, Nico, school, Gran. All gone. Fate didn't care whether you had enough. She just kept handing out more.

"They've both weathered a lot of change in their lifetimes, death of spouses, friends, a child in Jean's case. They've had plenty of good change as well. Career success, homes, three generations of family after them. Their attitude is awesome. I want to be like them when I grow up."

His hopeful attitude grated on Emma's fear, wearing it down.

Well ahead of them, Nana Jean and Horace stopped. Horace

laughed at something Nana Jean said. She placed her hands on his chest and continued to talk, making him laugh harder. As if he'd done it a hundred times, Horace drew Nana Jean into a tight hug, rocking her from side to side. They stopped laughing and grinned. Their joy in each other glowed brighter than the stars.

Emma gazed up into Asher's dark eyes. She took his other hand in hers and put his hands at her waist. His smile seeped into her, unfurling hesitant blooms of hope.

So far in her life, change had been a beast, with spurs. Could change be a good thing? Was she brave enough to take a risk?

She raised her face, inviting a kiss. Maybe it was past time to find out.

He kissed her softly, a gentle touch of his lips against hers, once, twice, and eased back. "Okay?"

"Oh, yes." She rose on her toes, wrapped her arms around his neck and dove head first into his welcome. Heat rose in her, slid through her veins and warmed every cell in her body. He hummed deep in his chest and pulled her flush against him. Desire lit her soul.

Change could go take a long walk on a short pier.

"Nana Jean, Nana Jean! I'm here!" Hayley's shout preceded her charge up the outside staircase. The energetic thirteen-year-old bounced into Emma's apartment and flung her arms around Jean's shoulders.

Jean steadied herself against the happy onslaught of her great-granddaughter's hug.

"Yay for Saturday! We did muffins two weeks ago and cake last week. Are you ready to make Dad's butter tarts like you said?"

"Yes, everything's all set for this perfect day for your lesson."

"What makes it so perfect? Aren't all days the same?"

"The lard and butter in pastry like a cool breezy day."

Hayley tucked her chin, her brows pinched with scepticism. "That's silly. Butter can't tell what temperature it is."

"What happens when you put cold butter on hot toast?"

"It melts."

Jean waited.

Hayley tipped her head. "So, when you make pastry you want the butter to stay cold? Why?"

"Your pastry will come out flakier if the fat stays hard."

"What do you make on a warm day?"

"Bread. The yeast likes it cozy."

"So, we go with the dough." Hayley twinkled for a bit then her smile faded. "You didn't get my joke."

Jean thought fast and hard. "Oh, go with the flow. Of course. How clever you are."

"Lindsey and I are writing down our word jokes."

"They're called puns." Jean immediately wished she could take back her teacher-ism. No wonder some people got tired of listening to her.

"Thanks, Nana Jean."

Jean regarded her granddaughter suspiciously, expecting teenaged sarcasm. "For what?"

"Teaching me stuff and making me smarter." Hayley tapped her temple.

Jean's jaw slackened. "You don't mind the lectures?"

"Well, sometimes you go on about it a bit much, but only because you want me to be smart. I want to be smart, so, it's all good."

Tears pressed against Jean's eyes.

"And I'm so glad you're at Emma's, and not at the Cedars, so we can go with the dough and make pastry because it's a perfect day for it." Hayley hugged Jean quick and hard before scooting into the small kitchen and started pulling bowls from the cupboard.

Jean stood, blinking and stunned, as gratitude swirled through her. Giving herself a shake, she followed Hayley at a more moderate pace. She took two aprons off the hook on the back of the pantry door, swathed her precious Hayley in one and they got down to work.

Several hours and many laughs later, two dozen raisin butter tarts cooled on the counter. Flour dusted the floor at the base of the cabinets and floated through the air in a victory dance. Hayley slumped at the table with her chin propped atop her hands, her elbows splayed and her eyelids drooping. Jean hooked her great-granddaughter under the armpits, scooped her from the chair, and guided her to stretch out on the couch. She covered the sleeping teen with the afghan and stroked the sandy curls.

Love overwhelmed Jean for this girl she hadn't known until two summers ago. Tears of deep joy and aching sorrow clogged Jean's throat. Hayley resembled her daughter, Francie, who'd succumbed to cancer shortly before the girl had been born. For years after Francie's death, Jean had existed in a grey limbo of grief. Then Cathy had come back to Clarence Bay with Hayley, and everything had changed. Hayley's bright curious spirit had stuck restless fingers into the murky waters of depression, stirred them up and lifted Jean into the everyday light. Myra's death had threatened to send Jean back to limbo. Ryan's two children reminded her of the life she had stopped living.

She was a long way from dead, and she wanted more. More life, more living.

A knock sounded at the outside door. Through the large glass panel, Horace waved and beamed a greeting. Jean's melancholy dissipated like a sour stench in a fresh breeze. A grin creased her face, and she crept over to open the door to the more of everything she had in mind.

"Shh," she warned, finger at her lips. She stepped outside to the landing, closing the door behind her. "Hayley's snoozing."

Horace peeked past her shoulder and through the door. "What'd you do to her?"

"We made raisin butter tarts. And a huge mess."

He rubbed his hands together and boyish greed glinted in his dark eyes. "May I have some, please?"

"You can take four for you and Asher. Now don't pout. Be happy you get so many because they're meant for my grandson Ryan."

An awkward stillness bloomed. Jean hadn't seen Horace since she'd impulsively kissed him on the dock after the sunset dinner on Wednesday. Did he want another kiss? Did she want to give him a kiss?

He reached out, released the fabric of her apron from the torment of her twisting fingers, and took her hands in his. The gentle stroke of his thumbs feathered goose bumps up her arms and neck.

She sighed at the release of tension.

Smiling, he pulled her closer and wrapped her arms around his waist until she clasped hands in the small of his back. He circled his arms around her and stepped a little closer.

He heaved a hugely satisfied sigh. "Now tell me how much you missed me."

"I didn't miss you at all."

He pressed a soft kiss to her temple. His moustache tickled her forehead.

"Well, maybe a bit."

He nudged her head to one side and nipped her earlobe.

"Okay, some. I missed you some."

She rose on her toes and gave him the deep kiss she wanted all along. She was twenty years old again, a hot young thing plastering herself against her man with total abandon.

He broke the kiss on a loud gasp for air, steadying her as she swayed. "Damn, but you do that mighty fine. I've a mind to take you home for some afternoon loving."

She grinned up at him like a young fool. "I think I just might take you up on your offer." Then she laughed at his stunned expression. "Did you think I was going to give you some stupid argument about being too old?"

His jaw flexed, but no words came out.

"Is Asher home?"

He appeared so puzzled, Jean smiled. When the name came to him, he blushed with chagrin. "Yes, he is. And so is the piano tuner."

She pouted playfully. "Shame that. We'll have to make it another time."

Below the couple, Emma stopped with one foot on the bottom stair and a hand on the railing. The sound of voices drifted down from the deck outside her apartment.

Jean and Horace were up there smooching.

A spurt of envy tweaked her stomach. What was Asher up to at the moment? Would he be interested in a bit of smooching? She grinned to herself. If his response to their kisses on Wednesday was any indication, it was a very stupid question.

But she had to get upstairs. "Make what another time?" she called up to interrupt them. She chuckled as the older couple sprang apart. "As if I couldn't guess." Emma climbed the stairs and checked out their oh-so-innocent yet horrendously guilty expressions. She questioned Nana Jean with a look. "Weren't you supposed be making butter tarts with Hayley today? Instead of sucking face like a teenager?"

Emma laughed aloud at Nana Jean's affronted false modesty.

"None of your business, my girl—"

"I dropped by to ask Jean on a date," Horace interrupted. "Now, if you don't mind?" He pointedly opened the door for Emma to pass through.

Still grinning, Emma squeezed past the pair and into her apartment. "Horace, after Jean says yes, join us for coffee and those tarts I can smell from here."

Julia minded the shop today, so Emma had gone to her favourite boutique. By the time she dropped her bag of new clothes in her bedroom and used the washroom, Hayley was sitting up in a sleepy-eyed stupor. "Hi, Emma."

"Hi, sweetie. Did you have a nice nap?"

The teenager yawned hugely and stretched. "Yeah. Can we have some butter tarts?"

"I'm putting the coffee on. Would you like some milk?"

"Can—may I try some with you guys?" No doubt about it, the girl had definitely spent time with Jean.

"Uh, sure." Emma took down a demitasse, a tumbler, and three mugs.

Hayley yawned her way to the washroom.

Emma would have an early dinner then take over shop duty at six until the doors closed at nine o'clock. While setting the round table, Emma threw quick glances out to the landing. Though Jean and Horace kept their physical distance, a wall of intimacy had sprung up around them. They shared a joke about a paper in Horace's hand. Their low laughter rippled through the nearby open window.

If Emma weren't so happy for them, she'd be jealous; but only for a moment. She knew where to find kisses of her own. A smug little smile hitched a corner of her mouth.

The couple entered, and Horace handed her a flyer for the grand re-opening of the drive-in theatre.

"You want to borrow my car?" she guessed.

Horace smoothed his moustache and Jean blushed. "Your car's a little cramped for a fellow my size. We want to borrow your person."

"Huh?"

Horace and Nana Jean exchanged glances. "We want you to come with us tonight to keep Asher company in the front seat."

Emma shook her head and backed into the kitchen. "Ah. That would be a no, heck no."

"We want to use his SUV, but I hate driving the monster. Please come so he won't feel like a third wheel."

"Take who where?" Hayley asked as she returned to the room. "And can I come?"

"Asher and Emma to the movies with us, and no, you can't come because the movie is rated for adults."

Hayley pouted for a second or two then eyed Jean and Horace's clasped hands. "Are you guys dating?"

They exchange twinkling smiles. "Yes, I suppose we are," Jean said.

"Are you getting married? Can I be your flower girl? Before I get too old."

Emma suppressed her laughter at Hayley's obsession. Even though she'd been a flower girl for her mother and father, she still wanted more.

"Umm." Nana Jean hedged.

"None of your business, young lady," Horace said.

Hayley gave a sage nod. "That's what people say when they don't actually know."

Yep, thirteen going on thirty with a psych degree thrown in for extra measure.

Jean turned to Emma. "So, please will you come?"

She dawdled over a precise pouring of coffee. "You're not playing tricks again, are you?"

"Asher said he'd take us wherever we wanted to go."

"Don't you like Asher?" Hayley asked.

Only enough to want to unbutton his shirt, run her hands over his chest and down— she shut off the streaming video in her head and sipped her coffee to cool down. "I'm not sure. I guess he's okay." *Liar, liar, pants on fire.*

Nana Jean and Horace were only slightly successful at keeping their laughs under wraps.

"Then go to the movie. It's just sitting in a car. Right?" Hayley sipped at her coffee, black like her dad took it. She grimaced and took another sip. "Like me and this coffee, if I hadn't tried it, how would I know if I liked it? Same with you and Asher. If you don't try him—" She broke off and stared around the table at the three adults weak with laughter. "What's so funny?"

Tears streamed down Emma's face. Never had the thought of

change, of trying out a new future, come with laughter.

"You did it again, didn't you?" Asher faked a frown at his grin-ning grandfather. "You arranged a date for me." They both knew Asher was happy about it, but the correct form was that he shouldn't be. Asher stood outside Granddad's bedroom while the older man rooted in a dresser drawer.

Asher glanced at his watch. "Time for us to go." He hurried down the stairs, heading for the garage. So what if they were go-ing to be early. He wanted to maximize his time with Emma.

"Hey, wait up!" Granddad hustled after him.

"What movie are we taking the ladies to see?"

"*From Here to Eternity*," Granddad informed him as they climbed into the SUV and pulled into the street. "The classic with the hottest beach scene ever."

Asher turned onto Bay Street and stopped in front of the closed shop. "Emma knows about this date, right?"

Granddad winked. "Jean says Emma wants to get to know you better."

"Seriously?" Asher still didn't have a crystal-clear idea of what Emma expected between them. He was still nervous she might pull back like she had before. With all the summer people de-manding his medical attention and her shop time, they still hadn't talked about their differences. Asher suspected a little avoidance in the lack of a meeting as well.

"Yes. Did you think we'd force her to see you against her will?" Granddad slapped a hand to his chest. "What kind of man do you take me for?"

"Sneaky, manipulative, and bent on having your own way. And

I love you for it."

"Got it in one." Granddad got out and double-stepped up the stairs. For an *old man*, he could move when he had somewhere he wanted to be.

Beneath his grumbling, desire thrummed in Asher's blood. Maybe the evening wouldn't be so bad after all.

What a freaking nightmare. Granddad and Jean were wrapped around each other in the back seat. Deborah Kerr and Burt Lancaster were wrapped around each other on the screen.

Emma squirmed in the bucket seat beside him. Her denim skirt rode a little higher.

Lust wrapped around Asher, hard and tight.

He thrust himself out of the SUV, cursed when the remote drive-in speaker clattered to the ground. The occupants of the back seat didn't notice. Emma startled, pop-eyed and questioning.

"Sorry. Going for a walk. I'll be back."

He reset the speaker and sauntered along the rows of vehicles, headed for the line of trees surrounding the parking area. Foggy windows and the telltale rocking rhythm of a van tightened his gut.

If the wheels be a-rockin', don't come a-knockin'. Maybe if he found a cigarette somewhere and pretended it was all over, the pressure in his groin might ease up. Except he didn't smoke.

He settled on top of a picnic table, feet on the bench, and tipped back on his elbows to stare up at the star-packed sky. He picked out the brightest stars in the Big and Little Dippers and Orion's belt. A satellite moved through the heavens. An airplane blinked its route through the dark. Did anyone up there gaze down at the lights of humankind?

Footsteps in the gravel pulled his attention back to earth. He shoved up to a sitting position. The pressure surged back even stronger.

"May I join you?" Emma said. The flickering light from the movie screen backlit her figure, making her appear haloed, ethereal, as delicate as the china ladies she sold.

He moved quickly to one side of the table. Emma planted her delectable butt well apart from him and supported herself as he had done to gaze at the night sky. Soft deep shadows lay over her lovely face.

"Are you thinking what I'm thinking?" she asked.

About having my way with you under the stars? He propped his elbows on his knees to cover his body's response to his inappropriate thoughts. "Couldn't say. What are you thinking?"

"It's starting to feel like we're chaperoning a pair of horny teenagers around. Only, because they're old enough to know worse, we're supposed to not see."

He huffed a laugh. "Doesn't stop the sounds from the back seat though, does it?"

She groaned and rolled her eyes. "Lordy, so embarrassing. Never too old, etcetera."

He ran his palms along his thighs to steady his nerves. Sometimes the dark afforded the best place to ask and answer hard questions. He drew a breath and blew it out. "Why do you believe the differences between us should keep us apart?"

She sat up abruptly, wrapped her cardigan snug then wrapped her arms over top. "What do you mean?"

"You said we wouldn't suit each other because we come from

two different worlds. I think I get it, but I need to be sure."

She frowned. "Why?"

He clasped his hands. "Because I—" what were his precise feelings about her? "care about you."

"As a friend?" Her voice laced a hint of sarcasm in the question.

"No. More than a friend. I'm not sure how much more, but definitely more." He touched her shoulder. "What about you? More than a friend?"

She dropped her arms, dipped her head and nodded.

Hope swelled within him and warmed the nervous chill out of his blood. He picked her hand up from the table between them and intertwined his fingers with hers. Her arm tensed though she didn't withdraw. "Why don't we belong together, Emma?"

Her feet twisted side-to-side like windshield wipers. "You and your family are rich, well-travelled, well-educated. I'm not any of those things. I've seldom been out of Clarence Bay. I didn't finish college. I'm so far from rich it's ridiculous. Your mother was right. I don't belong with you." Crossing her ankles, she tried to take her hand back.

He held firm. "Would you let my mother choose where you live?"

She stopped pulling on his hand and gazed straight at him. "No."

"Would you let her tell you how to manage your business?"

"Of course not. She doesn't know anything about it." Indignation laced her voice and showed in her stiff back.

Hiding a smile, he paused. "Then why would you let her decide anything else about your life?"

Her chin rose. "Your mother has no rights in *my* life. She does, however, have rights in *yours*."

"My mother has definite opinions about my life and she's not afraid to express them." He acknowledged his mother's outspokenness with a wry tug of his mouth. "But my mother can be wrong. Very wrong at times. If I want to be with you, I will. Unless *you* tell me otherwise, here I am." He stood, opened his arms and prayed she'd jump into them.

Emma gazed at the tall handsome man before her, arms open in invitation. She was in his arms before her next breath, spun about in a fierce welcoming hug. His madly happy grin as he set her down twisted Emma's insides. Rising on tiptoe, she wrapped her arms around his neck and kissed him, passionate and open. She took his surprised breath into herself. He tasted of popcorn, root beer, and desire. He smelled of sandalwood, man, and passion; felt of strength, gentleness, and a raging hard-on. She flattened her breasts against his chest, swivelled her hips to bring them in line with his erection. She gulped down another of his surprised breaths. Did he think she was a virgin? True, it had been such a very long time.

His hand on her butt pressed her tighter against him.

Lust flared to life from its deep sleep, consuming her with fire. Some things were worth waiting for.

A prolonged horn blast from the rocking van startled every person in the drive-in. Even the people on the screen happened to turn and stare outwards. Laughter rippled from many vehicles.

Emma and Asher broke apart and joined in the amusement.

"Do you think the blast stopped the seniors in my car? Is it safe to go back?"

"Do we knock or what?" She started to walk forward, but Asher held her back.

"What do you say to ditching the seniors next time and going out just the two of us?"

She stared up into his eyes, seeking. What did she want from him? Trust, lust, affection, forever? Whatever.

What did she want from herself?

Good question.

Only one way to find out. "Yes, please."

CHAPTER 7

An Auction is Held

"Now you know how to download pictures, file them so you can find them again, and print them," Emma and Hayley sat side-by-side in Emma's office in the back premises of the china shop. "Next time, we'll talk about cropping your shots to make them look better. In the meantime, keep taking pictures and practicing the setup techniques I showed you yesterday."

"It's better to frame the shot in the camera than to crop the shot on the computer," Hayley summarized the lesson from yesterday.

She smiled at her young friend. "Right."

Emma's desk, a classic roll-top from her great-great-grandmother's day, sat at right angles to a modern table bearing a powerful desktop computer and oversized monitor. A barred door let in sunlight shaded by the upstairs deck. Down the hall was a tiny washroom and a storeroom for all the paraphernalia to support the shop. One shelf in the storeroom held customer orders, including the tureen for Horace to give Asher.

"Thanks for showing me, Emma." Ever since shopping with her mother and buying two *Bunnykins* bowls, Hayley had campaigned for photography lessons. "I'm gonna be an ace photographer, just like you."

Emma unplugged Hayley's flash drive and concentrated on getting the cap on just right. "I'm not an ace photographer."

Hayley pointed at the poster that had started it all, a tree about to be sizzled by lightning. "What's that then? Ugly?"

Emma glanced at the picture. "Not good enough."

Hayley popped her hands on her slender hips. "That's stupid."

"Excuse me?"

Hayley stabbed a finger at one of her own shots still displayed on the monitor. "Even I know mine isn't much. It's blurry, it's crooked, nothing to look at. You told me it had potential. And yeah, I know I'm a kid and you should be nice to me, but c'mon, I know useless." Hayley gazed at the framed photo. "Your picture is freaking awesome. It feels like I'm there. I wanna count the seconds until I hear thunder, so I know how far away the storm is. I know about another awesome picture, because I saw it. If there's two, there's gotta be more."

Emma pretended she had no clue what Hayley meant.

Hayley rolled her eyes and reached for the computer mouse. "Should I find it like you showed me? What day was it?"

"The day you decided we should all go for a swim in a storm," Emma said, hoping the reminder would distract her persistent pupil.

Hayley clicked on the file explorer icon. "Now I really gotta see it."

Emma pushed Hayley's hand off the mouse. "Stop that. If I don't want to show it, I don't have to." Emma rolled her eyes at her juvenile response. Who was the kid in the room?

"So, show me. I was there, I wanna see it."

"So do I." Asher's deep voice cut into the discussion. He leaned in the doorway, smiling widely.

Her face softened into a welcoming smile. "What's up?"

"I dropped in to let you know we have seats for tonight's performance." He pulled two tickets from his shirt pocket. "We're going to see Melody in *The Importance of Being Earnest*. Remember?"

"Yes, of course."

"And to pick up Granddad's order." He gestured at the monitor. "How did your lightning shots turn out?"

"Fine."

"Did you get more than the one shot? The one with the sheet lightning and bug lightning?"

She pulled her gaze from her hands clasped tightly in her lap. "You remember one shot? You saw so many, and you only remember one?"

He nodded. "It's an exceptional shot."

"I saw it. It's awesome," Hayley piped up. "Emma, show it to him."

"Yes, please show it to me." Asher gave her a surreptitious wink.

Emma glanced at Hayley then back at Asher, scolding him with her eyes. He winked again. She shook her head and clicked on the file. The image appeared on her huge monitor.

A prolonged silence from Asher and Hayley greeted the display.

"Wow," Asher said in a hushed voice. He bent over, brushing Emma's rigid shoulder, to get a better view. She pushed her chair sideways to accommodate him.

"Wow, what?" Jean asked from the office door.

"This," Asher moved aside. "Emma took this picture."

Jean stood staring. "Oh, that's wonderful." She turned and called out, "Horace, come and see this."

Flustered, Emma reached to minimize her photo-editing software. Her hand bumped into Asher's as it lay over the mouse, stopping her.

"Don't," he murmured so only she could hear beneath the noise of Horace's arrival. "You deserve the recognition."

Horace entered the room to stand beside Jean. "Incredible. Those *National Geographic* photographers are amazing. I love their website."

"It's not a website, Dr. Stockdale. Emma took it," Hayley said.

"Emma took it? Impressive."

"Yes, she did," said Cathy from the office doorway. "Quite the crowd in here. Let me see." She leaned past Horace to stare at the monitor. "Amazing work, Em." She slipped out of the room. In moments, she came back with Ryan. "This is the picture I told you about." Daniel squealed from the baby pack strapped to his father's chest.

"Wow, Emma, I have no words...."

The din created by all the people in her office pressed on Emma's ears.

No words, no words.

The phrase echoed in her mind. But it wasn't Ryan's awed voice she heard.

She heard Mr. Deacon. Thirteen years ago, the college teacher in Digital Media Studies, had stood at the head of the class, flipping through a stack of her prints. It was the first open critique day of the semester, when the teacher reviewed first-year student portfolios and offered constructive comments in public. The purpose was to toughen students for the real world where anyone and everyone had an opinion. Critique day was always well attended for the sport of watching the victims—students— squirm.

Today, Emma and two others were on the carpet.

She tipped back in her chair, waved to friends across the crowded classroom, and got smiles and a thumbs-up in return. At home, her bulletin board was laden with accolades and awards for her work, from her school, the *Clarence Bay Beacon,* and the college's admissions committee. She was confident of a good critique. Expectation hummed under her skin.

The teacher did a rapid review of the required twelve shots and went back to the beginning for a slower review. He paused a couple of times and waggled his head. Good sign. The best thing he'd ever done was to hold a photo up to the class and say, "Well done".

Emma slid forward in her seat.

He frowned. Bad sign. The worst thing he'd ever done was to tear a photo in half.

Emma absorbed the blow with a deep breath.

He nodded. Better sign.

Emma grinned at her friends. Their smiles anticipated the teacher's approval.

Finished, he tapped the edge of the stack of photos on his desk to square them up. He scanned the room until he found Emma. "They're all very pretty, Ms. Finn. You have an eye for light. Your compositions are nicely framed."

Emma sagged with relief.

The other students sagged with disappointment—nothing to gossip about this time.

"However...."

The class buzzed at the ominous word.

"Your choice of subject leaves much to be desired. None of these will incite a person to action. Where's the outrage, the drive to fix things, to make the world a better place." He riffled through them again. "Where are the people, Ms. Finn? There are no people in these images."

"I-I don't take pictures of people." *Not anymore.*

Mr. Deacon gaped at her. The other students turned in their seats to stare at her.

"Why not?"

"Be-because I don't." She pulled the right side of her upper lip between her teeth and bit down on her newly-acquired scar. The movement tugged at the other new scar beneath her eye. The disfigurement tortured her memory with the last time she'd taken a photograph of a person.

"How do you expect viewers to care about events if you don't show the human impact of those events?"

Struck dumb, Emma stared at him.

"No self-respecting newspaper or journal would give these a second glance. They're too trite, too trivial. I have no words...." He slapped the stack down on his desk. "But they would make a pleasant calendar."

Calendar. On campus, the word described the lowest of the low form of creative work.

The teacher picked up the next victim's submission.

Trite. Trivial. Calendar.

Shame burned its way through her skin to her soul. Shifted about and sat upon, the stack of her photos slithered apart. Several fell to the floor where the teacher trod on them. A cup of tea tipped over, smearing and rippling the images. The sodden mess was shovelled into the garbage can; her work effectively destroyed and dismissed.

She sat there for the remaining hour, numb, fighting back tears, too shocked to be outraged, too proud to storm out. At the end of the class, Emma pretended to be on the phone until the room emptied out. Then she went and pulled her photographs out of the garbage.

In the following weeks, Emma struggled to overcome the blow to her confidence. She ignored the first few times someone called her Calendar Girl. Then others picked up the mockery. As Emma's confidence shrank, so did her effort. By the time she'd left college to care for her grandmother Myra, failure loomed. It had taken years for her artistic soul to recover enough to pick up her camera.

And now, thirteen years later, more scrutiny.

Emma stared at the people crammed into her small office. Melody had joined the group now. All she needed was for her brother Grady and his family to show up and her entire world would be witness to her breakdown.

But the more she listened, the more she heard a difference in the tone of the voices.

No one had noticed her lapse in attention. A warm comforting heat stroked her shoulder. Asher had noticed. She smiled up at him. Apart from the desire always simmering there, she saw pride.

He was proud of her work. After seeing only two pictures and a stream of tiny images, he was proud.

"I remember when the tree on the front lawn at the Moreau place was struck by lightning. It split right down the middle from top to bottom. You could hear the crack in the next street," Ryan said.

"When the Red Rock lighthouse got hit, it burned to the ground. Back in the sixties before any of you were born," Jean said.

"I once saw the CN Tower struck by three lightning bolts at the same time." Horace added.

They were all talking about lightning strikes.

Inspired by her two photos? The possibility thrilled and humbled at the same time.

"You should put it in the auction to raise money for the Cedars renovation, Emma," Hayley's girlish voice broke through the adult chatter.

Dead silence.

In a room overstuffed with seven adults, a baby, and a teenager, silence hummed.

Until a babble-storm broke out; everyone voicing his or her opinion at the same time.

"A fabulous idea."

"About time you got recognized."

"Go for it."

Terror twitched up and down her spine. Emma shuffled her feet. Her head spun, and her palms sweat. Once again, a warm comforting weight settled on her shoulder, and she calmed.

"Okay people, you can stop talking. Should Emma decide to stick her neck out, she knows she has your support." Asher's resonant voice briefly silenced the babble.

They all started talking again. Giving Emma gratifying, terrifying encouragement. All expressing their belief in her.

Why was Emma Finn the only person who didn't believe in

Emma Finn?

Because Emma Finn was an idiot.

A faintly hysterical laugh burst from her. She touched the inside of her scar with the tip of her tongue. She'd made mistakes for which she'd never forgive herself. She accepted that, lived with it every day.

Could she have faith in herself despite her mistakes?

"Hi, Asher." Emma opened her door and sighed at all the male beauty before her. He smiled, and flutters broke out in her belly. No man had ever drawn a response from her like this man did.

"C'mon in, Asher. I'll be right with you." She stepped back to let him in to her apartment. As he passed by her, she admired his tight butt in light green chinos and his broad back under white cotton. A fine nervous tremor radiated out from the clench deep in her belly. As theatre-going was a casual affair in Clarence Bay, she wore her brand new pink flowered capris and a coordinating blouse. She also, currently, wore only one pink loafer. Her bare foot sported pink nail polish.

A smile kicked up one side of his face. "Need any help, Cinderella?"

Emma wiggled her toes. "I can't find my right shoe. I'm usually a very organized person. For instance," she indicated the glasses and wine bottle on the table, "would you like a drink before we walk to the theatre?"

"No thanks. Go find your shoe, and we'll take our time walking over."

Emma found her shoe hiding in the bottom of her closet. On the way down Bay Street to the theatre, hand-in-hand, she half-listened to Asher telling a story about his grandfather.

"And then Granddad climbed on the ostrich and flew off into the sunset," Asher said as he held open the plate glass door for Emma to enter the theatre.

"Hmm," Emma replied as she wandered to the other side of the lobby to stare out the window. Sensing herself alone, she looked around for her boyfriend.

Asher stood by the entrance, receiving their stubs from the ticket taker. He winked at her as he crossed the modern glass-and-concrete lobby towards her.

With shame prickling her cheeks, she gave him a quick apologetic hug. "I'm so sorry."

He stroked her temple, tucked a bit of hair behind her ear. "A little preoccupied, are you?"

She pressed her cheek against his warm palm. His strength seeped into her and settled her rushing thoughts. "Just a bit." She sighed and gave him a grateful smile.

"Do you want to talk about it?"

"I think so."

"Do you want to skip the performance?"

"No. You paid for the tickets. We can talk later."

The gong sounded, calling the audience to their seats. The set of an 1890s gentleman's room filled the simple wooden stage flanked by black velvet curtains. Soaring stone-veneered walls enclosed three levels of seating. The moment the lights dimmed, her mind started whirring like a pinwheel in a stiff breeze.

To show or not to show. Emma drummed her fingers on the arm of her seat. Safety or jeopardy. Obscurity or limelight.

Asher's hand slid over her busy fingers. "Stop thinking and enjoy the show."

On stage, Melody charmed the audience as an Englishwoman named Gwendolen who had a thing for men called Ernest.

Emma ran a fingertip over the scar on her right cheekbone. Her knee bounced up and down. To show or not to show.

"Emma, if I guarantee we'll talk about it later, will you stop making yourself crazy?"

Throwing him a sheepish smile, she forced her body to stillness and focussed on the stage.

The characters were in a house somewhere. The gentlemen kept changing their names, confusing her. A handbag looking more like a small valise was somehow important. Emma gave up trying to make sense of it. Someday, she'd ask Melody to explain it. A hearty round of applause with a smattering of standing ovation concluded the show.

"Did you want to go backstage and congratulate Melody on a performance you didn't see?"

"No, thanks. I sent her flowers on opening night." Once outside, Emma led the way to the pier. Streetlights and a full moon lit the way for Emma and Asher to stroll through the warm summer night to Emma's apartment. Jean was out with Horace, so Emma and Asher had the place to themselves.

She poured wine and they sat outside on her small deck. A citronella candle kept the mosquitoes at bay. A water-scented eddy of air danced with the tiny flame. Crickets chirped in the friendly dark.

She drew a steadying breath. "I'm terrified."

"To show your work?"

She nodded.

"Why?"

In fits and starts, her voice trembling, she told him of the college incident and its repercussions. She'd never shared the experience. The shame, pain, and humiliation had kept her silent all these years. The damaged photos, stuffed in the back of the bottom drawer of her desk, reminded her of what happened when she put her work on display.

He listened and didn't interrupt. When she uttered her last word, he stared at the cliff on the opposite side of the bay. He drank his last mouthful of wine and cleared his throat.

"The way I see it, you were trashed by a staff member with an overblown ego and then bullied by pathetic, small-minded students. The teacher should have been fired and the students disciplined. It's a wonder you even *look* at a camera, never mind pick one up, go on location, and come back with such amazing images. You are a strong, courageous woman, Emma Finn, and I applaud you."

She straightened from her hunched-over posture and blinked at him. Her fists loosened. The tight band twist-tied around her soul fell away. She drew a deep free breath, the deepest, freest breath since the event.

"What about before? Did you show before you went to college?"

"Yes. An art store, gone now, had a group show for local artists. I had a spotlight." She squared her shoulders. The lovely memory, once blurred by her pain, glowed again in her mind.

His gaze locked with hers. "You were a good photographer. And now you're a better photographer." The assertion in his voiced showed no doubt in his mind.

"Thank you. I know I should have toughed it out, but Gran needed me, and I took the easy escape route."

"I wouldn't call it easy to suffer like you did for all these years."

She huffed her agreement. Her mind replayed the event from her college days, reviewed her photographic endeavours in a new framework. The townsfolk must have thought her eccentric.

But she would worry about them another day. Right now, a gorgeous, wonderful, intelligent man deserved a great big kiss.

She rose from her chair and extended her hand to him. "Come with me."

His dark hair glinted in the candlelight. He looked from her hand to her eyes. A slow smile crept across his face. He clasped her hand. She drew him into her dark apartment and locked the door.

Wrapping her arms around his neck, she rose on her toes and took his mouth.

His surprise lasted for nanoseconds. His strong arms circled her waist and pressed her to him.

She slid her tongue over his plush bottom lip. With a sharp intake of breath, he parted for her and she swept forward to tangle with his tongue.

Needing to get closer, she wrapped a leg around his waist. He slid his hands down over her butt and lifted her, spreading her thighs. Her ankles locked at the small of his back.

Hands gripping her butt, he thrust his hips forwards, drove his hardness against her. With a soft growl, she arched into him, increasing the hot sweet pressure.

Panting for air, she broke the kiss, and dropped her feet to the floor. He cupped her head as she rested her head on his shoulder. The beat of his blood thumped under her ear. Lifting her head, she gazed into his dark eyes.

For better or worse, she was changed. No, not changed. With

his passionate soul and dispassionate view, he had given her back to herself. Reawakened her dormant confidence.

Enough to risk the change involved in her next step?

She smiled. From the depths of her being, with all the rekindled joy in her heart, she smiled. "Will you stay with me tonight, Asher?"

His answering smile softened the harsh lust in his face. "Emma love, I'd be delighted to stay with you."

Interlacing her fingers with his, she turned and led him down the hall to her bedroom. She snapped on the bedside lamp. Deep shadows enclosed them in the golden light.

Stepping out of her shoes, she tucked them under her bed.

"Remember where you're putting them," he murmured with a teasing expression.

"Ha. Ha." She let her gaze wander up and down his tall strong body, lingering at his zipper. When she met his eyes, an inferno raged in their dark depths. She slid the tip of her tongue over her bottom lip. His breath caught.

"I want you to take off—my shirt." She dropped her arms to her sides and straightened her posture to present the row of buttons down her front.

His shirt practically vanished, it was gone so quick. Crisp dark curls dusted his bare chest.

"I said *my* shirt," she scolded in her gentlest voice.

Asher glanced at the heap of white fabric on the floor then twitched his brows at Emma. "Shall I put it back on?"

Her eyes twinkled over her crooked smile. "No. I like you the way you are."

"While I'm working on me, why don't I finish the job?" He stepped out of his shoes and stripped off his trousers and briefs.

Naked, he stood proudly in front of her. Her eyes widened when her gaze landed on his cock, gratifying him. He caressed her face. Running his fingers through her soft chestnut hair, he released a light flowery scent.

"You are so beautiful, Emma, you stop my heart."

He planted a row of kisses across her cheekbones. Her eyelids fluttered under his kiss, her lashes tickling his lips. When he touched down on her soft willing mouth, she stole his breath, stopped his heart with an urgency he would never forget.

Buttons abrading his bare stomach reminded him of his task. Lifting his hands, he unbuttoned her shirt, pushed it off her shoulders and down her arms. His mouth watered at the sight of her lacy bra. Freckles dotted the skin of her chest and upper curve of her breasts.

His fingers trembled as he popped the front closure and slid the bra off her shoulders. Her lovely nipples puckered in the cool air. Cupping one breast, he measured its lush silken weight. He rubbed his thumb over her nipple and reveled in her light gasp. Repeating the gesture to raise a tight bud, he lowered his head and pinched the bud between his lips. Her small cry of pleasure echoed through his body. Addressing a ponderous inequality, he treated her other breast to the same pleasure.

He slid his hands down her bare back and encountered fabric. He stepped back. "What have we here?"

"Cap-pris." Her breathy hesitation pleased him no end. As did the fine quiver of her belly beneath his caress. He popped the button and slid down the zipper. A slow slide of his hands from waist to butt to thighs exposed her long sloping curves to his feasting eyes. Bending on one knee, he placed her hand on his shoulder, and together, they got rid of her final pieces of clothing.

He dropped his other knee beneath him, cupped her tight little butt, and drew her to his seeking mouth. Her hips pulsed as he flicked and licked her sweet folds until she grabbed a handful of his hair and came in a glorious back-arching thigh-trembling spasm.

The sight of her pleasure pushed him perilously close to the edge.

He laid his Emma in her bed, donned a condom, and came back in seconds. His breath hitched when she grasped his stiff cock and used it to tow him into place above her.

"You. In me. Now."

"Yes, ma'am. Our pleasure."

Her hot brown gaze locked with his, and a purely wicked grin spread across her face.

He slid in by slow degrees. At full depth, he stilled to absorb the feel of her, the scent of her. Her legs, wrapped tight around his hips, nudged him into a slow-riding rhythm. Her mewling, cooing noises pushed him to a quicker, ever quicker, pace. Her restless hands stilled on his butt, her fingers dug in, and away she went. Keening, soaring, flying. Taking him with her into ecstasy.

Jean blew a goodbye kiss to Horace from the deck, crept into Emma's apartment, and silently closed the door. If not for the mortifying prospect of a morning encounter with Horace's grandson, she would have stayed overnight. Exhausted, she collapsed against the back of the door. She was too old for all this sneaking around.

"Where have you been, young lady?"

Jean shrieked at Emma's sharp words from the darkness, then

blinked against the sudden light from the lamp behind the couch. A mock-stern pyjama-clad Emma closed her book and sipped her tea.

That girl had been lying in wait. "'I've been to London to visit the Queen.'" Jean sassed her with the old nursery rhyme.

"'Pussy cat, pussy cat, what did you there?'" Emma quoted back at her. "And don't tell me how you 'frightened little mouse under her chair.' The whisker-burn on your chin tells me more than I need to know."

Jean stroked a fingertip across her tender skin. Piffle!

"Whatever will the gals at the Stitch & Bitch have to say?" Emma grinned wickedly. "Or will you have a headache tomorrow? Or rather, today?"

The girl took entirely too much pleasure in teasing an old lady. Jean wandered into the kitchen for a glass of water. She flipped on the overhead light, got a clear look at Emma, and started laughing.

The girl sported her own patch of whisker burn. Emma kept grinning.

"Those Stockdale men grow a mean five-o'clock shadow, don't they?" Jean teased.

"That's not all they grow."

"Emma!"

"What? Am I too crude for your young and tender ears, Jean?"

Jean stood tall on the wobbly pillar of her dignity. "Piffle! I'm a great-grandmother I'll have you know."

"Shocking! A woman of your age sneaking around in the middle of the night and up to no good." Emma shook her head.

"Ha! It was very good what I got up to." Jean groaned and put her hand to her head. "What the heck did I just say? I'm so tired

I can't think straight. G'right."

"See you late tomorrow morning. I'll buy the makeup."

Jean shuffled into her bedroom and slid into a bubble bath. Her aching muscles thanked her for the hot water. She'd forgotten the athleticism of it all.

But she'd never forget the sweetness of "I love you" whispered among the pillows.

Emma hurried along Mary Street towards the town park. Today was the outdoor auction to raise funds for the Cedars. Almost every business owner and many residents had donated goods or services to the cause. The town council had expanded the event to include a market. The tented booths of local farmers and food vendors surrounded the grassy area reserved for picnic tables. Triangular pennants strung from trees to lampposts to flagpoles rattled as if participating in the celebration.

Many summer people had joined most of the townsfolk to form a respectable crowd of buyers and bidders. The whole community would do well today.

Emma reached the oak tree centred in the row of maples on the eastern edge of the park where she would meet Asher. Emma wasn't too troubled at his absence. Thanks to a faulty alarm clock, she was way behind schedule. She'd texted him before she left the shop. He hadn't replied yet.

Last week, she'd driven down to Barrie, gone to the printers then to the DIY frame store, and brought home a work of art with her name on it. Along the way, she gathered reassuring compliments. She hadn't told any of her encouraging friends, except Asher. Disappointment flared. Where was he? She so wanted to share this moment with him.

"Sold! To the lady holding card 138! The Cedars Retirement Residence thanks you for your generous donation." The auctioneer, a jazzed-up version of Margaret Thatcher, smacked her gavel on the podium and handed her sales note to her male assistant. The podium sat on the spacious stone platform at the base of the war memorial on the western side of the park.

"The rare and lovely figurine was donated by Finn's Fine China and Gift Shoppe. Thank you for your contribution." The auctioneer clapped her hands and the audience followed along. Distracted from her continuing search for Asher, Emma waved from her position.

"You are Miss Emma Finn?"

Emma turned at the question. An Indian woman with dark doe eyes, smooth brown skin, and bright red lips smiled at her. A red dot adorned her forehead between her brows. Dazzled by the shimmer of metallic embroidery on a gorgeous fuchsia silk tunic over matching trousers, Emma shook the outstretched hand.

"I am Prathiba Nayar, owner of the PK Gallery in Toronto."

The auctioneer's voice called the crowd to order. "Our final item on the block on a beautiful day here in beautiful Clarence Bay is, I'm told, even more rare than the figurine."

"Ah, the moment I have waited for." Ms. Nayar clasped her hands.

Fascinated, Emma caught the twinkle of a diamond nose stud and the gleam of multiple golden bracelets.

The assistant carried a large covered frame to an easel at the front of the stage, lowered it carefully into place, and stood to one side. He grasped the cover by one corner and nodded toward the auctioneer. She laid down her gavel, rested her arms on the podium and scanned the waiting crowd.

The Indian woman fairly vibrated with excitement beside Emma.

"Ladies and gentlemen," the auctioneer began in a conversational tone. "Lots of very fine art has come under my hammer over the years. As an auctioneer, I've been privileged to see many wonderful things. But, this—I have seldom been affected by a work like this one. It hit me right where I live." She patted her chest as if to soothe a racing heart. "Whew! The artist is unknown to the public, though I don't expect that to last more than thirty seconds. What I do expect, is bidding will be lively and reach those puffy white clouds up there."

"Oh, get on with it," Ms. Nayar muttered.

The auctioneer straightened and gestured to her assistant who whipped off the cover.

"This exclusive work entitled *Lightning Bugs* is by Emma Finn."

Her name rippled through the crowd. Faces turned her way. Fear froze the blood in her veins. Shaking like a leaf, she raised her hand in a timid wave.

"Incredible... amazing... talented... great job... well done." A flurry of clapping melded with the words.

"All right, ladies and gents," the auctioneer reminded them of why they were here. "Let's start the bidding at five hundred—a steal for something of this calibre." She pointed at the first raised paddle.

"Five-fifty on the left. Six from behind him."

Bids flowed fast and furious.

"Seven-fifty from the lady in silk, eight...."

"One thousand!" hollered a man from the middle of the crowd.

Emma snatched an astonished breath. Somebody would pay a thousand dollars for her work? She rose on her toes and craned her neck, scanning the crowd for the bidder.

"One thousand one," a woman called.

Emma's gaze snapped to the Indian lady, the gallery owner, waving her paddle like a crazy woman.

Emma listened to the increasing bids in a dizzying spin. The amounts were staggering. Even more startling were the people who put up the bids. Dahlia, Ryan, Greg the vet. Rocco the bar-keep? Some of the faces were as familiar as her own. Total strangers were also bidding for her work. Intent and determined, they all bid and bid and bid until each one bowed out with disappointment.

"Sold! To the lovely lady in silk holding number 162." The hammer fell, and the crowd cheered.

Ms. Nayar flipped her soft shawl over her shoulder and hurried off to collect her prize.

Twenty-five hundred dollars. Emma couldn't believe it. Ms. Nayar from Toronto had paid twenty-five hundred dollars for a photograph by her.

She needed to hug somebody, and dance up and down, and shout with glee. Melody rushed over and swept Emma into an affectionate hug. "You did it, you sneaky thing. I'm so proud of you."

Cathy swooped in next. "The picture looks incredible full size. Well done for being so brave."

Ryan added his congratulations.

"Will you teach me how to make a blow-up?" Hayley joined in.

Her friends continued to share in her triumph, laughed at how

Cathy and Ryan were bidding against each other at one point, and arranged a celebratory dinner.

"I saw Ms. Nayar with you. Did you like her?" Cathy asked.

Emma gave her a puzzled look. "She paid a fortune for my picture. Of course, I liked her."

"She didn't say why she came?"

Emma recalled the introduction. "She said something, but I couldn't hear her over the auctioneer."

Cathy glanced at Ryan. He gave her a brief nod. "She came because I called her. She's an acquaintance of mine from my days in the investment firm in Toronto. She owns an international art gallery, Emma. Asher asked me if I knew anyone and he called her. Don't be mad at us, okay?"

Replaying her friend's rushed words, Emma picked out the important message—without telling her, Asher had arranged for a knowledgeable person to view her work. Gratitude and resentment collided in Emma's stomach.

Cathy touched her arm. "I can see on your face what you think. I'm sorry. Before you get too upset, consider the whole incident may be nothing more than a purchase."

Disappointment joined Emma's turmoil. She rubbed her stomach; a foolish attempt to soothe it.

She needed to talk to Asher. Where *was* he?

In her office, Emma sat at her desk staring at her *Lightning Bugs* image on her screen. She had tried to sort through the sales receipts for Julia's shift, but her attention wandered. Excitement fluttered as she relived the auction in her mind. Asher's absence was the only flaw in a wonderful day. He'd texted by way of explanation.

> I'm in Toronto for a family emergency. Nothing fatal, just private. Sorry I can't explain more. Hope all went well at the auction.

She pinched back the small spurt of annoyance at his secrecy and prayed all was well for him and his family.

The ringing of the bell called Emma to the front of the shop. Ms. Nayar, the silk-clad Indian woman from the auction met her at the counter. She carried a Louis Vuitton attaché case. Her gorgeous high heels had red soles. The modern case and shoes clashed with her traditional garb.

"Miss Finn, please allow me to congratulate you for a wonderful auction result. Five times over estimate is an astonishing debut." Ms. Nayar's British-Indian accent charmed Emma's ears.

Emma wanted to hug the lady to bits but settled for a big smile. "Thank you for buying my photograph and giving the senior's residence fund a huge boost."

"It was entirely my pleasure to win such a coup. I will not sell this work. It is for my private collection. I shiver every time I look at the lightning in the sky and the lightning bugs on the ground. Such curious insects that glow to attract mates. I must try this." She laughed at her own joke. "Howsoever, I have great patience to wait for the precise moment when great talent reveals itself to me. Today I have my reward." She dusted her hands briskly, disposing of the emotion.

Emma walked around the counter to the same side as her visitor and held out her hand. "We have a mutual friend, Cathy Rossetti."

Ms. Nayar shook her hands. "We do. Cathy is very helpful to me with her financial advice, and I am most happy to return the favour. It is welcome to hear she is doing so well in her new home.

Please to say, Miss Finn, have you a portfolio of other marvellous works?"

"I have." Emma flashed back to the mockery of the college teacher. Her nerves tightened with the fear of exposure and rejection.

Ms. Nayar flipped her shawl. "Miss Finn, do you not wish to show your work?"

No sprang to the tip of Emma's tongue. She pulled her scarred lip between her teeth.

Artist seeking to touch people... you were good, now you're better... strong and courageous. Asher's phrases, ringing with pride in her talent, came to her.

She gulped down her fear, squared her shoulders, raised her chin. "Yes. I do want to show my work." Emma gestured, then stood aside to let Ms. Nayar pass through to her office. Emma tapped her computer to life and opened the file of shots she deemed worthy. She invited the gallery owner to sit in her chair and to scroll through the shots at her leisure.

Silence filled the room, punctuated only by Ms. Nayar's slight gasps and murmurings.

Emma stood at her shoulder, almost wringing the blood from her hands. The scent of jasmine wafted from her visitor's glossy dark hair.

After the final shot, Ms. Nayar sighed and stood. "Ms. Finn, you have a talent and skill of the highest order. It will be my honour to represent you." She dug into her case and extracted a large ornate business card and a sheaf of papers. "I came thinking this might be a false lead. I also came prepared for the best. Here is my card and my standard contract. Please to review the terms and we will negotiate to a happy conclusion. I foresee a most lucrative association for both parties." She picked up her case and extended her slim hand for a firm shake. "Thank you again for the privilege of allowing me to view your portfolio. Now, I must hurry back to the city."

The shop bell chimed, concluding a magical session. If not for the papers in her hand, Emma would have dismissed the whole meeting as a wild dream.

Flummoxed, gratified, terrified.

Emma couldn't pick just one emotion from the whirlpool swirling in her heart and head. One powerful emotion floated to the top.

Pride. Emma was proud of her work, her talent, herself.

CHAPTER 8

An Engagement is Announced

Jean sighed and rested her head on Horace's shoulder as they sat on the brown leather couch in Asher's living room. Asher and Emma were out for a Saturday night date. Dinner was over. Empty wine glasses sat on the small table. The coffee maker gurgled in the kitchen.

"The Cedars will be ready to move back in next month. Provided nothing else happens," Horace said. He crossed his legs one way, then the other, then left his legs apart. He tapped his thighs in a jumpy rhythm.

Jean tipped her head in question. He should be relaxed after she'd cooked his favourite meal. "I know. They've sure had their share of problems. Those carpenter ants spread far and wide once they get in."

Horace stroked his thumb over her fingers. "I can't say I'm looking forward to going back."

Soft tingles flowed up her arm. "You like living in a bachelor pad with Asher?" Horace had his own bedroom upstairs, though he had to share the bathroom.

"I do. Even more so when you come over." He gave her a half-hearted wink. "What about you with Emma?"

"I've been on my own for so long, I thought I'd have a hard time adjusting. But, no. Emma's lovely to live with and I'm delighted see her blossoming. Asher's been very good for her."

"They've been good for each other. Asher is happier than I've seen him in years."

The coffeemaker beeped. Her lovely man got up, took the glasses to the kitchen, and returned carrying a tray laden with full steaming mugs and plates of homemade pastry. He placed her things within easy reach for her.

Smiling her thanks, she took a bite of the pastry she'd made this afternoon with Hayley. "I've been trying to put my finger on why it's so different being at Emma's. I've never lived above a shop. You can't beat the commute down the stairs to work, especially when the weather is awful like today."

He sipped his coffee and wiped his moustache with a napkin.

She loved how fastidious he was about his facial hair. "I find it confining to never leave the building, physically and mentally."

"You put into words what I think about the Cedars and other places like it. Being in the same building with the same people all day, every day, isn't the best thing for people."

A thrill flew along Jean's nerves. He didn't dismiss emotions as touchy-feely nonsense. "Yes, yes. If you never even have to go grocery shopping, you turn into a vegetable." She huffed at his smile at her unintended word play. "You know what I mean."

"It's like we're stored in a warehouse to wait for our final move to heaven or wherever. They entertain us, and feed us, and organize us. It's depressing as hell." He dropped his hands between his knees, staring at the patterned area rug between his feet. His fingers twisted and twined around themselves.

Jean waited, holding on to her patience while he worked through whatever he wanted to say.

He took a bite of pastry and a sip of coffee.

Turning to her, he picked up her hand and kissed it. "What do you say we not go back?"

She blinked at him. "Pardon?"

"What do you say we move in together? Into our own house and take back our lives."

The unacknowledged cloud pressing down on Jean thinned and vanished. She straightened, the leather creaking at her sudden movement. "Do you mean that?"

He straightened also, a huge smile beginning to light his face. "Yes, I do."

"Then, yes, I will."

He took her in his strong warm arms and kissed her. Her heart beat the rhythm he had reawakened, pulsing heat through her in ways she never thought to relive.

He drew back and smiled sheepishly. "Umm... I'm doing this backwards. I have one other question for you."

"Bungalow or condo? In town or out?"

"No. Though we do have to figure it out." He slid off the couch, down to one knee and took her hands. "My dearest, loveliest Jean, the first time I saw you, you were so sad, all I could think of was cheering you up. Little did I know you would cheer me up so very much in return. I love you, dear Jean. Will you do me the honour of marrying me?"

Happiness filled every morsel of her being, flooding her with excitement. She leaned forward and tapped his cheek with a finger. "I did wonder if you were going to make an honest woman of me." She smiled. "I'm so happy you came into my life, Horace. Yes, I will marry you."

Many kisses later, Jean voiced her biggest worry. "What will our families say?"

"And now I'd like to propose a toast and make an announcement." Horace raised his glass from the dining room table at the end of the entrée. He'd asked Asher to arrange a family dinner. His grandson had given him a knowing smile, said nothing, and done his duty. He also asked if it was wise to have Jean present for what would likely be a difficult meal. Clever lad, his grandson.

"To Jean Wilson, my future wife," Horace toasted.

His grandson gave an enormous grin, tipped his glass and drained it.

His son Wallace, daughter-in-law Barbara, and granddaughter Tenley turned to stone, their glasses and smiles at half-mast. Horace exchanged amused glances with Asher.

Tenley thawed first. "To Jean Wilson. Whoever she is, I love her for the smile she put on your face." She tilted her glass towards Horace and then to her lips.

Wallace looked to his wife, ready to take orders whenever she decided what they would be. Horace grimaced and shook his head. His son needed to grow a pair.

Barbara set her glass on the pristine tablecloth and put her hands in her lap.

Wallace set his glass down, though he didn't let go. He gave Asher a long questioning look. Asher returned a discreet nod.

Wallace raised his glass to his lips with a slight extra upward lift—a sneaky toast at best.

Barbara scanned the table, pinning each person with knife-like glances. Her face and spine got more rigid with each person who wouldn't back down.

"Who is this person?"

To Horace's left, Asher drew a breath to speak. Beneath the table, Horace pressed on the toe of his grandson's shoe. Asher closed his mouth and sat back.

"Jean is two years younger than me. Retired, of course. A widow with two grandsons and seven great-grandchildren. She is also de facto grandmother to Emma, Asher's young lady."

"Where did you meet her?"

"At the Cedars."

"But who is she? Who are her family?" Barbara's face sank further into lines of disapproval.

"Her family is long-time members of Clarence Bay, not founding members." Horace purposely omitted Jean's grandsons' involvement in the prosperous Mill Lake community. He didn't want to appeal to Barbara's snobbery.

Barbara folded her napkin into a precise rectangle. "Absolutely not. At your age? Ridiculously inappropriate. I won't permit it." She turned to her husband. "Wallace, talk to your father."

Wallace shook his head. "It's not up to us."

"Asher, you must talk some sense into Horace."

"Tell my grandfather, a grown man in full possession of his senses, that he can't marry the woman he loves?" He shook his head. "I don't think so."

"Love," she scoffed. "At his age?"

"Yes, at my age. I'm only seventy-four. I'm not a doddering old fool. Far from it. Jean and I even have sex." Horace whisper-shouted the last word just to crank Barbara. He'd had enough of her.

Tenley choked on a morsel of roast beef.

Barbara's face puckered. "I did not want to hear that."

Horace pulled back his smile. "Too bad. It's a fact of life."

"What about your money?"

Insulted, Horace raised his brows.

"How do you know she's not some gold digger after your money?"

Sitting upright, Wallace directed a frown at his wife. "Barbara, you've stepped over the line now. Leave my father to his own life." Better late than never to grow some.

Barbara refused to back down. "It's a fair question, Horace, and one I'm sure Jean's own family is asking."

Across the street, around back, Jean sat in a Muskoka chair sharing baby-talk with her great-grandson Daniel. The infant, perched on her knees, blowing bubbles and chortling at her. Under her senseless prattle, tension lurked at her upcoming announcement. She sent a wish over the road to Horace.

"Peekaboo!" Ryan's daughter Hayley crouched on the grass beside them and encouraged her little brother.

"She's a funny girl, eh, Daniel?"

"Peekaboo!" On the other side of her chair, Mark's daughter Lindsey popped out from behind her hands.

Daniel flapped his arms and reached for Hayley's curls. She dodged with practiced ease.

Three generations of Jean's family milled about her grandson's yard. Her son-in-law Bucky and her two grandsons Ryan and Mark held a pow-wow around the barbeque. Mark's sons played soccer at the bottom of the yard.

Cathy came out and hefted Daniel off Jean's lap and into her arms. "C'mon now, my little monkey, time for a change and to join your cousin for a nap." The baby protested at being hauled away. His mom continued to talk as she walked towards the house. "You know if you don't nap, you'll be as cranky as the bear that chased Dr. Stockdale."

A glass of white wine hovered in front of Jean. "Oh, thank you, Emma. You're a sweetheart."

Jean sipped gratefully at the cool liquid while Emma sent the girls off to help Lindsey's mother Meg in the kitchen.

"You were telling me about your trip on the way over. Prathiba Nayar organized it?"

Emma, settling in the chair beside Jean, beamed at her. "Yes. I'll pay my share, but she arranged it. Three weeks on a cruise through the North Channel with David Chastain. He's a famous photographer who Prathiba believes would be a helpful mentor for me."

"What does Asher think?"

"He's so pleased for me. Calls it a great opportunity." Emma glowed with her feelings for Asher. "He gave me flowers to celebrate."

"I did wonder where those roses came from," Jean teased.

"You got roses as well. I wonder what for?" Emma teased right back.

Jean's granddaughters, Cathy and Meg, and great-granddaughters, Hayley and Lindsey, carried out bowls and platters of food, then joined them. The women relaxed into chairs. The teenagers flopped on a nearby blanket.

"Who gave you roses, Nana Jean?" Meg asked.

"Horace Stockdale, of course," Emma replied.

The men came up and stood behind their spouses. Except for Bucky, because his Francie, Jean's only child, had died thirteen years ago.

Jean took a sip of liquid courage. "I have an announcement to make."

Everyone stilled and glanced at the others. Small smiles passed between them. They'd already guessed and approved. Jean said it anyway. "Horace and I are getting married."

One and all, her family cheered. Then their loving concern started to flow.

"You're not getting married because you're both lonely, are you?" Bucky asked.

"My Terrence has been gone for many years now. His Erica passed four years ago. We were both lonely. Now we're not. But we're getting married because we love each other."

"Will you take a married suite at the Cedars?" Ryan asked.

"No. We hope you'll set aside one of your bungalows at the Mill Lake development for us. We'll stay with Asher until our new home is ready. Emma, if you don't mind, may I stay with you until the wedding?"

"Of course, you can stay."

Jean expected the response, but it still comforting to know.

"Will you have a housekeeper?" Meg asked.

"Whatever for?"

"To—uh—take care of you."

"We don't need a babysitter, Meg. A cleaner will come in every week to do the heavy work. I'll do my own cooking, thank you very much."

"Can we pay for the cleaner at least?"

"No, thank you, Cathy. Horace and I have more than enough between us."

"When's the wedding? Any idea where you'll hold it?"

"The Saturday after Labour Day in September. An intimate affair in Asher's garden."

Hayley and Lindsey squealed. "Can we be flower girls?"

What had he done to himself?

Tap-tap, tap-tap. Asher tilted back in his office chair and twirled his Montblanc pen around his hand like a tiny baton before he went back to his restless tapping.

This morning, bright and early, he'd seen Emma off at the dock for her three-week tour.

Rustle, rustle. His knee bounced the next patient's file where it rested on his crossed leg.

His ex-wife Sondra had always been, still was, incredibly focussed on her legal career. She travelled the world over by invitation of international governments dealing with children's rights.

Emma leaving for a tour didn't mean she was like Sondra... but it could. Emma seemed nothing like his ex-wife. She had given up college, stayed in her small town, and put her family first. She showed no inclination to chase a career. And yet, she was gone.

His gaze strayed over the patient file in his lap. He stilled and sat forward, placing the file on his desk. Familial... male line... inherited. A rare variation of Horner's syndrome. Huh. He called his receptionist.

"Send Tony Rassenti in, please, Pia."

"He's on his way," Pia's chipper voice replied.

"Hey, Doc." An eighteen-year-old Italian man swaggered into the office and sat in the patient chair. "How's it hangin'?"

"I'm fine. How have you been since the last check up?"

"Same as always, Doc."

"No changes in your depth perception, acuity, light sensitivity?"

"Nope, same as always, like I said."

"Okay. What brings you in today?"

"Same as always. To get my Horner's syndrome checked. It's not life-threatening or anything. What a pain in my ass." He sounded so put-upon Asher struggled to hide his smile. Granddad's lecture on how lucky we are to live in modern times echoed in Asher's head, but he held that in as well.

He pointed at the letter chart on his office wall. "Can you read out the fourth line for me, please?"

A while later, Asher got to the unique aspect of the young man's case.

"Your file says Horner's syndrome runs in your family."

"Symptoms are ptosis and anisocoria. No evidence of disease or trauma to cause the syndrome. There aren't any known risks associated with the syndrome. It just is. But I get checked every three years to document any changes."

Asher nodded. Tony had researched the syndrome to know the medical terms for drooping of the upper eyelid and pupils that dilated unequally.

"My grandpa, my dad, and kid brother all have it. My older brother had it. None of the girls have it."

"Your brother *had* it?"

"Yeah, Nico. He died in a car crash when he was twenty. I was five."

Asher checked Tony's birthdate. "Thirteen years ago."

Tony nodded. "Yeah, the whole family is still pissed off at him 'cause he was high on weed and drunk when he crashed. Killed himself and two other kids. Dad won't let anyone even say his name, like he's a ghost or somethin'."

"I'm sorry for your loss."

"Yeah, thanks. Mamma's always yakking at me to live up to my potential and not be like him." He hung air quotes around the last few words. "I dunno, I liked Nico. He was a cool dude who got wasted by a dumb mistake."

"So you don't do drugs?"

"No way. I have plans for my life." He sat up straight, his cool attitude burned off in his eagerness. "Say Doc, what's it take to be an eye doctor?"

"What are your grades like?"

"Straight A's. Maths and all the sciences. Mamma wouldn't have it any other way. I got accepted to the University of Toronto for science. Tell me the courses I should do."

"After your four-year Bachelor degree, write the MCAT, do four years in med school, apply for your licence, then a five-year residency. Only thirteen years. Keep up the marks and the extra-curricular and you should be on your way."

Tony gaped at him. "Wow, that's a lot of years. I'll be, like, thirty-one when I'm done." He shrugged. "Well, now I have some real plans."

"Goals, Tony. You have goals."

"Yeah, and I might even get rich and famous inventing a cure for something."

Asher offered the young man a handshake. Tony's exit from the office had none of the swagger his entrance did.

When he finished his case notes, Asher turned back to the window. A text from Emma came in on his phone.

Miss you already. Can't wait to get back. Going out of range. Take care. Hugs.

He grinned. Only gone for half a day and she re-connected with him. Sondra had never sent him such a note to remind him that he was important to her.

His smile faded when his mind whirled on to his other, bigger worry. He and Sondra had negotiated for a while and finally reached an agreement. Would she pull out at the last moment? Would he be left heartbroken yet again?

And what would Emma say if everything turned out the way Asher hoped?

Wednesday afternoon, Asher parked in front of Greg the vet's office with Pirate riding gunshot. Pirate's owners had come to claim him. Greg had warned him the people had sufficient proof to reclaim their dog.

Asher sat with his hands clenched on the steering wheel and his back teeth grinding. He wrestled with his urge to commit dognapping. Pirate pawed the door and whined a query at Asher. Why were they still sitting here when they could be outside having fun?

Asher took the dog on his lap, ruffled the black-and-white ears and scratched the furry head. He hugged the critter one last time, heaved a sigh, and opened the door.

Pirate jumped out and cavorted around on the end of the leash.

As they approached a grey van parked in front of the vet's office, the dog pulled back against his collar, his eyes rolling. He wanted to go back to Asher's SUV.

"I don't blame you for being afraid to go to the vet's considering what happened last time," Asher said in a soothing voice. "You'll like what happens this time. I won't, but you will."

The dog dug in his paws. Stiff legged, he wouldn't go forwards. Asher bent and rubbed the furry head. "C'mon little buddy, you'll be fine." Pirate tipped his head to one side, furrowed his brow in doubt and still refused to budge. Frustrated, Asher picked him up and carried him into Greg's waiting room. Once inside he placed Pirate at his heel.

"Spotikins!" A soft, round older woman with tight curls, dressed in pink sweats with "I ♥ my Doggie" on her sweatshirt, surged forward. She stooped to address Pirate. "There you are my naughty little doggie."

Pirate scooted up tight against the backs of Asher's legs, cowering and whimpering.

"Come to Mommy." The woman moved around Asher and extended a puffy hand laden with rings.

If Pirate clung any tighter, he'd become a tattoo.

"Mommy missed you so much. She was so upset when she couldn't find you. And now here you are again. Come see the sweet little plaid suit Mommy bought for you." She dug around in her huge purse and pulled out a hideous orange plaid outfit complete with a top hat.

Like that tempted Pirate? Asher's lip curled in disdain for owners who treated their pets like inanimate dress-up dolls.

"Get the damn dog and let's get out of here. I want my lunch." An older man, slight and wiry, rose from a chair and attempted to grab the leash from Asher's hand.

Asher dodged the grab. Pirate let out a tiny accusatory yelp. Asher glanced down to see if he was okay. Pirate crouched low, rolled sad brown eyes at Asher and uttered a begging whine.

"Teach the mutt who's boss." The man lunged with surprising speed and got a tight grip on the leash.

Asher aimed his sternest stare at the little creep.

Greg interrupted the stare down. "Asher, these are Mr. and Mrs. Smith, Pirate's owners. They responded to the monthly lost-pet ad in yesterday's *Clarence Bay Beacon*."

"Pirate?" The woman shuddered. "What a grubby name for my Spotikins. Isn't it, my precious?"

Asher winced at the grating coo aimed at the dog.

Mr. Smith jerked at the leash. "Precious nothing. That dog's ours, and we're taking the damn thing back. We got papers and pictures to prove it. Show 'em the damn pictures, woman."

Another rummage in the huge purse resulted in a prissy photo album jammed with pictures of Pirate as a puppy. What a cutie. The mistress held him in some photos.

Asher's heart seized, and his eyes burned. Forced to concede this awful couple were Pirate's rightful owners, he relinquished his hold on the leash.

The man tugged hard. Pirate backed up, growling and baring his teeth. Mr. Smith pulled harder, jamming the collar against Pirate's ears.

The leash cut into Asher's legs. Horrified, he moved out of the way before the man could hurt the dog.

"Hey, gently, man." Greg stepped forward.

The woman swooped in and scooped Pirate up to her chest. "Poor doggie. Look at this awful collar on you." She unbuckled the collar and held it at arm's length by two fingers in Asher's direction.

He took the collar and its dragging leash.

Cooing as if the dog were a child, Mrs. Smith forced the god-awful outfit on him. If Pirate protested, the man growled a threat at him. When done, she held the dog aloft. "There, now Mommy's little boy is looking like his old self."

Pirate cast one last begging look at Asher, before he was draped over the woman's shoulder and hustled out to the van. If only he'd listened to the dog's request to turn back.

The doors slammed shut and the grey van left in a cloud of road grit.

A sad-faced Greg approached and laid a hand on Asher's shoulder. "Damn, those are awful people. I'm so sorry this had to happen to you."

Asher gave a half-hearted shrug, wrenching his tight shoulder muscles. "It was the right thing to do," he croaked. His hands fisted against the turbulence in his chest.

Why did doing the right thing always hurt so fucking damn much?

Greg slapped his back. "Come have a drink with me. Drown your sorrows."

"No, thanks. Granddad's waiting for me to go out with him." He uttered the lie without conscience. He had to get the hell away from this place.

Asher climbed into his car and blindly headed out to... some-where, anywhere Without paying attention to the route, he ended up at the day use area in Killbear Park.

Unlike the last time, the area was packed with people. Down below on the beach, happy families with happy pets ate barbeque and played Frisbee. Kids and dogs swam and splashed in the clear water.

Pirate was gone. Hands fisted on the steering wheel, his rigid spine pressed into the back of his seat.

The relentless sun beamed through the open window, warmed his skin beneath the cotton of his shirt, seeped into his knotted muscles. Along with the warmth, some of the happiness rising from the beach, trickled into Asher's soul, and buffed the sharp edges of his loss. He sagged against the seat, hands loose in his lap, eyes closed.

Taking a deep breath and releasing it, he purged the emotion from his body. He detached the leash from the collar, coiled it up, and stuffed it in the glove box. He wound the empty collar around the gearshift and buckled it in place.

Possibly, maybe, someday he'd find another dog. Emma, on the other hand, was irreplaceable. He was an idiot to doubt her. She'd be back.

CHAPTER 9

Comings and Goings

Asher stood in the hallway in front of his ex-wife's door in an up-scale condo tower overlooking Lake Ontario. Sondra had hooked him, married him, given him a baby then yanked the hook out of his life and left him to die in the bottom of a sinking boat. He'd moved to Clarence Bay two years ago to find peace after the ship-wreck. Now Sondra sailed a life raft within an arm's length.

Asher tucked the stuffed moose under his arm, its antlers be-hind him to form some sort of surprise. He should have had the impulsive present gift-wrapped or bought a fancy bag. At least he'd cut off the price tag.

Would Brendan even like the beast? Was the boy old enough to see it for the icebreaker it was? Too bad Pirate was gone. He would have been a deal-clincher.

Annoyed with his dithering, he rapped the brass knocker. Heels clacked across the parquet floor then the door opened. "Hi, Asher. You're right on schedule. Come on in." Sondra moved back to let him enter. Her straight blonde hair flowed down her back in her at-home style. She'd lost weight she could ill afford, sharpening the features of her face.

Asher immediately scanned every corner he could see for Brendan. "Where is he?" he demanded and instantly regretted his sharp tone. He touched her shoulder, hoping to placate her. "Sorry, I'm nervous. Did you tell him?"

Sondra gave a warbling laugh. "I'm ridiculously nervous about this, too. So many what ifs. When I told him yesterday, he didn't seem impressed. But, this morning, it feels like he's been asking about you every second." She rubbed her hands up and down her crossed arms. "If it's all right with you, can I add a few more minutes to the months since you last saw him? I want to go over the forms. Then I'll take you to his bedroom."

He glanced down the hall leading to the bedrooms and looked back to his ex-wife. Her grey eyes betrayed how tightly she was wound, ready to explode if he so much as thought a wrong word.

"Yes, he really is down there, playing with his Lego bricks." She tipped her head to the living room and he followed her to the couch. Stacks of colourful plastic moving boxes lined the walls, each with its neatly written label. Legal documents lay tidily piled on a couple of boxes pushed together to form a makeshift coffee table. She handed one set of papers to him.

"These are your copies. I consulted my lawyer since we last met and researched precedents—"

He clenched the papers in a quick fist. "You changed your mind."

Impulsively, she grabbed his fist. "No. Not at all. I still believe this is the best course of action. Taking Brendan with me to New York is impossible. I simply won't have the time to look after him and attend to my duties at the United Nations. It's ridiculous. I'll be so busy taking care of all the world's children that I can't take care of my own."

He laid his other hand over hers. "Sondra, the fact makes you a selfless and giving mother. Incredible as you may think it, I admire you for it."

She broke his gaze and stared over his shoulder. She withdrew her hand.

"Thank you. When Brendan was born, you gave up your surgical practice and took an administrative position you hated so you could look after him. You agreed to gradually bow out of our lives when I moved on. I was so very wrong—" She halted, blinked rapidly against her tears then swallowed her emotion. "Enough maudlin nonsense."

She flipped through his stack of pages and pointed to an illegible scrawl of a signature. "His biological father has signed off all rights to Brendan. He never adopted him. He's perfectly fine leaving your name on Brendan's birth certificate." Her mouth tightened again. "He doesn't want anything to do with any of his four children. Or either wife. He's gone off to climb Mount Everest and find himself." The scorn she heaped on the last words rivaled the height of the famous peak.

"The fool deserves none of you," Asher said.

She brushed the words aside and flipped more pages to reveal her own clear signature, still using her maiden name, as recognized by the Law Society.

"My lawyer thinks I'm nuts—" she took a deep breath, "but as I'm leaving the country for an unspecified period—" Her voice pinched, and she ran a hand down her throat. "In Brendan's best interest, for the first time—" She stood and stared into the cold fireplace, her fist over her mouth. Her shoulders heaved.

Asher stood to move towards her, to offer whatever comfort he could. She thrust out a hand, palm outwards, to put Asher back in his seat.

Long moments passed. She straightened and turned a grim, pale face towards him. "In my son's best interest and because you don't need me haunting you with a threat to come and take him back—I, too, am surrendering all parental rights. To you. His father." The words spilled out, one on top of the other.

This time, Asher refused to leave her be. He folded his ex-wife in his arms, where she cried out her sorrow against his shoulder. He soothed her, as he'd never had to before, with soft nonsensical murmurs and pats on her back. At last, she raised a watery face to him and kissed his cheek.

"I hurt you dreadfully with my lies. And now you come to our rescue like the truly noble man you are. I was a fool to hurt you, to leave you."

"I'm not the least bit noble. I'm completely selfish. I'm here because I want the boy."

She laughed, wryly and watery. "Yes, you're a selfish beast. Always have been. Not." She patted his chest and stepped back, reached for the box of tissues on the mantel. "You see, I knew I would need these." She mopped up her tears and blew her nose. "Okay, one ordeal over." She forced a brave smile. "Sign the papers." She waited while Asher completed the task. "On to the next step. Come and get him."

Asher grabbed the toy moose and followed his ex-wife down the hall to Brendan's room. He took her arm and halted them in the hallway, hushed her with a finger to his lips. He stepped around her to stand in the doorway and simply watched a four-year-old boy, in jeans and a striped T-shirt, carefully select a red brick and lock it into place atop a yellow brick. Boxes jammed this room as well.

"Brendan." He savoured the feel of the name on his lips and tongue.

The little boy turned, a blue brick held in mid-air. His dark eyes widened. His mouth trembled. The brick clattered to the pile beside him.

"Daddy?" The boy climbed to his feet. He ran over, stared way up, and hesitantly patted Asher's leg. "Is that you, Daddy?"

Behind Asher, Sondra sobbed and ran to her room.

Asher went down on his knees, opened his arms. "Yes, it's me, Brendan."

"Daddy!" the boy crowed, threw his arms around Asher's neck and clamped his legs at Asher's waist. Asher hugged the child closer than close. Tears coursed down his cheeks and soaked into the dark curls. He filled his soul with the precious scent of his little boy.

After Sondra had revealed Brendan's true paternity, divorced Asher, and married Brendan's biological father, Asher had never expected to see the child ever again. He rose to his feet and rocked side-to-side, comforting himself as well as his boy. Would he ever be able to let go of him?

Brendan recovered much sooner than Asher. He levered back, wiped his own eyes before he wiped the tears from Asher's face. Tears welled again.

"Daddy, you don't hafta cry anymore. I'm here now."

Asher smiled the wobbliest smile ever and blew a raspberry in his son's neck.

His son squealed in delight, wriggled with joy. "I love you, my Daddy." His boy planted a smacking kiss on Asher's cheek.

"Is he for me?" Brendan pointed at the fallen and forgotten moose.

With Brendan still in his arms, Asher knelt, picked the critter up and presented it to his son. His son—what incredible words. "He's yours all right."

"Do I get to take him with me?" His lower lip trembled. "You won't leave him here, will you?"

Asher cringed at the backhanded accusation from an innocent bystander to adult melodrama. "Both of you are coming home with me. So are you bricks, and books, and bed, and everything else. You're coming to stay with me forever and ever."

"Forever and ever," Brendan repeated, relishing the words. Asher hugged his boy tight until he squirmed for release.

Once his son was steady on his feet, his held the moose at arm's length to begin the buddy-naming ritual they'd devised. "Hi, moose. I name you Horny."

Asher's laughter burst from him on a wave of stress-busting relief. "Those are antlers, not horns."

Brendan squeezed the body part in question. "Antlers."

"Why don't you try another name?"

He raised the moose again and screwed his face in concentration. How many stuffed animals did his son have now? If he recalled correctly, they'd stopped at thirteen.

"Hi, moose. I name you Marty." He peered at Asher. "Is that okay, Daddy?"

Asher ruffled the dark curls on his son's head. "Perfect. Why don't you pack your bricks while I go talk to Mommy?"

Brendan grabbed a fistful of Asher's trousers and stared up at him. "You won't leave without me, will you, Daddy?"

Asher's throat closed. How long would it take the worry to re-
cede? Would his son ever trust him again? "No way. Cross my
heart and pinky swear." He suited his gesture to his words and
Brendan mimicked him. They joined pinkies and shook hands on
a solemn vow. Brendan grinned confidently and started to tear
down his tower. He chatted to Marty the Moose as the bricks
clacked into their bin.

Asher found Sondra in the kitchen, packing the last of the
dishes. A bunny dish sat on the counter and brought Emma to his
thoughts. He resolutely set her aside. She was on her North Channel cruise, the first step in her journey to the acclaim she so well
deserved.

Sondra pointed at the dish. "He doesn't use this anymore, but
it's his, so you take it."

"Thanks, but no. Your mother gave it to him, so you keep it."

She turned to lean against the counter. "You're the only man
Brendan has ever called Daddy. In his mind, you're his father.
Ca—the other guy—was never his father. Brendan never called
him anything. Drove him nuts."

"Thanks. I think."

"Anyway... I told Brendan all about moving with you to your
new place. I'm not sure he understands what's going on. He'll par-
rot the words back at you, but...." She shrugged helplessly.

"I'll watch out for any signs of trouble."

"Daddy? Are you still here?" Brendan's fast footsteps echoed
down the uncarpeted hall.

"In here, little buddy." The nickname fell from his lips with
ease.

"Are we going now?"

Asher looked to Sondra.

She bent down. "Yes, you are, my bumblebee."

Brendan rolled his eyes. "Mommy," he complained.

"Come give me a hug and kiss goodbye."

Brendan ran to his mother and graced her with a huge hug and a smacking kiss.

Tears leaked from her eyes and her mouth trembled. "I'll see you at Christmas. I love you, B."

"I love you too, Mommy. A whole lotsa bunch." Brendan kissed his mother's cheek and slid from her grasp. He ran to Asher and took his hand. Brendan's hand didn't feel so small and defenseless in Asher's larger palm. "Let's go, Daddy."

Asher climbed from his car and stretched his back. He opened the back door and shook his son's shoulder to coax him from his deep sleep in the car safety seat. "Brendan. Wake up, buddy. We're here. This is our new home."

Brendan woke bit-by-bit and stared at Asher in wonder. He placed a palm on Asher's cheek and rubbed the stubble. A huge smile lit his small face as he reached out. "Daddy!" He lunged forward, wriggling for escape.

Asher released the harness and scooped his son into his arms for a fierce hug. There'd been many such hugs exchanged over the past two days at his parents' home while Asher and Brendan got used to each other again. Though Asher was certain he'd never get used to the burst of transfiguring joy whenever Brendan smiled at his daddy. He put his son down on the front lawn. The boy leaned against him; an arm wrapped around Asher's leg, and stared at his new surroundings. The sun helped make the most of the moment by shining cheerfully down on them.

Asher cupped the back of his son's curly head.

Brendan peered upward, his brown eyes full of questions.

Asher winked at him, drawing out a grin. His wave encompassed the world. "Go ahead and check the place out while I unload some of your things."

With Marty the Moose tucked under his arm, Brendan inspected everything in the front yard giving Marty a play-by-play of each item capturing his attention. After unloading the smaller things to the driveway, Asher leaned against the SUV and waited. Every few minutes, Brendan would stop to look at Asher, grin, and carry on with his inspection.

Across the road, the curtains at Mark Chisholm's place twitched. How many minutes—uh, seconds—would it take Meg to spread the story? Which of the Gossiping Grishams would make first contact?

"Asher, why are you dawdling on the lawn?" Granddad opened the front door and came out to the porch.

Asher tilted his head to where Brendan stood transfixed by the goldfinches at the bird feeder, chortling at their feathered antics.

Granddad gaped then laughed for pure joy. "Benny-boy, is that you?"

Brendan turned and ran to his great-grandfather who scooped him up and spun him around before bringing him in for a hug.

"GeeGeePa! I'm here! And so is Marty!" Brendan showed off his newest friend. "I wanted to call him Horny, but he has antlers, not horns. See?" He shoved the moose in the older man's face. Granddad guffawed at the innocent story.

"I have to take a whiz," Brendan announced.

"Well, let's go inside and take care of business," Granddad said to his Benny-boy. Asher got a narrow-eyed glance. "Then your dad and I are going to have a chat."

The moving van pulled up and the next couple of hours were consumed with installing Brendan's furniture in the third bedroom. By lucky chance, Asher had chosen a complimentary paint color and Brendan could settle in right away. Then there was supper and bath time full of endless little-boy questions about his new world.

To close the day, Asher propped himself on his son's bed to read a book. Brendan snuggled under Asher's arm, warm and trusting with Marty against his side. Asher's throat closed on a lump of gratitude. Granddad sat in the chair beside the bed. His eyes glistened with moisture he didn't bother to hide. Brendan fought valiantly but succumbed to sleep after only three short pages. Asher eased out of the boy's grip, tucked him in, and then bent over to kiss the rounded cheek. Closing the door part way, Asher faced Granddad, a weary smile on his face.

Granddad cleared his throat and clasped Asher by the upper arm. "Tonight, we need The Macallan."

After he poured the aged whiskey into crystal tumblers and they settled into the front parlour, Asher told the tale of Sondra's second divorce, her new job, and her decision to return Brendan to his father.

"Why the secrecy, Asher? Not that I didn't enjoy the incredible surprise."

"I didn't know for sure if the arrangements would go through. Her parents were willing to take him, as well. But in the end, Sondra decided on me. For which I will be eternally grateful."

"Where's the son of a bitch new ex-husband, now?"

Asher dropped his head to the high back of the couch. "Everest. To find himself. Left behind his other ex and her three children, too." His disgust of the man rang loud and clear.

"Shit on a stick."

Asher raised his head. "Yeah. Now will you ease up on Sondra?"

"She put you and the boy through the wringer, for which I will never forgive her." Granddad sipped. "But she did the right thing in the end and the boy is where he belongs."

Asher gave him a grateful smile.

"Did you tell your parents, your sister?"

"Yes. But I prefer to keep the information in the family. If Brendan ever has questions about—that guy—Sondra will deal with them."

"Fair enough. How did your parents take the news?"

"Mother and Dad are overjoyed to have him back. I told you we stayed with them while Brendan's things were packed?"

"You did. Where's your sister Tenley these days?"

"Vacation in Denmark. I emailed her. No doubt, she'll visit when she gets back."

"Can't keep a loving auntie from her favourite nephew." Granddad raised his glass. "I said it before and I'll say it again. You're a good man, Asher. I'm proud to have you for a grandson," Granddad said, his voice rough with emotion.

"Thanks, Granddad."

The two men clinked glasses, sipped, and turned away from each other, pulling themselves together.

When Asher turned back, Granddad stared into his glass. "Does Emma know?"

Asher sagged into the couch and closed his eyes. "Not yet."

"How do you think she'll take it?"

"Our relationship isn't quite to the place where we've talked about having children. She loves Ryan's kids and her nieces and nephews, so I assume she wants some of her own. I just don't know. If she's not into kids, that's a deal breaker for me."

Three leisurely days of sailing past spectacular vistas of pine forest and granite ridge brought Emma, David Chastain and the two-person crew to an overnight berth in Little Current on the eastern shore of Manitoulin Island. For the first time in those sunny days, they were within range of cell towers.

David was the successful photographer who Prathiba Nayar had arranged to mentor Emma while on the cruise. Fifty-something with thinning hair, blue eyes, and a slight paunch, he did not wear his success well. He strode the decks and ladders of the rented boat, issuing orders to Mike and Tina as if he had superior knowledge of handling the large vessel.

Emma sat in the common room at the only table on the boat. A fine rain blurred the windows. Clouds hid the moon and stars. If not for the twinkling lights of the small town, outside would have been pitch dark.

After dinner, Tina and Mike had gone ashore to visit family. They'd be back to spend the night on the boat.

Emma and David had gone ashore during the sunny afternoon to hike and shoot the incredible Cup and Saucer Trail. The older and less-fit David had taken one of the easier trails. Emma had climbed to the cliff tops for a panoramic view.

Emma had downloaded the images from her camera to her laptop to view the thumbnails. Most of the shots were pretty; a couple were reasonable; one she liked a lot. And one was spectacular.

Dramatic angles of light and a tight field of vision reduced a recognizable landscape to a moment of pure abstract colour. Her second choice was of a slender birch sapling appearing to hold up a gigantic limestone boulder—a scrawny Atlas carrying the world. The humour of it tickled her fancy.

Two shots in one day. She danced in her chair. What a great beginning to her first long-term photographic field trip.

"Okay, Emma, I've left you to your own devices long enough. Let's see what you've done so far." David slid onto the bench seat beside Emma. The gold leather creaked under his weight. Without asking, David slid her laptop from beneath Emma's hands and scrolled through her images.

"Yes, yes." He pursed his lips and made a funny kissing noise. "Nice of a deer to wander into the shot. Very pretty." He frowned over the shot Emma considered her best. "No, this won't do. Too impressionistic. Where is it? What's around it? Objects must have context." He snapped his fingertip against the delete key. He jumped at Emma's horrified gasp. "You didn't think I would allow you to keep such garbage, did you?"

Emma stared at him, too horrified to think of sufficiently polite words for his high-handedness.

Then he deleted her best shot.

"Stop." He barely got his fingers out of the way before she slapped her laptop closed and snatched it out of his reach. "Your job is to teach. You may comment on my work. You may *not* delete or destroy my work."

David smiled and shook his head, *tsking* the whole time. "Emma, Emma, Emma. Ms. Nayar tells me this is your first field trip. Yes?" His tone of voice added a pat on the head for her, the ignorant child.

"Yes."

"And you have had no formal training in photography. In fact, no training at all. Yes?"

"Yes." Emma wouldn't be telling Prathiba of her disastrous time in college.

"I have years of experience. I have sold my work all over the world. Yes?"

"Yes."

"So, I am the better judge of the merits of a work. Yes?"

"Yes." Couldn't argue with experience, fame, and money.

"So, if I say a shot is garbage, then it is garbage. Yes?" He reached for her laptop.

Garbage.

Emma flashed back to the nightmare day in college. Her sodden photographs slopping into the garbage can. Dismissed. Destroyed. Shamed.

Trashed and bullied... should have been fired and disciplined. Asher's voice echoed in her ears, stating a different viewpoint.

Those rejected photos, in the bottom drawer of her desk, cautioned her to stay hidden, stay safe.

You are a strong, courageous woman, Emma Finn, and I applaud you.

Resolve flowed through her, boosting her fragile confidence. She firmed her jaw and tightened her grip on her laptop. "You may have authority and experience on your side. However, it is not your prerogative to declare what is garbage. Nor can you destroy any image I have created."

"But how will you learn if you don't participate?" He favoured her with a benevolent smile.

"Depends on your definition of participate."

David pushed his stiffened back against the bench, his eyebrows rising up his forehead. "What do you mean?"

"An equal and open exchange of our opinions on a work—yours and mine."

He reared back. "Mine? What do you have to teach me?"

Emma relaxed her white-knuckled grip. "I don't have a clue. But we won't know until we try. And I certainly won't be hitting delete on one of *your* images."

He huffed loudly. "You certainly won't." With that, David got up and went into his cabin for the night.

Emma recovered her images from the trash file, embedded her signature, and saved them. Once done, she stared out at the night. A curious emptiness echoed in her chest. An emptiness where pain had festered and poisoned her vision of herself as an artist. She might not be famous or rich, but she had a wealth of talent. Talent she would nurture and grow. Talent to make herself proud.

During the long northern twilight on the Friday of the first week out, at harbour in Gore Bay, Emma settled in the cushions on the aft deck to catch up with her messages. She scrolled through the list, searching for one name before any other—Asher's. She opened an email, dated today.

Emma,

Remember the family emergency I couldn't talk about? The one that took me away from the auction? Which I'm still sorry I missed. My ex-wife called about our son. I had to go. I didn't want to say anything at the time in case it all fell through. Didn't tell my family either. If you look at the attached photo, you'll see the family in the emergency. My

son. I have him back. His name is Brendan. He's four. I can't wait for you
to meet him.

Miss you,
Asher

The photo showed an adorable child with dark curly hair, dark
eyes, and a huge, happy grin. Brendan held a stuffed moose in his
arms and sat on the lap of a grinning Asher.

Emma's hand dropped to the cushion. She stared out at the
lights strung in rows up the dark slopes of the town. Sunset filled
the sky with glorious colour. It would have been an incredible
shot.

Emma didn't see it. Instead, she turned inwards to the war
raging between her fear and her reason.

He'd deserted her. At a time when she needed his support, he
ran off to his ex-wife.

For his son's sake. His son was more important than holding
Emma's hand at an auction.

He'd betrayed her.

He hadn't told his family either.

Could she deal with the complications attached to a single father?

She loved children; wanted her own someday.

And so on. And so on.

She heaved a deep, sad sigh. Tired of the emotional seesaw she
went down to the ship's galley and made herself a cup of tea.

David came out of his cabin with a book under his arm, poured
himself a bourbon, and sat at one end of the couch. Emma sat at
the other end with her tea and read Asher's email again. Before
David opened *Mystery of Depot Harbour*, he peered at the smiling
faces of Asher and Brendan. "Handsome guys. Your family?"

They could be. "My boyfriend and his son." Warm affection softened her face as she smiled down at them. Her imagination supplied Asher's supportive wink. *You can do it. We can do it.* She paused, listened to her internal ramblings, and surprised herself. Her fears had gone. Her anxiety quieted. Affection had won the day and silenced them both. She had the courage to face this change. She replied to Asher's email.

Dear Asher,

Brendan's adorable. I can't wait to meet him when I get back.

Hugs,
Emma

On the final morning aboard ship, Emma gripped the rail on the foredeck and loosened her knees to absorb the pitch and toss of the waves. A light spray dampened her hair into a mass of curls. She laughed into the wind. There hadn't been a single thunderstorm during the entire trip—no way for her to share with David her techniques for capturing vivid images of lightning. Now a storm headed for Clarence Bay. The breakwater stretched across the opening to the marina. The slightly calmer waters of the harbour beckoned. She hung her wet jacket on a hook in the shelter of the cockpit and went below to collect her gear.

"Good morning, Emma." David stowed the last of his equipment in his bag on the table. Emma had maintained a cautious distance for a couple of days after he deleted her photos, while he'd held his offended stance. Gradually, his attitude had shifted from offended, to neutral, to friendly. No further images had been trashed.

David zipped the bag shut and set it at the bottom of the stairs. "I wanted to thank you for sharing the journey with me. I hadn't realized my teaching methods were so offensive." He paused then shook his head as if to clear it. "My mentor worked with me that way. I hated it, and yet, I perpetrated the same on my students. I apologize for doing it to you."

Speechless at his humility, she grabbed the back of a chair to steady her shock.

He gave her a sheepish smile. "I'm as surprised as you are. It's been quite an experience."

She laughed at his wry tone. "Yes, it has. Though, you must be doing something right for students to keep coming to you."

"It's kind of you to say so." He held out his hand. "Thank you."

Emma shook his hand. "I had a wonderful time and learned so much and feel so much more confident now. I hope to see you again."

With a concerned expression on his face, he clasped her hand between both of hers. "I'll give you one final instruction. I noticed you exclude people from your subject matter. Even though your focus is nature, you will learn so much from photographing people. Your framing will become quicker and your judgement sharper."

Emma ran her tongue behind the scar on her lip. "I have my reasons."

He touched her shoulder. "I imagine so. If you can find a way around your difficulty, your work will benefit from it. And you'll have the skill to manage animals when they venture into your shots."

Emma only nodded.

The two of them went on deck. The ship approached Clarence

Bay from the north. First came Silbow Rock sheltering the town beach. Then a stretch of forested slopes hiding most of the town. Once around the breakwater, the town dock came into view. A long freight train whistled as it traversed the trestle spanning the Seguin River. Emma glimpsed her shop across the street from the marina park. Finn's couldn't hold her attention for long. She scanned the park for Asher and Brendan.

On shore, two guys waited for Emma's ship to come in. A gull screeched from the top of a bollard at the marina, bobbing its head and showing off the red inside its mouth.

"Daddy, are the seagulls laughing at us because we can't fly?" Brendan asked. A stiff breeze tugged at his clothes and tangled his curls.

"It sure sounds like it." Twelve precious days had passed since his son's arrival. It still felt too good to be true. Every morning when Brendan bounced out of bed to greet the morning, Asher counted the blessing of his son's shining eyes and curious nature.

"Is it time for our picnic, yet?" Brendan tugged the strap of the backpack Asher carried.

Asher scanned the harbour. "Not yet." They continued their walk along the concrete pier.

Brendan tried to encircle the hawser wrapped around the gigantic cleat to hold the *Island Queen* at dock. "Look, Daddy, I can't put my hands around the rope." Asher bent to try the same. His fingertips barely met. "Yep, a huge rope for a huge boat."

Brendan repeated the last phrase, entranced by the cadence.

"Swings, Daddy." Off ran Brendan, Asher close behind. They played at the swings until Brendan wanted to slide. All the while,

Asher scanned the water for incoming vessels. Clarence Bay Harbour was wide and deep, and the boats were so small. *Finally.* Anticipation swelled. Emma was back. Even with the major distraction of his son, he missed Emma more than he thought possible.

"C'mon, Brendan. There's a lady I'd like you to meet."

"Okay, Daddy. Is she special?"

Hand-in-hand, they sauntered in the direction of where her boat would dock. "Very special." He glanced towards his heel then remembered Pirate wouldn't be there. He sighed. A fly in the ointment made the honey sweeter—or some such thing.

Emma waved with both arms while still a ways out.

Asher waved back. Joy spread from his smile to his entire body, expanding his chest and setting his soul on fire. He squatted beside his son and pointed. "She's on the green and white boat right there."

Brendan let go of Asher's hand and ran towards the dock while trying to wave at the same time. He dropped the ever-present toy moose and stumbled over it, doing a face-plant into the soft grass. Distraught, he picked up the animal and hugged it tight. Asher hurried over and scooped them both up.

Tears streamed down his son's face. "Are you okay, Marty? I didn't hurt you, did I?" Hiccupping, he thrust the moose at Asher. "Daddy, give him a 'xamination."

"I will. But first, I have to check you out." Asher did a quick survey. The only harm done, a scuff on Brendan's palm, was more grass stain than skin damage. Brendan hovered like an anxious parent while Asher squeezed Marty's arm to take his pulse, touched the back of his hand to Marty's forehead to take his temperature.

Keeping his smile under firm control, Asher nodded and tucked Marty in Brendan's arms. "He's as fine as you are." He used a handkerchief to mop up his son's tears then handed the cloth to his son to do the same for the moose.

"Is he okay?" Emma called from aboard the boat now alongside the dock. A crewman eased down the hinged gangplank to span the gap from ship to shore. The rough water lifted the vessel and dropped it, lifted and dropped. The gangplank pitched steeply and levelled, pitched and levelled.

Asher took an instinctive step towards Emma and nearly bowled Brendan over. He scooped up his boy and moose with a hasty apology and ran down the pier. His backpack thumped against his spine.

Emma, still on board, concentrating on the rhythm of the waves, obviously preparing to jump.

Asher's heart slammed against his ribcage. "Wait!"

She glanced defiantly at him.

Time turned sticky. His legs refused to work as fast as his mind drove them.

Her body rocked back and forth, synchronizing with the rise and fall of the vessel.

"Emma, no!"

She gathered momentum and with a joyous shout, she leapt. Her hair streamed out above and behind her. Her feet hit solid ground. She stuck her position like an Olympic gymnast, arms high, chest proud, laughing aloud.

Asher tightened his grip on his son and charged up to her, ready to shout her ears off. Did she know she could get badly hurt? Every summer weekend, the ER was jammed with the results of such lunacy.

Oblivious to his terror, she took her bags from the crewman.

"I'll give you a perfect score, Emma," the guy said.

"Thanks, Mike. I haven't done that in ages. I wonder why?" Emma said. Mike handed down her gear as the waves allowed.

Asher stared back and forth. They discussed the impending weather and smiled expectantly back at him.

He shook his head and forcibly swallowed his complaint. He only wanted her to stay safe. "You people are nuts." He hitched Brendan higher on his hip.

Emma and Mike exchanged glances and shrugs at his comment, answering with a non-verbal "clueless city people".

"Bye, Mike, Tina. Say hi to your family for me. Bye, David. Let me know the date for your next show." The three people gave Emma fond goodbyes.

Emma slung her backpack and camera bag over her shoulders and turned to Asher. She appeared different. Sure, her face was tanned from three weeks in the sun, but she looked taller, more confident.

The world drew to a pinpoint focus on her happy face, her glowing eyes. His heart stalled, stuttered, slammed against his ribs. A surge of longing slugged him in the gut. She stared back at him, her russet eyes wide and tender, a soft smile hovering on her lips. He rubbed his chest.

"Hi." Brendan shattered the trance.

Emma blinked a few times and colour filled her face. Her smiled broadened before she shifted her gaze to his son.

"Hi, there, Brendan, I see your daddy's fixed up you and your moose." Emma smiled at the little guy, charmed by him.

"You're Emma, the picture lady."

"Yes, I am." Emma shook hands with his son. "And who's your

friend?"

"He's Marty the Moose. My daddy gived him to me." Emma said hello and shook hooves with the moose.

Brendan reached over Asher's shoulder and patted the backpack. "She's here, so now can we have our picnic, Daddy?"

Asher bent a little more than necessary to put Brendan down, so he could hide the hot sting in his cheeks. "Yes, now we can have our picnic. Why don't you get a table for us?"

"Okay." Brendan turned concerned brown eyes to Emma. "Don't worry, Daddy made extra sammiches for you." Then off he ran, leaving behind an awkward silence.

Asher took the full force of Emma's gaze again. Silence flowed around them.

Emma cleared her throat and gestured at Brendan. "How's he settling in?"

He gratefully accepted the conversational redirect. "Terrific. Though he might be a little too attached to his moose." He lost his power of speech again listening to her chuckle at his lame joke. "I took two weeks' vacation to stay home with him. So far this week, he's been happy to spend the day with his Geegeepa while I go to work."

"Does he miss his mother?"

"I'm not sure. He Skypes with her every night but seems to forget about her the rest of the time. Is that a good thing or a bad thing?"

"I wouldn't know." Emma shrugged. "You could always check with the paediatrician."

"My backup plan." They started to walk towards the table, hands clasped.

"How was your trip?" he asked.

She stared out over the horizon to the north for a while then turned back with a sheepish grin. "I've lived my whole life in Clarence Bay, taken a million pictures, and have never viewed this part of Canada like I did these past weeks. I'd never paid attention to the water, rock, and forest shaping this town. Never noticed the granite is so varied. Or how many sounds the wind makes in a forest. Or how many smells water can have." She took his hand, captured him with her gaze. "I love it here. I don't ever want to leave." She chuckled. "Okay, the occasional trip is appreciated, but never permanently. I'm not leaving this place. Or you."

He stopped walking and took her in his arms. His hands bumped against her backpack as they slid around her waist. She softened against him with a sigh and raised her face with a smiling invitation.

Asher's phone rang, startling them both. He reached for it and checked the number, surprised to see James Garven, the Chair of Ophthalmology at the University of Toronto. "I have to answer this. Sorry," he said to Emma.

She nodded and strolled off to join Brendan at his chosen table.

Asher put the phone to his ear. "Hello, James."

"Hi, Asher. How are you?"

After some chat about the weather, James got down to what Asher sensed was the point of the call. "Have you heard about Sam Shepherd way up there in the boonies?" Sam was a Professor and Director of the Postgraduate Committee.

"Nothing new. What's Sam up to?"

"He's taken a post at Queen's University out in Kingston." James *tsked*. "I don't understand the appeal of these small places."

Asher scanned the spacious park, the green water laced with white caps, the high cliffs cradling the town. "Country living has its benefits. Clean air, clear water, forest at my doorstep."

James' shuddered audibly.

"Admittedly, Kingston's a lot bigger than Clarence Bay. I'll bet Sam gets a nice salary increase," Asher continued.

"Yeah, money talks. So, I've been chatting with the Executive Committee and they seem very interested in you stepping into Sam's shoes as Director. Do you think you might be interested?"

"I'm honoured and surprised." And confused.

"Don't be surprised. We need you down here. You can schmooze money out of donors like nobody else can. You know we need every one of those research dollars."

Asher grimaced. Yes, he could schmooze with the best of them, but he'd hated that part of his job. All those supporters with deep pockets and trembling hands needing to be flattered and cajoled into making donations. All the begging among the thousands of alumni of such a large university.

"It's an honour to be considered, James...."

"Ah, a young lady's involved?"

Asher maintained silence.

"Well, you bring her along. What kind of career can a woman have in a little town like—where is it you moved to?"

"Clarence Bay."

"Cottage country district hospital, right?"

"Permanent residents add up to sixty-five hundred. Summer folk increase it tenfold."

"Well, doesn't beat the five million people in the Greater Toronto Area. I do have an intriguing new development for you. The Moseley family has bumped the Foundation's research endowment up to two million a year. The matriarch has been diagnosed with dry macular degeneration and the family wants a cure."

A wish list flashed in Asher's mind as he fantasized about all the benefits reaped with a budget of that magnitude. A budget he would control.

"There'll also be a considerable increase in status and the salary to go with it. You'll have to move back to the city, of course."

"Of course."

"Why the hesitation? The young lady?"

Emma and Brendan sat at the table, chattering and focussed on each other. Brendan said something, and Emma laughed at his son's quirky humour. Asher couldn't hear the words; just see the expressions on their faces. Instant bonding.

Emma's words on the beauty of the country echoed in his ears. The faces of his new friends clicked through his mind. Horace and Jean as a couple—what a hoot. The half-hour rush hour—a joke compared to four hours in the city, one way. People talking about, and caring about, each other. He had a house larger than anything he could afford in the city with a huge yard and a hideout for his son. He gazed at Emma's china shop. She had deep roots in Clarence Bay. Asher, growing roots of his own, could not tear up hers.

"Asher? Are you still there?"

"I'm not."

"Huh?"

"I'm not applying. I don't want to leave here. This is our home now."

CHAPTER 10

A Fly in the Honey

Horace sat on the back patio sipping his last cup of breakfast coffee and reading the Saturday morning newspaper. Brendan, in his pint-sized version of Horace's Muskoka chair, sipped at his own mug of milk with a drop of coffee and read a board book to his moose. Well, the little fella recited the words from memory. The moose didn't know any better.

Horace's phone, seldom far from his hand, chimed with a text message from Asher.

How's Brendan?
Perfect, reading. How's the canoe trip?
Excellent. See you at 6.

Then his phone told him Asher had gone out of reach. Nothing unusual in cottage country. The new cell tower scheduled to be built would be great for service. If only the town could decide where to put the darn thing. There was a bad case of Not in My Backyard going around.

"The end." Benny slapped the book shut and gazed around for the next thing to do. He spotted the playhouse halfway down the backyard. Painted white with a blue door, yellow-checked curtains hung in the blue-framed window. Benny had seen it before and ignored it. Now he was entranced. Kids were funny that way. "GeeGeePa, can we go inside the little house?"

Horace tried to recall any reason not to and found nothing. He shrugged and hauled himself up out of the chair. "Sure, I guess."

Benny tore off down the dewy grass with his moose stuffed beneath his arm, easily beating Horace to the playhouse. He pulled on the door, pushed on the door. It didn't open. "The door is locked," he hollered. "Open it."

"Let me see if there's a key somewhere. Come and help me find it."

"'Kay." The little guy raced towards the house, passing Horace on the way. For having such short legs, his great-grandson could sure make tracks. The screen door slapped behind him.

Crikey, where was the boy going? A horrible image of Benny rifling through Asher's desk speeded Horace's steps. Amazing what a smart kid could figure out.

Sure enough, he'd turned out the center drawer of the roll-top desk, dumping the contents any old place. Horace hurried forward and grabbed his small hand as Brendan grasped the handle of the side drawer.

"Hey, hey, hey, Benny-boy, take it easy." Horace sat in the desk chair and started scooping things up off the floor and putting them back. He'd explain the mess later and let Asher put stuff where it belonged. He searched through every unlocked drawer and came up empty.

"No key?" Benny's bottom lip quivered. He wrapped both arms around his moose and tucked it under his chin.

"I'll call your daddy and ask him, okay?"

"Where's Daddy?"

"Gone out," Horace replied absently as he scrolled through the contact list and pushed the button for Asher. "Blast it, still no reception." Horace continued scrolling for the number of the paddling centre on Cole Lake. "What the heck is the name of that place?"

"Gone to work?"

"What? No, gone out with Emma. Remember he told us this morning?" Horace tried calling again.

"Daddy's gone?" Benny flew out of the room. His small sneakered feet ran through the two parlours. "Daddy! Come out, come out, wherever you are!" His voice rang clear then muffled as he ran further away.

Phone at his ear, Horace followed his great-grandson's commotion into the dining room.

The little boy charged around the dining table, then crawled through the maze of chair legs. "Daddy?" he called, panic edging into his voice.

Horace grabbed him by the shoulders as he zoomed by on his way to the stairs. The poor kid was getting sweaty. "He's not playing hide-and-seek, Benny. He's gone out. He'll be back for supper."

"Daddy's gone without me?"

"Yes, but he'll be back."

Benny squirmed from Horace's grip and headed to the stairs, calling for his daddy. Horace captured him halfway up.

The boy crumpled into tears. "I want my Daddy to come back and get me."

Horace turned and sat on the stairs. "Don't worry, Benny-boy. He'll be back. Your daddy will be back in time for supper."

"No, he w-won't. He won't c-come b-back. I w-want my da-daddy." The little guy wailed like his heart would break.

Horace tried everything to soothe his great-grandson; he offered him ice cream, cookies, video games. Nothing worked. The poor little boy was inconsolable.

Horace wore out his thumb calling Asher. He made the canoe-rental guy crazy. Still nothing.

At last, Benny cried himself to exhaustion. Hiccups wracked his small body. Horace hugged him close and let loose with a few tears of his own.

"Asher, look, over there, along the shore," Emma whispered and pointed to the left of the canoe at the base of a high rock wall. A group of common mergansers fed in the shallow water. They dove repeatedly, flicking water from their rusty-coloured head feathers when they surfaced.

In the bow of a rental canoe on the clear green waters of tiny Cole Lake, Asher turned a little too quickly, setting up a precarious wobble. His shout rang out over the water. As a group, the mergansers took flight into the clear mid-morning air, all the while complaining about the disturbance. In the stern, a laughing Emma steadied the small craft. This was their first time alone in the fifteen days since Emma's return.

Asher dipped a hand to scoop water and throw it backwards and ended up with a soggy sleeve for his efforts. And, of course, she laughed harder.

He gazed over his shoulder at her lovely face filled with the beauty of her laughter. She was a sight for sore eyes. A sight he could easily gaze upon for the rest of his life.

"Do you want to continue on around the lake, or head back to shore?" He waggled his eyebrows, hoping she chose to head back to her bedroom for one last tumble before their day together ended.

"I want—" She stopped, surprise on her face. Her jaw moved a couple of times though no words came out. Her paddle hung in mid-air, dripping water.

"Emma?"

Her puzzled gaze locked on his eyes. "I want—I want to not be afraid of you."

Slowly, he turned around in the canoe. "Afraid? Why? We spent time together this morning making incredible music." He cringed at the awful cliché. "Sorry. Blame the piano-player in me."

She drew a deep breath. "I love the piano-player in you. I love the doctor in you. I love the father in you." Her words tripped over one another. She breathed deep again. "I just plain love *you*." She rested her paddle across the gunnels and stared into the bottom of the canoe. She curled in on herself as if preparing for a blow.

A crazy doubtful hopeful joy lit in his heart and vibrated out along every nerve until his body sang. Reaching forward, he took her hand. "I love you, Emma. From the moment I walked into the ER cubicle, I've loved you. I wanted to kiss you so badly, but you were my patient. I nearly went crazy waiting for my divorce to finalize so I could ask you out. I've wanted to hear you say that for so long. Say it again."

She straightened and lifted an ecstatic face to him. "I love you," she shouted.

The words echoed back from the rock face. A flock of small birds burst from the trees and flew off in an undulating cloud.

The canoe set to rocking with laughter again.

She deftly turned the canoe and together they put their backs into a return ride taking half the time of the outbound journey.

Within metres of the dock, the phone in Asher's pocket chimed with endless missed voice mails and texts. Alarm skittered down his spine as he pulled it out. He dialed immediately.

"Granddad?" He barely recognized his own voice for the tightness in his throat. "What's wrong, is Brendan okay?"

"Everything's fine. Except Brendan is beside himself wanting you."

Asher hauled in a steadying breath. "Let me talk to him."

The canoe bumped into the dock. Asher climbed out and ran for his car. Behind him, the oars clonked on the wooden boards. He turned to watch Emma tie up the canoe then race towards him, an oar in either hand. She stopped at his side, panting and gasping.

"Daddy?" His son's voice warbled through the phone.

Asher tucked Emma beneath his arm, snug against his side. Her strength settled the raging fear, calmed his voice. "Hey, little buddy. Your GeeGeePa tells me you're upset."

"Are you gone, Daddy?"

He swallowed hard against the guilt clogging his throat. "No, Brendan, I'm not gone."

"Are you coming to get me?" He glanced at Emma. They weren't due home until the early evening.

"Of course, you are," Emma whispered in his other ear.

He gave her a grateful smile. "I'm coming home to you right away, little buddy." They walked to the lakeside office to turn in the oars.

"You're coming?" A world of doubt and hurt filled Brendan's

voice.

Asher put extra reassurance into his own voice. "Yes. I'll be there before supper. I pinky-swear."

"He pinky-sweared, GeeGeePa. He's coming home. I hafta tell Marty." The phone clattered to the floor. Small footsteps retreated.

Granddad's voice came over the phone. "Asher, I'm so sorry. I don't know what set him off."

"We'll talk about it when I get home. Gotta go, Granddad. See you shortly." He disconnected and tucked the phone in his pocket. How could he apologize enough?

Before he could speak, Emma raised her hand as a stop sign. "Don't you dare apologize for cutting our day short. Brendan needs you, so we go."

He hugged her close, so grateful to her. "You're an amazing woman. No wonder I love you."

She preened under the compliment. "For what?"

"Putting a child, who's not even yours, before your own pleasure."

"Love you, love your child."

As soon as Asher climbed out of his car after he dropped off Emma, a small body hurtled towards him from the front door. "Daddy! You came!"

Asher lifted Brendan up into his arms. His son buried his face in his neck and started bawling. His small arms gripped his neck; his small legs gripped his torso. Asher cupped the back of his son's head and murmured soothing words. "Yes, I'm here. I'm not going anywhere. Hush, little buddy. Hush." He rocked back and forth, murmuring and stroking the dark curls and small back. "Hush."

Granddad came over and patted Brendan's back as well. "What happened, Granddad?"

"One minute we're looking for a key, and the next minute he's tearing the place apart looking for you. I think he thought you were gone." Granddad smacked his forehead. "Gone. Damn it. That's why."

"Why what?"

"Benny-boy went nuts when I used the word *gone* more than once, with your name attached." Granddad groaned. "I'm sorry. I'm an insensitive old coot."

Asher touched his Granddad's shoulder. "Don't worry about it. He's been so comfortable. No one could have known the trigger."

Brendan released Asher's neck and twisted in his arms. "Daddy's not gone," he scolded Horace. "He's here."

He kissed his son's cheek. "That's right. I came when you needed me. I promise I will always come when you need me."

Monday evening, after Brendan was sound asleep, Asher climbed Emma's outside staircase, heavy with dread over the outcome of the next few minutes. Emma's beaming smile faded as she let him in and saw his morose face.

"What's wrong?"

He led Emma to a seat on the couch and sat beside her. He propped his elbows on his knees. "Brendan and I visited Dr. Bauer, the consulting child psychiatrist at the hospital, about Brendan's separation anxiety attack. She feels the month since he came home may not have been enough for him to feel secure. Granddad and I thought we were in the clear, but I guess not."

Emma laid a hand on his shoulder, giving him comfort and strength.

"The doctor feels your presence may have upset him."

"She thinks we shouldn't see each other?"

Before she could retreat, Asher drew her hand through his arm and between his palms. He turned to her and nodded. His dread deepened at the serious look on her face. "I don't want to surrender my life to the control of a four-year-old. I love you too much to say goodbye. I'm asking to keep our relationship separate from my relationship with my son. Only for a little while. Until Brendan can be completely sure of me."

When Emma straightened, he had to do the same. Her pale face frightened him. She drew a deep breath and her shoulders dropped. "I was terrified you were breaking up with me. But you're not. I'm not going to lose you right after I got you." The smile she gave him lit his hope. "I love you, too." Her smile took on a mischievous edge as she waggled her eyebrows in an over-the-top tease. "I've always wanted to try nooners."

Laughing aloud with relief and gratitude, he swept her into an embrace. He held her tight against his chest, treasuring the warm, soft feel of her. He slid his tongue across her lower lip. With a sigh, she opened her mouth to let him in. After many heated kisses, she stood and tugged him to a standing position. She ran her hands up his chest to his collar. "I'll tell you a secret. This pretty pink shirt of yours turns me on." She started undoing his buttons. "It looks very sexy on you." She tugged the shirt from his waistband. "But it looks even sexier lying in a heap on my bedroom floor."

The second Saturday in September was a perfect day for a wedding: blue skies, soft breezes, warm temperatures. Asher's backyard, groomed and pruned to within an inch of its life, was the venue for both the service and the reception for Jean and Horace's wedding.

"Okay, everyone. Smile!"

The bridal party, Jean and Horace, Cathy and Asher, formed an unusual composition with the gorgeous grey-haired couple beaming with happiness from the centre of the group instead of relegated to the periphery. Jean's silky dress in blue and pink jewel tones contrasted beautifully with Horace's navy suit. Clicks rattled like frantic crickets from professionals and amateurs, young and old alike. Except for Emma—no picture taking for her. She stroked her scarred lip and trembled at the mere thought of aiming a camera at the group.

"Thank you, ladies and gentlemen." The official photographer released the wedding party from their poses.

Emma's gaze lingered on Asher, gorgeous in his custom-made suit, as he went about his hosting duties. Absence makes the heart grow horny. She huffed at herself.

"The buffet is now open. Enjoy." Asher directed the guests to the long table set to one side. Two lines of hungry folk formed, and they shuffled their way through their selections. Emma stepped into line behind Ryan, Cathy and Hayley. Daniel, now nine months old, rode in a carrier on Ryan's back. His hair had grown to a mop of sandy curls like his big sister and his father. The baby boy bopped his dad repeatedly on the head with a soft alphabet block. Emma reached to take it from him.

Ryan stopped her with a raised hand. "Please don't take it

away. If you do, he'll pull my hair, and I've already shaved my head practically bald."

"And I have to put my hair in a braid or wear a hat, so he won't pull mine," Hayley piped up.

Over the summer, Hayley had shot up in height and added a few shy curves to her boyish figure. She was now taller than her mom and so pretty in her budding womanhood.

Emma smiled at Hayley. "I see you talked your mom into the heels."

Hayley pouted. "Yeah. But not as high as I wanted."

"They're high enough for a thirteen-year-old girl." Cathy joined their conversation. "And you got the dress you wanted."

Hayley smoothed the soft purple fabric of her A-line cap-sleeved dress, a perfect adaptation of her mother's grown-up little black dress.

Cathy looked beyond Emma's shoulder. "Hi, Asher. The yard is gorgeous, just like you."

"Hey there, wife, who are you calling gorgeous that isn't me?" Ryan protested much to Hayley's amusement.

"Emma. Who else?" She gave him an innocent look.

"Dodged one, didn't you?" Ryan grinned at Emma. "You're gorgeous today."

Cathy poked Ryan in the ribs. "Hey there, husband, who are you calling gorgeous that isn't me?"

Ryan pointed. "Umm—Asher."

"Exactly what I said. I'm so glad we agree." Cathy tucked her hand into Ryan's elbow and rose on her toes to kiss his cheek. Daniel made a grab for his mother's hair. Hayley giggled, spoiling her young woman aura.

Cathy and Hayley glowed at each other, treasuring the shared moment. Ryan and Asher exchanged knowing glances. Both of them understood the tender magic of loving their children.

Asher ran his hand down Emma's bare arm and clasped her hand. Heat flared under her skin. "Someday, I hope we'll have children."

Emma bumped her hip against his thigh. "I hope so, too."

The Chisholm family moved ahead. Emma and Asher lingered. Leaning in close, he murmured in her ear. "I've missed you. May I come over tonight? Mom, Dad and Tenley are staying so Brendan is taken care of."

"Yes, please."

"Planning a tryst, are we?" Melody fell into line behind Asher. He politely stepped beside Emma and surreptitiously laid his hand at the small of her back. She shifted her weight to increase the contact. He lowered his touch a thrilling inch and spread his fingers.

"You're not invited," Emma teased.

Melody pouted. "Aw. I've always wanted to try a threesome. Asher, do you have a willing friend?"

Emma snickered. Melody was all talk and no action. Well, hardly any action.

Brendan ran full tilt into Asher's legs. "Daddy! Daddy! Help me get food."

Asher shuffled to maintain his balance, and his hand separated from Emma.

"Of course." He grabbed a couple of plates. "Let's see what's available." He gave her a look of apology and moved off. The absence of his hand left a chill on Emma's back and an ache in her heart.

"What will the girls do when he hits puberty, or possibly

sooner?" Melody fanned herself with a hand. "If the boy grows to be half as hot as his father...."

Emma elbowed Melody. "Stop ogling my man."

"Spoilsport. C'mon, chicky, some food needs eating." Melody handed Emma a plate and started down the line. "Did you get your photos sorted from your cruise?"

Emma finessed a spoonful of slippery Asian noodles to her plate. "Yes, I did. I whittled a pile of twelve-hundred down to sixty-three. I'm much faster at getting the best shot on my first, well third, try. I even deleted some as soon as I took them." She scooped up some eggplant in tomato sauce without spilling a drop. "It will save me so much editing time. I used to keep every shot I took. I'm more aware of muted tones thanks to David." She turned to Melody, surprised to find her several feet back, simply staring at her. "What?" Emma examined her flowered silk dress to make sure she wasn't wearing her lunch.

"You're talking about your photography." A proud-mama smile broke across Melody's face. "You're not afraid anymore. You've grown into your artist self."

Why did people think Melody a ditzy gossipmonger? Couldn't they see it she acted as surely as any role she played in the community theatre?

"Ask me again when I have my first show." Emma shuddered.

Melody started making her selections. "Ah, stage fright. I know it well, the fiend."

When their plates were full, Melody touched Emma's arm. "I see the perfect spot to eat. Right at the table with the hot dad and the cute kid. I'll play chaperone, maybe distract the little cutie. Then nobody's alone."

Later in the evening, at a table as far from the portable dance floor as she could get, Emma swayed to a slow country ballad. "Please may I have this dance, Miss Finn?"

Emma gazed down into Brendan's flushed face, his adorable mini-tux rumpled and grass-stained. The bottom button hung by a thread. Did his bright hopeful smile mean anything to her and Asher's relationship? "Of course, you may."

He took her hand and led to the edge of the dance floor, turned with a puzzled frown. "I forget what comes next."

Emma hid her smile and offered her hands. Brendan placed his grubby palms in hers. She stepped from one foot to the other in time to the music. Brendan followed along.

"I'm dancing with a lady," he crowed, so proud of himself.

A laugh bubbled in Emma's chest. "Yes, you are."

"My aunt Tenley teached me, but I forgot. Except for the asking part."

"You did very well." Emma turned him from the path of a dancing couple.

"She said I should ask a girl, but I like you better." He grinned up at her with all the charm of the Stockdale men in his cute face.

Whew, that was some powerful spell. "Thank you."

They step-swayed a few minutes in silence. Guess Tenley hadn't got to the small talk part. Was Brendan into dinosaurs or space or both?

"Do you like my daddy?" he asked solemnly.

More than you want to know. "I do." She went with a safe answer.

"Then why don't you dance with him?"

"Because he hasn't asked me." Another safe answer.

His face fell. "Does that mean he doesn't like you as much as I do?"

Things were getting tricky. Mercifully, the song ended, and Brendan released her hands and bowed solemnly. "Thank you for the dance, Miss Finn."

She dropped him a curtsy. "You're welcome, Master Stockdale."

"Hey, Benny-boy. Well done." Tenley ruffled his hair. "Now you've had your dance, it's time for your bath." She grinned at Emma as the boy tore off shouting for his father. "Asher's been telling me all about your sacrifice for Brendan."

"I don't know if I call it a sacrifice, but you do what needs to be done. I want them both to be happy. If giving up some of my time with Asher makes them happy, then it's all good."

Emma laughed when Tenley pulled her into an impromptu hug. "Asher's an awesome dad, and I can see you'll be a great mom. I hope you have a herd of kids for me to spoil."

At the patio door, Asher scooped up his son and spun him around. The boy squealed in delight and hugged his father tight. She couldn't hear their words over the music, but she saw the love between the man and his boy.

As they entered the house, Brendan peeped over his father's shoulder and blew a kiss to Emma. Asher spoke to Brendan, who pointed at Emma. Asher glanced between them, uncertain how to respond. Brendan nudged his dad's shoulder. Asher nodded and blew Emma a kiss as well.

She caught one kiss in each hand and patted one on each cheek.

Tenley clapped her hands in joy. "Brendan's seal of approval. Do I hear more wedding bells?"

CHAPTER 11

Repercussions

"Why are we going down this road?" Emma asked from the passenger seat in Asher's SUV on the day after the wedding. She stared out the window at the trees and rocks passing by. Tension coiled through her every nerve and muscle.

"To get to the beach. Like we talked about this morning." Asher cocked a questioning eyebrow. "I was told this was the most direct route."

"You didn't say which one. If I'd know you meant Gerry's Beach, I would have picked another one. The area is littered with beaches." Emma never drove along this road.

He turned a puzzled glance her way. "When I asked around, everyone in town said it had the best sunsets."

"If you turn up here on the left, you'll get a better road." For thirteen years, she'd detoured around The Spot where her life had changed in the flash of a camera. Now she was headed straight for it. The tension wound a little tighter.

Asher carried on past the turn-off. "Jacques Corbeau said

they're digging out the ditches, tearing up the roads in parts. He advised me to stay on the main road."

Emma had to accept Jacques knew what happened on his own road. Didn't mean she had to like it. Not one little bit. Her heart pounded against her ribs.

At one time, this stretch of road had been as familiar as her young lover's smile. More than a decade later, she still knew every curve around every massive rock formation in every light. Then, as now, the slanting rays of dusk sharpened the edges of the granite and sparkled off embedded quartz and mica.

The swamp on the left was dry now in early September. A red-tailed hawk swooped from its perch on the power line. Here was the private lake on the right. A monster of a cottage had replaced the small log structure. A raft floated on the glassy surface.

They were almost there.

Emma's body stiffened. Her back pushed against the seat. Her foot drilled into the floor where a brake pedal would be.

Almost—

The next curve snaked right, then hard left.

There—

Great slabs of bare rock like a fallen Stonehenge—

Look out! Look out!

Emma screamed, clamped her arms over her head, and curled forward over her knees.

Keening.

Rocking.

Crying.

Asher skidded to a stop on the side of the road just beyond The Spot. He jammed the car into park and reached for her. "Emma! What's wrong?"

Frantic, shaking her head from side to side, she pushed his hands aside and thrust pointing fingers down the road. "K-keep g-going! Don't s-stop!" She forced each individual consonant and vowel through her terror. "Oh, G-God, d-don't stop!"

Bewildered, his movements agonizingly slow, he put the car in gear, checked for traffic, and pulled out.

Well into the arrow-straight portion, Emma dragged her hands from her hot, wet cheeks and pressed them between her knees. Rocking back and forth, she struggled for control.

His concern rippled across the space between them. She absorbed his strength like dry lichen sucking up rain. With each turn of the tires away from The Spot, her terror subsided, and her tremors stilled. She heaved a restorative breath and dared to peek at him.

He sat tense and white-knuckled, focused on driving. His eyes, when he glanced at her, were huge with worry.

She covered her own eyes in acute embarrassment. "Sorry."

"What happened, Emma?"

His caring only deepened her shame. "Could I ask you to forget about it?"

He blew out an indignant breath. "How can you expect me to ever forget seeing the woman I love in the middle of a classic panic attack? I did a rotation in a Psych ward and I never saw an attack so extreme. Do you know what caused it?"

His words blocked her argument before she could form it. He was right. People who loved each other owed each other honesty. She rubbed a fingertip over the scar on her lower lip and the scar on her cheekbone. "Yes. I know what caused it."

They arrived at Gerry's Beach. She scrambled out of the car, dragged the picnic gear from the back, and hustled across the grassy area to the sand. She spread the blanket, flipped open the hamper, and started dealing food and plates at a crazy pace.

Asher strolled over and grabbed her by the shoulders. "That's the site of the car crash when you were young, isn't it?"

She nodded. Shame and guilt bent her head. "People don't talk about it."

"Emma, look at me."

She stared at his chin.

"Emma."

She met his dark compassionate gaze.

"You don't have to tell me if you don't want to. It was a traumatic experience. If you can't bear to relive it, that's okay."

He drew her into his arms. His loving support warmed her like she didn't deserve. She stepped out of his embrace long before she wanted to and carried on with the picnic preparations.

All during the meal, as they chatted and pretended nothing had happened, she waited for him to nudge her to speak. He repeated the gossip buzzing around town, told her Brendan's latest quirky joke.

The sun dipped below the horizon with a final blazing show of colour and surrendered the sky to the full moon. Asher lit the prepared fire. Flames danced among the logs, sparks snapped high into the darkness. From a thermos, he poured hot chocolate into thick mugs.

She peered up at him. Didn't he want to hear what had turned her into a crazy crying nutcase?

Emma scanned the beach then back to Asher. The scent of wood smoke drifted into the nooks and crannies of her mind, drawing out suppressed memories, happy and sad.

She crossed her legs and stared into her mug. "His name was

Nico Rassenti."

At her side, Asher stiffened. She turned towards him, but he shook his head and relaxed. He gestured for her to keep going.

"We'd known each other all our lives, grew up together. He was a classic bad boy. Trouble on the outside, scared and vulnerable on the inside. I wasn't quite as bad, but bad enough. We loved each other so passionately. Like only teenagers can love." She huffed a sad little laugh, raised her arm and pointed. "We lost our virginity in the clearing where those trees have grown in." Sadness dragged her arm back to her side. "We called this our beach. We came here to be alone, to skinny dip, make out. Nineteen and twenty years old, we thought we owned the world. We were going to backpack all over Europe."

She swirled the last of the cocoa in the bottom of the mug, drained it and set it down. Back in the day, they'd drunk cheap booze.

"One night we were headed out here with another young couple. We were going to get drunk and spend the night on the beach. We crashed off the road at that spot."

"Was Nico drunk?"

"A drunk driver killed my parents, so he promised he would never drink and drive." She rubbed the scar bisecting her upper lip. A slow-motion replay started in her head, and her hand trembled. She tucked both hands between her knees.

"Emma. You're safe now."

Asher's insistent voice penetrated her panic. She drew a deep breath and calmed her nerves. He wrapped an arm over her shoulders. "You don't have to keep talking if you don't want to."

She nestled into his warm body. "I want to tell. I've never talked about that night."

"Not even to the police?"

"Yeah, them, but I didn't remember much at the time. I was banged up quite badly, in a coma for six days, then in and out of consciousness for a couple of weeks. When I came to, the others were gone. Dead and buried. I missed all the funerals. I didn't get to say goodbye." She took his strong hand between hers. "Today is the first time I've been back to the spot."

He kissed her forehead, his lips warm on her night-chilled skin. "No wonder you suffered a panic attack."

"For some unknown reason, out of four young people headed out for a good time, I was spared. Why?"

He laid back on the blanket and she snuggled into him, borrowing his strength to finish telling the final bit of truth that would turn him away from her.

"Emma, I heard about what you did for your grandmother. How you came home from college to care for her. Gave up your dreams for your family. Isn't that reason enough?"

"I owed her. She took me and my brother in after our parents died. And I gave her nothing but grief in return."

"Except at the end of her life," he added.

"Anybody would do it."

"No, they wouldn't. Don't diminish your goodness, Emma love. It doesn't suit you." He turned to peer at her. "Why do I get the feeling you're suffering from more than survivor's guilt from the crash?"

She stood from her comfortable position, walked beyond the reach of the firelight. Tears stung her eyes, but she wouldn't allow them to fall. She didn't deserve the relief. Stalking back, she stood before her inquisitor.

She jammed a finger into her breastbone. "I caused the crash.

Me, I killed three people."

"But—"

"No excuses. Me and my stupid camera."

"But—"

She thrust a hand eastward. "I took a picture as we turned the corner. The flash went off. And we crashed."

"But—"

She threw up her arms and let them drop. "Stop butting me. I killed them as sure as I pulled out a gun and shot them dead." She ran away, heedless of her direction. Shallow water, still warm from the sun splashed up from her running feet.

He came after her, grabbed her arm, and spun her about. She slammed into his hard chest; his strong arms banded her against him. Frantic, she fought him, fought the emotion roaring in her ears. He held her tight. Forced her to feel her pain, her loss, her lover's death. He murmured senseless soothing words of comfort, cushioned her head on his shoulders, and sopped up her tears with his shirt. He rocked her until her racking sobs quieted and she hiccupped her last. With an arm over her shoulders, he led her back to the blanket.

"Go on, say it." She ordered him, hands clenched against the far more horrific loss of him. "Say I'm a horrible human being and you don't want to be involved with me. I get it."

Asher cupped her face and wiped a tear with his thumb. "Emma love, didn't anyone ever tell you what really happened that night?"

Emma opened her door to Jean whose arms were laden down with serving platters. "Thanks for the loan for our open house."

Emma took the stack and set them on the table. Envelopes filled the top dish. For a fanciful moment, the uppermost letter, thick and scary, vibrated before her eyes.

Jean tapped it. "I met the postman at the bottom of the stairs and brought his delivery up for you. I couldn't not notice this one's from the hospital. Are you okay?"

Emma shoved the mail onto the table and took the platters into the kitchen, hoping Jean didn't see the quiver of her hands. "Thanks. And yes, I'm fine." Thank goodness, she lived in a small town where the bureaucratic wheels rolled quicker. Still, it had taken a couple of tense weeks for her Freedom of Information Act request to process and spit out her medical records.

"Are you sure?" Jean stood at her side, wringing her hands with worry.

Emma pushed a smile across her face. "Yes, I'm sure. Now get going. Horace is waiting."

Still her friend hovered.

Emma let out an exasperated breath. "Do you think a doctor in this day and age would snail mail me any results of any tests, especially bad ones?"

Jean let out a relieved sigh and touched Emma's shoulder. "You're right. Of course, they wouldn't." Jean picked up her jacket and purse, said a quick goodbye, and hustled down the outside stairs.

Emma laid her hand on the thick envelope. Her tongue slid over the scar through her lip. What did it matter about events of more than a decade ago? The past was over and done, immaterial. Yet Tony, via Asher, had raised doubts. Had they somehow been high?

Her last lucid moments had been of the flash of her camera,

the huge slabs of rock in the headlights, the horrific pain.

She didn't need an official report to tell her what she knew. She no longer took photos of people because of the crash. Rocks, trees, and water didn't die and leave behind grieving families.

Emma left the envelope unopened on the table and went down to the shop. Julia Westover, her part-time employee, smiled a greeting from the central table where she laid out a place setting for a customer.

Emma slipped into her chair in the back office and booted up her computer to go through her latest shots. She clicked through the fifty images three times without making a single decision.

"Piffle to hell and back." Surrendering to the vibes put out by the envelope, she locked down her computer and stomped back upstairs. She grabbed the envelope and tried to rip it open. Made of modern fibres, the envelope resisted her fingers and her teeth. Growling, she went to the kitchen, grabbed the scissors, and forced the envelope to deliver the goods.

A harmless-looking file folder slid to the table along with a covering letter acknowledging her request. Blah, blah. Blah, blah, blah.

Taking a deep breath, she sat down and started to read.

She skimmed backwards past her boring present and delved into her turbulent past. Months of physiotherapy after six days of coma; the painful effort to force broken bones to bear her weight. Bandages around her head, scaring the life out of her. She touched the scar beneath her eye, touched her tongue to the scar bisecting her lip and continued reading. Plastic surgery to mini- mize the visible damage.

She found the emergency report and read the paragraph de- scribing the accident. Phrases jumped out at her.

Single vehicle. Hwy 559 west of intersection with Corbeau Rd. Approx. 11:30 PM Saturday June 3, 2000. Driver, male 20, measured BAC .0173, evidence of THC. Passenger, female 18, DCA, BAC .002. Passenger, male 21, BAC .096, died in OR. Passenger, female 19, BAC 0, survived, only one wearing a seatbelt.

Survived.

Three friends had died and been buried while she lay unconscious in hospital. A simple strap of fabric had prevented a fourth death; saved her for payback months later when Gran needed her. She shook off the grim thought of Fate's machinations.

BAC—blood alcohol something? How bad was that number? THC—marijuana?

Asher had said Nico's brother Tony mentioned Nico had been high that night. This was the medical evidence. Google time would confirm the details.

But where and when had Nico gotten high? A memory forced its way out of the recesses of her mind.

Kids had been dancing and goofing around in the moonlight on the football field. She, Nico, and a few others hid in the dark shadows between the gym and the admin offices. Emma had come back from college to celebrate Nico's graduation.

"C'mon, Em. It's freedom night." Nico had shoved a glass bottle with a few ounces of clear liquid into her hands. "No more teachers' dirty looks," he chanted the old rhyme. Though a year older than Emma, he'd fallen a year behind her in school. He'd squeaked through his courses, begging for extra marks, making one excuse after another, never really doing the work. He had a highway construction job lined up, holding the stop sign.

She took the bottle of vodka, sipped and choked on the fiery liquid. She was used to beer. This stuff was awful. She accidentally on purpose dropped the bottle on the grass. The last ounces of vodka glugged into the dirt.

"Hey, that's my share you dumped out," Nico hollered. The other kids laughed uproariously.

"I'm sorry. The bottle was wet, and it slipped out of my hand." Emma prayed it was too dark for him to see her fingers crossed against the lie. She laid a French kiss on him. "I'll pay you for it later," she purred. Whistles and catcalls came from the peanut gallery.

"You bet you will, darlin'." He grabbed her butt and tried to haul her tight against him, but her camera came between them. He swore at her, rubbing his ribs. "Why the hell do you always have that damn thing around your neck?"

"To pay for college." He opened his mouth to complain like he always did about her leaving and about how if she loved him, she would stay with him. She stopped his predictable rant with another kiss, leaving him grinning.

"I have to take a few more pictures for the newspaper, then we can go swimming. Are you coming inside?"

"Nah. I'm gonna stay and watch the moon rise. Hey, you got any munchies on you? I'm starving."

"You ate tons of food for supper."

"So? I'm hungry again." He stared up at the moon, seemingly fascinated by it.

Her nose curled at the smell of him. "How much have you had to drink? You promised you wouldn't drink and drive."

"Well, thanks to you, I'm not drinking at all."

She sniffed again. "Are you smoking pot?"

"Nah." He flipped his hand at some other kids standing nearby in a tight circle. "It's them. It musta got in my clothes." He slapped her on the butt as she turned. "You go get us some money, darlin'. I'll stay out here and celebrate my freedom."

She jerked back into the present, the remembered smell of pot in her nostrils. All three of her friends had smelled of pot in the car. Nico had glugged down a Coke as he slid into the driver's seat. He'd thrown the empty can on the ground. Emma had thought littering was his worst offence that night.

Her hand rested at the spot on her chest where her camera typically struck. She hadn't shot them dead with her camera. She'd done what she'd always done—recorded dozens of precious moments, with and without the flash, of Nico doing every little thing. He'd gotten to the point where he no longer noticed.

What had happened to her camera?

She didn't want to know.

She read on.

Spontaneous abortion. Fetal development, eleven days. D&C performed. Blood transfusion.

She read the words again. And once more, before she understood their meaning.

Pregnant?

She'd been pregnant?

More words grabbed at her.

Resulting infertility.

She pressed a hand to her abdomen, once covered with bruises. Why hadn't Gran told her? Had she thought it best not to? No way to find out now. Would the knowledge have made a damn bit of difference to her life? Is that why Gran had always encouraged her to think beyond being a wife and mother, to think big?

Getting up, she walked into her bedroom. Nico smiled at her

from his place of honour on her dresser. Three kids had died from his celebrating. Three kids, and a baby, and her nebulous dream of a family had died under the influence of alcohol, drugs, speed, and the bravado of youth.

Stupid, stupid boy.

Carefully, she took the frame in her hands and stared down at Nico. She'd taken the photo days before his death and had treasured it ever since. She had thought she would love Nico forever.

Stupid, stupid girl.

A rueful smile tugged at her lips. For the first time in ages, she noticed the pull of the scar. She turned the frame over and slid the photo out. She placed the empty frame back on her dresser. Gazing at his face, she tore Nico's smile in two, four, eight, sixteen tiny pieces. She carried the shards outside and dumped them in the compost bin. She took a shovel, and carefully buried the fragments under the garden refuse.

Quietly, she returned to her room and perched on her bed.

Her clasped hands found their way between her knees.

Rocking, rocking, rocking.

Whisper, hum, sing.

No good, nothing worked to stop the crash of emotion.

Tears streamed down her cheeks to splash on her forearms. Grief swamped her. Collapsing face down in her pillows, she sobbed for a long time.

She awoke feeling like death warmed over. The soggy pillow under her head chafed the skin of her cheek. Yuck. She flopped to her back and stared at the ceiling. For some bizarre reason, she expected to see cracks in the plaster due to the shift in her world.

Once upon a time, she'd dreamt of motherhood. The dream had receded over the years to nothing more than a shiny bauble of might-have-been. Asher and Brendan had brought the dream close enough to grasp. Now, the pretty bauble dangled just out of reach and she wanted it more than ever.

How did Asher feel about adoption? They'd never discussed it. He didn't seem the type of man who would insist on a blood relationship. He already had a son of his own.

Another wave of deep regret rolled over her. She rubbed her barren belly to soothe the emptiness.

What would Asher say?

Asher let himself into Emma's apartment and dropped his bags of food, wine, and flowers on the table. The lasagna he'd begged from Jean went into the oven.

"Hi, Jean. Make yourself at home," Emma called up the stairs.

Grinning, Asher pushed his voice into falsetto range and replied with a brief "Okay". Then he got busy preparing for a memorable night.

An hour later, he lit the candles as Emma climbed the stairs. Anticipation danced along his nerves.

Her steps slowed as she reached the landing.

"Oh, Asher, what have you done?" Her voice wobbled, and her eyes shone with pleasure. She quick-stepped over and flung her arms around his neck. "You darling man. What a perfectly lovely surprise. How did you know what I needed?" She laid a kiss on Asher that curled his toes. The chiming of the stove clock interrupted the hot make-out session.

"Why don't you freshen up while I rescue the first course?"

She gave his butt a playful pat and scooted off down the hall.

Oh yeah, he could so do this for the rest of his life. Whistling his latest piano piece, he plated broiled oysters and poured a crisp Ontario Gewurztraminer. When Emma returned, he tucked her into her seat, and so began the perfect meal of delicious food and even more delicious company.

The closer confession time got, the higher his shoulders went until they were intimately acquainted with his ears.

Eventually, the meal wound to a gracious close, and Emma laid aside her cloth napkin. "Thank you for a wonderful surprise. And it's not even my birthday or anything."

Asher held out a hand and escorted her to the couch. They sat close together. Emma melted against him with a deep sigh of contentment.

The longer they sat, the more Asher sensed a tension in Emma. Had she somehow guessed his intentions? In a way, he hoped so.

First, he had a truth to reveal.

If she received it well, he had a specific question to ask her.

"You're very welcome." He reached for the envelope he'd tucked between the couch and side table earlier. "Hayley gave me a photo she took at Jean and Horace's wedding. I want to give it to you. I didn't frame it, because I know how fussy you are, but I will pay for the framing."

With a curious expression, Emma took the envelope and slid out the photo.

A tiny gasp greeted the shot of himself and Brendan seated side by side on a swing. Brendan, in partial profile and wearing his tiny tux, shared the secrets of his universe. Excitement lit his eyes and showed in his hands. Asher had gazed directly into the camera at Hayley's approach. His expression, on the cusp of intense focus and warm welcome, invited the viewer to share his son's secrets.

"Wow. I'm impressed. I was all set with some kind and encouraging words for a first attempt. But this... stunning. I want to lean in and listen, too. Remarkable." She tore her attention from the composition. "She has a true gift."

"We all asked for copies. Hayley's quite pleased with herself."

"I would be too." Her face echoed the wistful note in her voice.

"The crash is the reason why you don't take pictures of people, isn't it? Do you still blame yourself after finding out about the state of your boyfriend?" he probed gently.

"Not as much. I think there'll always be some guilt, but not quite as... debilitating as before. In fact, I just might aim my camera your way," she lifted a hand, "but not while you're driving."

They shared a wry laugh.

Emma captured his gaze. "You're so tense. What's up?"

"Nothing." He rolled his eyes at his own cowardice. "Well, yes. I need to tell you something and I've been putting it off."

She jumped a bit, almost a bit too much. "Why?"

He took his arm from around her shoulder to rise and pace the room. "I'm afraid you'll think less of me."

"Have you committed a murder? Robbed a bank? Done a hit and run?"

Her words stopped his pacing, and he relaxed. "God, no."

"Then I'm good." She patted the cushion beside her. "Come back and sit down and tell me what you've done."

He settled beside her and handed her the photo again. "What do you see here?"

Mystified, she stared. "A father and son sharing a very special moment?"

"Look again. Who does the little boy look like?"

"His father?" Emma turned her palms up, asking for clarification.

"I'm not his father. My name is on his birth certificate. But I'm not his biological father."

She continued blank-faced.

He grit his teeth, and restated the point. "My ex-wife had an affair, got pregnant, and told me the baby was mine."

Her eyes widened and filled with an unholy blend of anger and pity. "The bitch!" She clapped a hand over her mouth. "Sorry," she muttered through her fingers.

"Don't be. I've called her much worse, and everything in between."

"Does your family know?"

"Yes, but I've told no one else. Except you."

"Why wait to tell me now?" She laid a hand on his thigh. "Don't say it. I understand. You didn't want to be seen to be a cuckolded dupe. Can't say I blame you, and there's no hint of the fool in you. You loved her, and she abused your trust, broke her marriage vows. She lied and lied and lied. Good grief, what a bitch."

Her defense of him warmed the cockles of his heart.

"When Brendan first arrived, you told me your ex had surrendered him to go to New York, now tell me all the rest. How did you find out?" She tapped the photograph lying on the coffee table. "Because he is clearly your son. No child ever loved a father more."

Tears scalded his eyes. He blinked rapidly to stop their embarrassing escape.

"She didn't know, until after Brendan was born, who the father was. Without telling me, she had a DNA test done. Since the guy was married, she kept the information to herself. Until the guy left his first wife—and took *my* wife and *my* son." His hands clenched into fists at the remembrance of the other man's smug face. "I was supposed to do a fade-out, so Brendan would forget me. I hadn't seen him for months before Sondra called out of the blue."

"What an awful dilemma for you. You chose to do the right thing though it cost you so much. That's why you moved all the way up here."

He unclenched his fists. "No sooner were they married than he ran off to find himself on Mount Everest, leaving behind two wives and four children."

"There are no words to describe such a man. I hope he finds his way to the bottom of a crevasse."

Her outrage soothed his lingering resentment. "When Sondra was offered the job with the United Nations, she didn't feel right about dragging Brendan away from the only family he had left, only for him to spend most of his time with a nanny. So, she called me to meet her in Toronto on the day of the auction, to—"

"Dump her child when he became an inconvenience."

"Do the right thing by her son and give him to someone who'd never stopped wanting him," Asher said.

Emma hunched at the gentle chiding. "I'm sorry. Brendan's a lucky boy with you for a dad. It's the only hope for him to overcome having a bitch and a bastard for biological parents."

His snort of laughter surprised him. "No wonder I love you so much. You make me feel like a hero."

"You *are* a hero."

"You just earned yourself a kiss." Suiting actions to words, he scooped her into his arms and kissed her with his heart bursting with gratitude. Why had he been so afraid? He kissed her a while longer, nearly losing sight of his second goal for the evening. Determined to carry on, he loosened his grip enough to watch her face.

"Now I've unburdened myself and you made me feel like a hero, I have a question for you."

Her face shuttered. A dull premonition filled him, but he kept going. "Will you marry me? Be Brendan's kind and beautiful stepmother? Maybe bless him, and us, with siblings for our son?"

Emma pressed a hand to her abdomen.

He knew what the gesture meant.

"You're pregnant?" He scooped her into another hug and a passionate kiss. "What an awesome mistake. We'll have to get married soon. Yes. The sooner the better. I hope she's as beautiful as you are. A sister for Brendan. Wonderful."

Emma's stiff posture broke through his haze of joy. Her face was not wreathed with the joy dying in his chest.

He released her altogether. "You have doubts?"

She blanched. "I can't—I won't—I—oh!" She tore herself from his arms. "Please—"

Her cell phone interrupted her fractured speech. She rose and ran across the room, grabbed the phone like a drowning sailor grabbed a lifeline, glanced at caller ID, and threw him a hugely relieved and apologetic look.

He scowled in return, shamelessly eavesdropping, and determined not to leave until she stated her reasons for not marrying him and he'd swept them all aside and taken her to bed.

"Hi, Prathiba." Emma eyeballed him and turned her back. "Yes, I remember David from the cruise."

Asher recalled the story Emma told of staking her claim on her work during her tour of the North Channel.

"That's awful. His poor wife. I'll send him an email. Thanks for letting me know."

Asher assumed Emma would hang up and share the news.

"Yes, I remember you mentioning the trip as a possibility for next year." Excitement began to glow from her. "Yes, of course I'll take David's place. It's a wonderful opportunity. Let me grab a pen and paper."

She hunted frantically for a few moments. "Okay. Air India, flight 1999, leaves Thursday. In four days. Got it."

"Okay, I'll watch for your email. Thanks a million. See you at the airport. Bye." She thumbed off her phone. She drooped briefly, then squared her shoulders, and turned to face him.

He dropped his gaze to her hand, now fisted against her belly.

She moved her hand to her hip. "No, I'm not pregnant. I—"

"For your sake, I hope not. Because if you are, I will not allow another woman to take a child of mine away from me."

"Is Emma joining us?" Horace leaned against the kitchen counter as his grandson as he prepared the roast beef for Sunday dinner.

"No." Asher stabbed the tip of the knife into the hapless roast and jabbed a chunk of garlic in the hole.

"She's sick?"

"No." Asher stabbed and jabbed.

"That time of the month? Your grandmother suffered quite a bit."

Asher made an odd choking sound. The full length of the blade went clear through the roast and struck the cutting board beneath. He pulled. The blade stuck fast. He slapped his other hand on the meat and yanked at the knife.

"Asher, stop." Horace stepped forward and grabbed Asher's right wrist, halting the action. "Your hands."

Asher released the knife and thrust Horace's hand away.

Horace stumbled back.

Asher reached again for the hilt. He yanked the knife free and aimed it towards Horace. "I'm fine!"

Horace lifted his hands in surrender, his eyes wide. He stepped back. "Okay, son. Whatever you say."

Horror convulsed Asher's features. He tossed the knife into the sink and stormed out the back door.

The clang of metal on metal, the slap of wood on wood, echoed in the startled air.

Horace shook off his scare, finished preparing the roast, and put it in the preheated oven. He followed Asher out to the back-yard. His grandson strode the length of the yard and back again. It didn't take many seconds.

"I'm sorry, Granddad. I don't know what's got into me—" He shoved out a snarling sigh. "I lied. I know but I don't want to talk about it."

"If you're pointing knives at people who love you, you desperately need to talk, whether you want to or not."

"It's—damn—I've been such an idiot. Why can't I see what women are?"

"Emma, I take it."

His grandson gave a tight nod. Horace waited, hoping the silence would prod Asher into speech. He had never been this angry before, not even at the worst moments of his relationship with his ex-wife.

"I proposed to Emma last night. She never answered. But she did accept an invitation to go to India, on Thursday, for six weeks.

I think she's pregnant even though she says she's not."

Horace reeled with the onslaught of information. "Wow I don't know which part stuns me the most."

Asher grunted and took off for another march.

Horace stared into the thin forest backing the lot. The fall colors were beginning. "What are you going to do?" he asked the next time Asher was within earshot.

Asher threw up his arms in angry frustration. "What can I do? I don't want to carry another marriage all by myself. Brendan needs a mother *and* a father. Hell, she couldn't even be bothered to answer my question with actual words." He curled his fingers into his hair as if he could pull the thoughts out through his skull. "What a fucking mess!"

"Should Jean talk to her?" It was the only offer making any sense.

"No. Yes. No." Asher slid his hands down to clasp his nape and stared up at the sky. He spun a couple of times and dropped his arms to his side. "I have to know. I *need* to know if she's got my child in her."

"Hi, Emma. Sorry I'm early for our lunch date. I got through my appointment sooner than I expected," Jean told Emma when she answered her knock.

Emma opened the door wide. "No problem. I only have a few more things to sort out before I take the bus down to the airport hotel tomorrow. I'm leaving the day after."

"I know the plan." Jean moved through the chaos of Emma's living room and into the relative calm of the kitchen. She filled the kettle and got down mugs for tea.

Emma continued to bustle around her place, scooping up items to put in the suitcase. She added to a shopping list, paused to think then zipped off to her bedroom. On her return, she tossed in a box of tampons. So much for Asher's offensive theory. Emma went to rummage in her closet by the sound of things.

While the tea steeped, Jean stacked the outdated newspapers and magazines strewn across the coffee table to make room for a plate of biscuits. The beautiful photo of Asher and Brendan fluttered to the floor. Did Emma not plan to take it with her? Was she going to recycle it?

Checking the coast was clear, she slid the photo into the bottom of Emma's suitcase. The kettle screeched so Jean had an excuse to avoid an argument with herself. The photo would stay put.

Jean grabbed Emma as she whizzed by and pressed her into the couch. "Sit and catch up to yourself." She put the mug in her hands.

Emma settled with a huge sigh. "Thank you." She sipped her tea and seemed to pull herself together. "How goes married life?"

Jean dipped her head to hide her huge grin. "Fine. Lovely." Heat flowed up her face. "Terrific."

Emma squinted at her. "Why are you really here so early?"

Jean thought fast. "To see if I could help Julia in the shop while you're gone." Huh. She hadn't known she wanted it until she said the words.

"Won't Horace object?"

"Why should he?"

"Because you're his wife and he wants you with him."

"True. But there is such a thing as too much of a good thing."

"He won't stand in the way of your career?"

"I'd hardly call helping out a friend a career move." Jean put down the mug. "What's going on?"

"Asher doesn't want me to go to India. He wants me to stay home and be a good little wife and mother."

"I understand he proposed. And you said no."

Emma grabbed a biscuit and took a fierce bite. "Yes."

"He told you not to go to India?" Jean didn't believe it for a second.

Emma finished off her biscuit and started on another. She sipped her tea and added more milk. "Oh, all right. He didn't say any of that. He's been nothing but encouraging to me."

"Then why are you running away? Why won't you talk to him? I know he's been calling and coming over."

Emma's hand spread over her belly. "Because I'm not good enough for him."

"Piffle! He never said that either."

"Doesn't make it any less true. His mother hates me." Emma's hand fisted, still on her belly.

Jean's curiosity caught on the gesture. "You're afraid."

"Terrified. I've had too many changes in my life. Too many people have died on me. I can't do it again. I don't want to hurt so bad again."

Jean stroked Emma's arm. "Yet you survived it all and are stronger for it."

"I can't, Jean. This is the perfect opportunity to put some distance between me and Asher."

Jean glanced from Emma's clenched fingers to her distraught face and tried to change the subject to the weather in India.

Maybe Asher wasn't nuts after all.

Jean doubted if Emma was pregnant, but something was not sitting right with her dear friend. She laid her hand on Emma's fist. "Emma, what's happening here? You can tell me anything, and I'll understand."

Emma pressed her hands to her mouth and shook her head. Her hair flew around her face.

Jean's eyes welled for Emma's torment. "Okay, I'll leave it until you come back. While you're gone, think about if you're doing the right thing by letting your fear stop you from having the life you want."

A red maple leaf, spinning by on the fresh fall breeze, gave Asher's nose a playful flick. Startled, he quit ruminating to see Brendan run straight through the neat pile of leaves Asher had just raked together.

"Daddy! I'm flying!" Near the patio, Brendan banked his wide-spread arms and zoomed back through the pile. "I'm the plane Mommy went on to Darfur to help all the kids."

Sondra had called from the airplane. In the three months since Brendan had come home, Sondra had yet to miss a weekly phone call. No matter where she was, she kept her promise. Their son had reason to feel safe and happy. On this gorgeous October weekend as his family celebrated Thanksgiving, they would all have something for which to be truly grateful.

Except for Emma. The ache of missing her prowled like a beast in his chest, never resting, always clawing. The scent of her lingered in his nose, the touch of her burned in his palms. His music had deserted him, deepening the hollow agony.

Brendan swooped around him, his fingertips brushing the back of Asher's knees, tickling him. A rusty laugh creaked out.

The little boy hugged Asher's thighs. "Don't be sad, Daddy.

Come and play."

His vision blurred, and he squinched his eyes to clear them. "Lay down on your tummy and stick out your arms and legs." After Brendan eagerly complied, Asher picked him up by one arm and one leg then twirled around on the spot. The little boy squealed his delight at being airborne. Asher raised and lowered his flying son as they spun, getting more shrieks. He landed him in a pile of leaves, scattering them everywhere.

"More, Daddy, more!"

A sound came from the woods. Asher bent to put a finger over Brendan's mouth. "Shush a minute. I heard something."

Man and boy stood stock still, listening. There it was again. A whining noise from the woods on the other side of the creek.

"Is that a doggy?" Brendan whisper-shouted.

"I'm not sure. Might be. Shush again, so we can tell where it's coming from."

It was unmistakable this time.

"We have to save it, Daddy." Brendan tore off towards the gate in the newly installed fence leading to the creek and the woods beyond.

Asher hustled after him and grabbed his small hand. "It might not be a dog. It could be a skunk or a fox. So, we have to be careful. You hang onto my hand, little buddy, and don't let go. All right?"

Eyes wide and full of excitement, Brendan shushed them both and nodded. The intrepid rescuers passed through the gate. Asher picked up his son, hopped across the shallow creek and put him down again. They moved through the forest, stopping every few minutes to trace the whine. After roaming the woods, getting soakers and gathering burrs, they found the poor critter. A familiar black-and-white body was caught on a broken branch hooked through the sleeve and collar of a hideous frilly lime-green jacket. Blood from abrasions caused by the jagged edge of the branch matted and stained the black fur of his chest.

"Pirate, old man. What kind of trouble have you gotten yourself now?" Speaking low and soothing, Asher bent to investigate. The dog whimpered at the sight and sound of his old master.

"Is he your dog?" Brendan squatted beside Asher's bent knee. "Can he be our dog?" He cautiously pat the dog on the head.

The poor beast was in a sorry state. Muddy fur, bloody paws, underfed. "Okay, little fella, I'm going to break this branch, and then you'll be free." Asher freed the dog and tucked him against his chest. Pirate wriggled in delight and licked his cheek.

"Can I hold him, Daddy? Can I, can I, please?" Brendan continue to pat the bedraggled head.

"Let's get him back to the house and check him out. Then we'll see, okay?"

Brendan pranced all the way home, tripping a dozen times because his gaze stuck to Pirate. At the creek, Brendan splashed through the water, soaking his shoes and cuffs, and not caring a bit. Once inside the yard, with the gate safely closed, Asher put Pirate down and ran his hands over him. No major harm done. He took off the hideous jacket and dropped it to the patio stones.

"Can I pat him some more?"

"Sure. But be gentle, he's likely got some bruises and it will hurt if you're too rough."

Brendan stroked Pirate's rough coat and got a lick on the face for his gentleness. Both small bodies squirmed with joy.

"Can we keep him? Please, Daddy?"

"No, I'm sorry we can't. I know who his owners are, and we can't keep him."

Asher wanted to pout right along with Brendan. He loved the dog and missed him foolishly. "It might be a couple of days before his people can come and pick him up, so you can borrow him. What do you say we give him a bath and some food?"

Brendan's smile wobbled on his sweet face. "Okay, Daddy."

Hours later, with Pirate fed and pampered, Asher reluctantly called the vet for contact information on the Smiths. Yeah, he should have done it sooner, but he just plain didn't want to. Greg gave him a number and Asher dutifully placed the call and dutifully pushed a voice mail out of his mouth. No knowing when they would call back. Hopefully they wouldn't.

Pia knocked on his office door during a patient visit and stuck her head around the door. "Dr. Stockdale, Horace is on line three. He says it's extremely urgent."

Fear licked up his spine and raised the hair on his nape as he picked up his phone.

"Yes, Granddad?"

"Those god-awful Smith people are here to take Pirate. Brendan's barricaded himself and Pirate in the playhouse."

"When?" Asher stood and started shutting down his office.

"Twenty minutes ago."

"I'll be right there."

"Sorry folks, gotta go." He rushed through the waiting room, leaving his wide-eyed patients to find their own way out. He arrived home in what seemed like hours. A grey van parked in the middle of the driveway forced him to park on the street. He flew into the house shouting for his grandfather. Granddad waited in the foyer and dragged him into the kitchen. Jean stayed in the front parlour with the Smiths.

"That woman oozed cutesy goo all over the boy and the dog and—" Horace began.

"I don't give a flying fuck about her. Where's Brendan?"

"Benny excused himself and ran off with the dog. He's still in the playhouse and he won't come out. Got himself tied in. I didn't think it right to force my way in."

Asher flew out the back door before Granddad stopped talking. At the playhouse, he heard Brendan weeping. Asher propped a hand on the roof to steady his own thundering heart and loosen the painful clench of his muscles. As the adrenalin receded, his legs wobbled, and his head swirled. Damn! Drawing a deep breath, he called softly to Brendan and knocked on the door.

"Go away!"

Asher tried the door. It opened a couple of inches and stopped. He peered around the edge of the door. Like Granddad had said, his son had looped a jute string around the inside handle and tied the other end to the built-in bench.

"Brendan, it's Daddy. Will you untie the rope and let me in?"

"No!"

"You don't have to come out. Just let me come in."

Long minutes passed before there was some rustling and the string fell. More rustling sounded and then silence. Asher gave his son a few moments to settle before he opened the door. His son huddled on the bench as far away as he could get. Asher stooped his way into the little house and squeezed into the space left on the bench. Brendan clutched Pirate tighter and buried his face in the dog's neck. Pirate threw Asher a look pleading with him to make this right.

"I want to keep him." Brendan threw himself against Asher's

chest, dragging the dog along.

Asher pushed his grief down deep. "I know you do. So do I. But he's not ours." Asher pulled boy and dog onto his lap, soothing and stroking.

"I d-don't ca-care!" Brendan hiccupped and banged his head on the underside of Asher's chin.

The sharp pain of his teeth on his tongue halted the escape of Asher's grief. He wrestled it down and shoved it back in its cage. "How would you feel if you had something very special and you lost it, and somebody found it, but they wouldn't give it back to you?"

Brendan sulked profoundly. "I dunno," he grouched.

"I think you'd expect them to give it back to you."

"But Pirate's mine. He said so."

Asher hid a smile. "People rules override dog rules. Pirate isn't ours. The Smiths have a license."

"A license?"

"Yes, a legal paper saying he belongs to them, like the license I showed you for my car."

Brendan buried his face in soft fur. Asher stroked his back. "Come on, Brendan. Let's go give Pirate back to his rightful owners."

"Do I have to?"

"It's the right thing to do."

Without further fuss, Brendan climbed down off Asher's lap and left the playhouse.

As they walked towards the house, anger boiled in Asher. For once, just once, he'd like to fuck the rules. He concocted an elaborate plan of hiding Pirate in the playhouse, then Pirate would "escape" into the forest never to be found, the Smiths would leave, and Pirate would belong to them.

It would be doing the wrong thing for the right reasons.

Lying to make his son happy.

When they got to the screen door, Asher grasped the handle. His fingers refused to work the lever while he studied the lie from various angles.

"Daddy?" Brendan piped up, hope blooming in his dark eyes and on his tear-stained face.

Ashamed of the example he set for his son, Asher opened the door. The hope faded in Brendan's eyes, and he dragged his feet into the house. Pirate paused and showed Asher a face of deep disappointment.

Asher took Brendan's hand, and they slouched into the front parlour. Pirate moped along. Granddad brought up the rear. Jean stood and joined them, forming a camp of Stockdales against Smiths.

Mrs. Smith jumped up, grabbed the dog under his forelegs, lifted him high and shook him. "Spotikins! You're a naughty, naughty doggie, sneaking off from your mommy and daddy again. Shame on you. I'd spank you if I wasn't so happy to see you." She kissed the dog on his lips and waggled him from side to side.

Pirate begged with his dark eyes. Brendan drooped, a forlorn weight on the end of Asher's arm. Doing right by the rules versus doing right by his son warred in Asher's chest.

"I'll give you five hundred dollars for the dog," Asher blurted out the offer.

Mr. Smith's beady eyes lit with avarice. "Make that seven-fifty and the critter's yours."

Pirate's legs dangled as Mrs. Smith tucked his torso under the arm on the far side of her husband. "How dare you sell my dog!"

He turned on his wife. "I bought and paid for him. He's mine. I'll do whatever I want." Mr. Smith scanned the house, stared at the grand piano in the back parlour, and scowled at Asher. "You're a rich man. I changed my mind. You can have him for a grand."

Asher's molars squeaked a protest at being clenched so hard. "I'll give you three-fifty."

"Hey! That's not how it works." The short scrawny man puffed up like a bantam rooster.

Asher shrugged as if he couldn't care less. "That's how it works for me." Beside him, he sensed his family straighten in hope and support.

"All right, six-fifty."

"Two-fifty."

"Okay, okay, five hundred. My final offer," the little man crowed angrily.

"Three-fifty. Take it or leave it."

"Daddy?" Asher's face softened as he gazed down at his son's brightening face. He stroked the messy curls from his forehead.

The squint Asher fired at Mr. Smith dared him to disappoint his boy.

Mrs. Smith pressed her free hand to her chest and sighed dramatically. "Your sweet little boy can have my Spotikins for three hundred and fifty dollars. Cash." The sentimental face hardened. "But you can't have any of his outfits. The creature never appreciated them anyway."

"You have a deal."

Mrs. Smith put Pirate on the floor. He sprinted into the middle of the legs of his new family. Brendan, gurgling with joy, squatted to hug his dog.

That evening, Brendan and Pirate slept in a heap in the little boy's nautical-themed bed. Asher stood in the doorway watching them.

Jean sauntered by with a cup of tea. She peeped into the room and smiled. "All you need now is a wife."

Asher raised quizzing eyebrows.

"You have the house, the dog, and the boy. All you need now is a wife. And we both know what her name is."

Asher cast a wary glance at Jean. "How is she? Does she ask about—Brendan?"

She rubbed his arm. "I'm glad you swallowed enough pride to ask. Unfortunately, there's nothing personal in her emails, only a travelogue. Beautifully written, lots of interesting tidbits. But nothing about any of us."

"May I read them?"

"Of course. Come to my room, and I'll set you up with my laptop."

Asher peeped again at the sleeping boy and dog, reassured himself all was right in his son's world and followed Jean.

He paged through email after email. The photos were breathtaking and the stories accompanying them brought Emma's sense of humour vividly to mind.

Damn his idiot hide for letting her go so easily. Jean was right. He had all but one element to make his dearest wish come true. Screw doing the right thing. The second Emma got back; he was pulling every naughty and nice trick out of his sleeve to bring her home to Pirate, Brendan, and himself.

On second thought, he refused to wait the four weeks until she got home. He was going to start now.

CHAPTER 12

An Expedition

In the early morning of her third consecutive day of travel, Emma awoke with the change in the sound from the tour bus's engine as it switched from uphill grind to downhill coast. The other passengers stirred, talking amongst themselves. Through the window, ranks of dark-green mountains surrounded a placid lake. Bluish mist billowed in the valleys.

India.

"A lovely morning, everyone." Prathiba's voice came over the microphone. "Below us, you will see Ooty Lake located in the Tamil Nadu state of southern India. We are on our way to the town of Ooty where we will reside at Roseneath, one of the few remaining Hill stations still in private hands. The surrounding mountains are the Nilgiri, which translate to The Blue Mountains."

To Emma, the hills didn't look anything like the Blue Mountains at home in Canada. Curiosity and discovery buzzed in

Emma's veins. Was Blue Mountain pottery from Ontario anything like Nilgiri pottery in India? She couldn't wait to explore.

"When we arrive at Roseneath, we will partake of brunch and retire for a much-needed rest. Thank you." Prathiba clicked off the microphone.

The final curve revealed a sprawling two-storey red-stuccoed house. Their hosts, Rosemary and Stephen Hetherington, stood at the top of the stairs flanked by two young Indian women garbed in cayenne-coloured saris with gold embroidery. They greeted the exhausted photo tour group with quiet smiles and a generous meal. The group lapped up the refreshments and headed off to their assigned rooms in the mansion to unpack and rest.

The window in Emma's room opened over the forecourt and down the slopes to the lake. The scent of eucalyptus floated in. A big change from the white pine at home.

Big changes for a woman who feared change.

Guess I'm not afraid anymore.

After sighing over the view, Emma dragged her jetlagged self into the shower. Somewhat refreshed, she turned to her suitcase to unpack for the first two-week's stay. At the bottom, beneath her bras and panties lay Hayley's photo of Asher and Brendan. Sudden, hot longing flowed through her, warming her from the inside out. She held the picture in trembling fingers. The love between Asher and Brendan was palpable. She'd seen such a welcome in Asher's eyes, though for her, his eyes always held desire as well as welcome. Except for the last time she'd seen him. His eyes had been flat, hard, suspicious. She shivered.

Hold on. How had the photo gotten into her suitcase? She certainly hadn't done it. After fighting with Asher, she couldn't even remember where it had gone. When had her suitcase been out of her sight?

"Jean." She scolded her dear friend from afar. "You couldn't leave well enough alone, could you? You just had to meddle. Again."

Now what to do with it? She moved to tuck it into the inner pocket of her suitcase where it would remain unharmed and unseen. Her fingers refused to release it. She tried to tuck it in her expanding file folder crammed with trip information. No luck.

"What am I going to do with you?" she asked of the handsome man.

Emma was so tired she could have sworn Asher winked at her. She propped it on the bedside table and crawled into bed. Those beautiful brown eyes were the last thing she saw before she passed out.

And the first thing to greet her sleepy smile when she awoke the next morning. Her first whole night with Asher. To escape the bitter regret, Emma rose and dressed for the day. In the dining room, Emma selected Indian items from the breakfast buffet.

What was Asher doing now? Clarence Bay was ten-and-a-half hours behind, no ahead of, Ooty—seven-thirty plus ten-thirty—nine o'clock this evening. Brendan would be sound asleep with Marty in his grip. The three older Stockdales would be reading or watching television. Maybe Asher played his piano. She chuckled ruefully at herself. Jean's scheme had worked.

"Is something amiss?" Her hostess Rosemary asked in her upper-crust English accent.

Emma took a seat at Rosemary's table. "Absolutely not. It all looks and smells wonderful. Will you tell me what I've chosen?"

Rosemary pointed to each item on Emma's plate. "The puffy white cakes are *idli*, the crêpes are *adai*, and the tea is grown in lower elevations down the mountain in Kotagiri. I'll warn you now to taste a small amount of the chutney—you chose something quite spicy. Smart to have yoghurt to cool your mouth if you need it."

They chatted for a few minutes about what flavours Emma could expect in Indian cooking. Then Rosemary said, "You're one of the Canadians in the group?"

Emma nodded.

"My oldest son went to Canada for a career in banking. Do you live anywhere near Toronto?" She raised a hand to her cheek. "What a silly question for so vast a country."

"No silliness this time. My hometown is a couple hours north."

"In cottage country."

"Yes. Does your son own a cottage there?"

"Indeed, he does." Rosemary gestured to a framed shot of a large log home, surrounded by the mixed forest common in her area and beyond.

"I recognize the Canadian Shield topography, but the Shield is a huge area. I don't recognize the spot."

Rosemary chuckled. "It's near Huntsville."

"About an hour's drive east of my town. Have you ever been to Canada?"

"Not yet."

Prathiba called the diners to order for a breakfast meeting regarding the schedule for the days ahead. Mornings were for travelling to local beauty spots, most afternoons and evenings were free to roam about the estate and its neighboring villages. Evenings were for convivial company.

"Each evening after supper, we will have a slideshow. We encourage everyone to submit three to five untouched photos a day, and we will discuss. On Saturdays, we'll compile your best retouched shots for what I call our Saturday Show. Sunday week, we move on to our next destination. For today, we will take an easy trip. The bus will leave in one hour for the Ooty Botanical Gardens."

On the following Friday, Emma ventured into the tiny estate village. It was Thanksgiving Day back home. Or was that yesterday? Emma aimed her camera at the more unusual buildings for a couple of shots each. The sunlight at this time of day raked across surfaces at a sharp angle, highlighting unexpected textures. A golden Buddha smiled benignly from his shrine, his hand up in blessing.

A little footsore, Emma sat at the fountain in the square. Tourists wandered by and tossed coins to make wishes. Peering into the water, Emma recognized Canadian loonies and American quarters. Some coins had holes in the middle or were octagon in shape. Gold, copper, and silver gleamed up through the clear waters.

A young girl in a saffron skirt and top climbed up the steps of the drinking fountain burbling to one side. Her long glossy dark hair slipped forward as she bent into the constant-flowing stream. Her huge brown eyes gazed unflinchingly over the spouting water.

Emma's shutter-finger twitched, startling her. For years, the small reaction only occurred at the sight of transcendent natural beauty.

Did she dare?

She positioned her camera with trembling hands. Carefully, she framed and focused the child in the viewer. Paused. Dared. Pressed the shutter.

Took her first portrait of a human being in thirteen years.

Drawing a deep steadying breath, she grinned at the child who grinned back, showing a gap where baby teeth had fallen out.

Emma pressed the shutter again a split second before the child's mother called and she vanished. Emma bent to review the shots, her thumb hovering over the delete button.

It was bad luck to take pictures of people.

No, it wasn't.

It was bad luck to get in a car with a reckless young driver under the influence of drugs and alcohol.

She shifted her grip on the camera, ready for the next person.

Back in her room, Emma uploaded her favourite shots to her laptop. She came to the young girl. Her great big eyes stared straight into Emma's soul, shaking her, demanding to be shared with someone who knew the meaning behind the photo.

Before she could second-guess herself, Emma attached the photo to an email, put "I did it!" in the subject line and sent it to Asher.

Saturday, the final full day at the Hetherington villa, Emma answered Rosemary's knock and invited her to enter the room.

"Afternoon, Emma. Did you have any pictures for the slideshow this evening?"

"Almost. Have a seat while I save the final changes to my last shot." Emma sat down at the desk, embedded her copyright on the shot then saved it to her laptop, the jump drive, and the Internet cloud.

Rosemary bent to peer at the photo on the bedside table. "Such a handsome family you have there."

A wistful smile tugged at Emma's lips. How she wished her hostess's statement was true. "He's just a friend."

"But you wish he were more, I surmise." Rosemary wagged an admonishing finger. "Don't worry. Things will work out as they're meant to."

Emma shrugged.

"I see you're dressed for dinner. You're quite lovely. I'm sure the merchants had great fun finding the perfect green to go with your colouring."

Emma smoothed the *churidaar* and *dupatta*, an outfit of trousers with a short-sleeved tunic and shawl, purchased today. "Thank you. I had a lot of fun as well."

"Won't you join Stephen and me for drinks?"

Emma hesitated. She wanted to read the latest email from Jean before the party.

"Please, do. We'd love to chat with you about our son's new home."

How could she resist? Emma pulled the jump drive from her laptop and together they went down to the Hetherington's private suite of rooms on the first floor.

Stephen poured drinks, and Rosemary gestured to a tray of delectable Indian appetizers. After chatting about Canada and immigration problems, Rosemary cleared her throat.

"If it's not too intrusive, would you tell me why the handsome man is just a friend when you hope for more."

Emma's hand touched her belly. Could she tell these kind strangers? What was the likelihood she'd ever see them again?

"He asked me to marry him and I had to say no."

"You don't love him?"

"I love him very much. I don't think I'll ever stop."

"He doesn't love you?"

"He did. I'm not so sure now." Emma's gaze fell to the empty glass in her hand. "I can't have children and he deserves one of his own. The little boy in the photograph isn't his—well, he is, but he isn't."

"Adopted?"

"Yes." No need to go into the details of Brendan's parentage.

Her hosts exchanged dire glances. "You feel adopted children are less valuable than natural children?"

"No! Heavens no," Emma blurted. A little voice in the back of her head poked at her declaration. If she adopted Brendan, would she treat him differently? No, not at all.

Stephen stood and got a large photo album from a bookshelf behind the door. He invited Emma to a seat between him and his wife on the sofa. Emma was bidden to open the book.

"These pictures are from our fiftieth wedding anniversary."

The first shot showed her hosts, beaming with joy. The second was a large family group spread out over the grand staircase.

"This is our family; children, grandchildren, and the little fellow on Rosemary's knee is our first great-grandchild. Three more have been added to the family since this picture was taken last summer."

Stephen pointed out two tall Indian men standing to his left. "These are our sons, Fahad and Sanjit. They married Bella and

Preety." Beside Rosemary, he indicated a young African woman and a white-blonde woman. "These are our daughters, Aisha and Hannah. They married Xian and Helmuth." And so on went the naming of individuals from every continent on the planet. Some of the people were familiar to Emma as staff members in the villa.

"When Rosemary miscarried our first child, the damage to her was irreparable. Rather than be childless, we adopted four children who needed us as much as we needed them. Between them, we have seventeen grandchildren, six of whom are also adopted."

"I don't think we could have been more blessed if any of them had been born to us." Rosemary wiped a tear from her eye.

Emma turned the pages. A young girl sulked in her mother's arms while being offered treats by her grandmother. An infant snoozed in the tight space between his father and his grandfather. A bride and groom waltzed amid their extended family.

Videos unwound in Emma's mind. Asher hugging Brendan. The proud claim in Asher's voice as he said, "my son". The endless patience and love he bore his child.

She paged back to the family group. "No," she said to her hosts. "Blood makes no difference at all."

When she returned to her room that evening, Emma logged on for yesterday's email from Jean. She reported the purchase of their bungalow had gone smoothly. Melody had gotten a kitten from the Humane Society and tweeted too many pictures. The Stitch & Bitch group had started a project of toques for cancer patients. Then came Jean's daily dose of Asher and Brendan stories. Pirate had come back. Emma wished she been there to see Asher's reverse bargaining technique.

Jean was persistent if nothing else.

Emma sighed and went to the next email. Up popped a photo of Brendan, Marty the Moose, and Pirate sound asleep on Brendan's bed. Aww. Her insides went all mushy. Then she read the text.

My darling Emma,

I have a house, a dog, and a son. My life is incomplete without you. Please, come home to us.

All my love, Asher

A sob exploded from Emma. She clapped both hands to her mouth. Her chest juddered with more sobs. Tears slid from her eyes and over her fingers. With trembling hands, Emma reached out to respond "Yes." Instead, she shut her laptop down for the night.

She couldn't reply. Not until she confessed all to Asher in person and he sent her packing, or... Emma dared not think of the or.

Asher's heart practically leapt out of his chest and boogied down the stairs ahead of him, arms spread, lips a-pucker.

Emma was here.

He halted at the top of the stairs, repeating his mantra to be gruff and stoic. She hadn't answered his plea, only copied him on the chatty travelogue emails for Jean.

Stoic, remember.

She'd also sent him, only him, a portrait every day. No words, just an incredible photograph of an Indian. Sometimes up close, sometimes within their milieu, always emotionally touching, always personal.

Asher proceeded at a more normal pace, reconnected with his assorted parts at the bottom of the stairs, and reined them in.

Stoic.

Emma stood, shy and hopeful, beside a smiling Jean and Horace and a squirming Brendan. Even Pirate and Horace's new white terrier Petticoat, were there as part of the welcoming committee.

Screw stoic.

He swept Emma up and hugged her tight, groaning with the delight of having her in his arms again. She squealed as he spun her around and kissed her for all he was worth.

"I missed you," he said, his head still whirling.

She stroked his cheek. "I would never have guessed."

"Spin me, too, Daddy." Brendan wedged his way between them, lifting his arms.

Asher ruffled his son's curls. "Later, little buddy. Right now, Emma and I have important things to discuss."

"Are you gonna ask her to be my new mommy? That's the bestest thing in the whole world. Can I call you Mommy even if I gots a mommy?" Brendan bounced on his toes, glancing from Asher to Emma, his anticipation spilling over.

He crossed his arms. "Granddad, Jean, what have you two been telling him?"

Jean laughed in Asher's heated face. "Nothing he doesn't already know. You're not so good at keeping your emotions under wraps." She hugged Emma. "If you don't say yes, I'll disown you." Her carefree smile disarmed her threat.

Horace scooped Brendan out from between them. "C'mon,

Benny-boy. Let's take the dogs for a walk. Leave these two to their business." He turned to Emma. "You say yes now, you hear. My grandson's been a misery-guts without you." The three of them donned jackets and left with the two dogs.

In the quiet of the empty house, the furnace cycled on, sounding like an airplane coming in for a landing. They both jumped then grimaced at their nervousness. The scent of coffee reminded Asher of Jean's earlier preparations.

"Would you like some coffee?" he said. "Jean made pinwheels."

"Yes, please." Emma's shoulders dropped, and her smile widened.

They settled at the kitchen table, fiddled with the cups and plates and utensils, cake, and coffee. A persistent drip pinged into the stainless-steel sink.

Asher sighed. "Are you feeling as awkward as I am?"

"Yes, but not, I think, for the same reason?" She stared out the window at the barren yard.

Brendan had been upset at the closing of his little house for the winter. Trepidation settled between his shoulder blades, pulling the muscles tight. He rolled his shoulders and subtly tilted his head from side to side, waiting for the axe to fall.

She cleared her throat, nibbled and sipped.

"Emma just say it."

"What?"

He swallowed his impatience. "Whatever it is you're worrying about."

"It's not another man."

He blew out a gigantic sigh of relief. "I wouldn't have thought so after your greeting."

Her responding smile didn't quite make it to her eyes. She

shifted in her seat, picked up her cup and put it down, crossed her arms, uncrossed them. Then met his eyes. "I have to confess something I don't think you want to hear. Something that might change your mind about me and our relationship."

He pushed his lips into a rough approximation of a smile. "Have you smuggled drugs into the country? Failed to declare an import."

The corners of her mouth kicked up at the playback of herself when Asher had revealed Brendan's paternity. Her tension ebbed a pinch. "Do you remember when I told you about the car crash? The one that killed Nico and two of our friends?"

He sat back at the swift change in topic. "Yes."

"I got my file—a copy of my medical file."

He had no clue what to expect, so he simply waited.

"I read the emergency report. You were right. Nico was drunk and high. He killed himself and those two kids. Not me. He was so used to the camera flash—mosquitoes bothered him more." Her shoulders drew up around her ears. "He also killed someone else."

Asher's jaw slackened. "A pedestrian?"

"A baby."

"A mother was walking—?"

"My baby. I miscarried because of the crash."

"Oh, Emma. I'm so sorry." He went around the table and tried to pull her into his arms.

She pushed him back and rose. Scooting around him, she stared out the window. "I—I—" She swallowed audibly and turned to face him. A woman facing the firing squad. "The report said there won't be any more children." She pressed a hand to her abdomen. "I'm infertile. Nico killed all of my children. All of *our* children."

He stood like a statue, his blood cooling in his veins. His mind whirled in sickening arcs. Hopes and dreams crashed and burned. Is this what it felt like to be shot through the heart?

She walked over and stroked his arm. "I won't expect you to ask your question again." She stared up at him, tears brimming over her glorious eyes. She stood on her toes and pressed a kiss to his mouth.

He couldn't respond. He stared at her stricken face.

A soft sob broke from her. She slid around him, headed for the front door. Time stretched to mark the beat of her footsteps. A metronome of grief.

The front door opened and shut.

The click of the lock clanged in his emptiness. The echo rattled through him. Swept away the fragments of his shattered dreams.

"Emma!" He shouted though he knew she didn't hear. He spun about, raced through the foyer, yanked open the front door, leaving it ajar. "Emma!"

He sprinted across the lawn and into the street, paused long enough to spot her blue mini-SUV.

She sat in her car, her head on her arms folded on the steering wheel, her shoulders quaking.

His sweaty hands fumbled the door latch.

She jumped and turned a face soggy with misery to him. "Asher?"

Finally, his fingers made the necessary connections. He pulled opened the door and snatched her from the seat and into his arms.

"I don't care about babies. I have a child. I don't have you. It's you I want. Only you. You're all I'm missing."

He kissed her madly, deeply, with all the joy in his heart. She wrapped her arms around him and kissed him back. The glorious heat of his Emma brought Asher back to life.

"Don't go, my darling Emma. Come inside. Tell me everything."

Arms around each other's waists, they returned to the house, to the front parlour. "I told you everything."

"The report was over ten years old. Things may have healed."

"Is it important to you?" she asked.

He tipped her chin up, wanting eye contact with his precious love. "It's important to you and that's what counts. Have you been to a gynecologist?"

"No. The report was fairly conclusive."

"I still think you should have the report confirmed." An idea struck him. "Heck, I don't have any proof I'm not infertile as well. We'll both get checked. But regardless of the outcome—" He shoved the coffee table out of his way then got down on one knee in front of her. "I love you as you are. The future will take care of itself. Will you marry me?"

She gave him the crooked smile he loved so dearly. "Could we adopt?"

He huffed and tipped his head. "Not quite the response I expected. I'd like you to adopt Brendan. If we decide we want more, we'll adopt more. Now to repeat my question, my lovely Emma—will you marry me?"

"Yes, I'll be happy to marry you." She melted into him and pressed a kiss to his mouth. The kiss deepened, tongues tangled, arms drew tighter.

Asher toppled backwards to the carpet. He refused to loosen his grip and Emma sprawled across him, laughing and kissing at the same time.

Driven by the need to feel her skin, he slid his hand under her shirt. She hummed her approval.

"Let's take the celebration upstairs, shall we?"

The front door opened, and Asher's family poured in. They took one peek at their faces and leapt to the correct conclusion.

Asher rose from the floor and extended a hand to his fiancée.

"Congratulations." Granddad clapped him on the back then hugged Emma. "Welcome to the family, Emma."

"Good for you, Asher." Jean kissed him. As she hugged Emma, she murmured in her ear making Emma blush and smile.

"Did she say yes, Daddy?" Brendan wrung his small hands. On either side of the young boy, Pirate and Petticoat barked the same question.

Asher lifted his son and kissed his soft cheek. "Yes, she said yes."

His son bounced in his arms. "Yay! Two mommies. Can I have a cookie?"

Emma ruffled her son's hair. "Of course, you can."

Brendan ran off to the kitchen, the dogs in hot pursuit.

Emma spoke ruefully, "Your—our son is a sight for sore eyes, but he sure can holler."

Laughing together, they went to join their family at the table.

Epilogue

Reluctantly, Emma opened the last cardboard file box from her apartment above the shop. Inside, were the contents of her roll-top desk. The file folder of wrecked photographs from that day in college lurked in the back of the box. She withdrew the folder and laid it on the desk now installed in the fourth bedroom of Asher's—their—home. She hadn't seen the photographs in fourteen years.

The shock and shame of that day rippled across her skin. Emma shivered. She wrapped the soft cashmere folds of her *dupatta* around herself, drew a breath, and flipped open the folder

"Emma, what are you doing in here? The party's about to start." Asher rounded her desk and peered down at the warped image. He laid a warm hand on her shoulder, instantly giving her support.

She squared her shoulders and turned over the first image to see the second. Silently, all twelve images were exposed to the light of day. A muted sadness filled Emma's eyes with moisture.

"You were right, Asher. I was a good photographer." She sighed and gazed up into dark eyes filled with sympathy.

He stroked her cheek. "Yes, you are good. What will you do with them now?"

She closed the folder and spread her hands across it. "I used to keep them to remind me never to show my work, never to risk the mockery." She opened the bottom drawer and slid the folder back where it belonged. "Thanks to you, I've gone beyond that."

"Then why keep them?"

She shut the drawer, stood and moved into the circle of his arms. "To honour the work of my younger self. To remind me to stand up for myself and others, so the bullies don't win." His kiss chased away the last of her sadness.

Down below, in the front hall, the doorbell rang, signalling the beginning of a party celebrating a housewarming and Emma's first one-woman show. Emma led the way downstairs to greet their first guests.

Within minutes, the crowd of combined Finns, Stockdales, Chisholms, plus a few extras, filled the first floor of Emma and Asher's home.

Posters from Emma's India trip lined the walls. In pride of place, hung the image of the little village girl at the water fountain. Among the personal photographs in freestanding frames sat a photo of Brendan, Hayley and Daniel munching on Popsicles.

The dining-room table groaned with a buffet spread.

Prathiba Nayar arrived and greeted Emma with a gift box wrapped in India silk. "Don't open it now, but it's for good luck in your career. We have a highly profitable new offer to consider." She waved her hand around the room. "These photos are making a splash even before your show. My cousin read your posts on your website and he loves your words. How would you feel about a coffee-table book about your travels in India?"

Prathiba cut off Emma's enthusiastic response. "Before you get excited by this offer, there is an addition. He wishes also to produce, with only your photos, a deluxe calendar. We will sell millions of them and be rich and happy. Your work will be seen all over the world."

Calendar.

Emma's thoughts snagged on the word.

Seen all over the world. Rich and happy.

She laughed and hugged a puzzled Prathiba. "Yes, let's get rich and famous with a calendar and coffee-table book."

"Excuse me, I don't mean to eavesdrop, but did you say a coffee-table book, Ms. Nayar?" Barbara Stockdale interrupted.

"That is correct." Prathiba flipped the drape of her yellow sari over her left shoulder. The dense golden embroidery gleamed in the light. "You know of this form of book?"

"I do. I have a collection of several hundred." Surprise rippled through Emma. Asher's mother didn't seem the type to appreciate the art form.

"Is Emma publishing one?" Mrs. Stockdale glanced between them in anxious query.

"This is so," replied Prathiba.

Asher's mother touched Emma's arm. "Emma dear, tell me the moment it comes out and I'll buy a copy."

"Of course. But no need to buy, I'll give you an autographed copy for your collection."

Mrs. Stockdale gave Emma her first honest smile then turned to Prathiba. "Ms. Nayar, may I ask about your sari? The fabric is beautiful. How do you wrap it?" The two women moved away, deep in discussion about the intricacies of the Indian sari.

David Chastain arrived next. Emma gave him a brief hug. "How's your wife?"

He kissed her cheek. "Much better. Thank you. Your emails meant a lot to her." He hesitated then squared his shoulders. "I want to thank you for standing up to me on our North Channel cruise. I've changed my whole approach to mentoring and have more students than ever. My own work is better than ever. But I still can't catch a decent lightning shot."

"It took me a lot of years to perfect the technique so give it time. By the way, has Prathiba told you about the gallery we're putting together?"

"No, but tell me more." Interest shone in his blue eyes.

"You remember I have a family business?"

"Yes, a china and gift shop down by the marina. You pointed it out to me when we got back after our field trip."

"I've cleared the apartment above the store to use as a gallery featuring local artists and artisans, including the First Nations in the area. I also want to show works done around here. Here's where you come in. Would you be interested in showing some of your North Channel work in our gallery?"

A smile swept across his face. "Absolutely. We've rented a cottage for next summer near Killbear Park, so that would be the perfect venue. Thank you."

"Excellent. I'll send you the details in an email."

David kissed her cheek again and wandered off to the buffet appearing much happier.

Asher slid a hand around Emma's waist, and gave her a quick kiss. "Hello, my wife. How did it go with David?"

She took another kiss. "It went very well, my husband. He's

agreed to show."

Hayley and Lindsey rushed up. "Asher, if your grandfather is married to my great-grandmother, are we cousins?"

"I don't know. Ask Emma. It's time for me to play." Asher grabbed another kiss for luck from his lovely wife and walked into the back parlour. He sat at the piano, hands loose in his lap.

Emma called everyone to order. There was a mad, brief scramble for seats before silence fell.

Off to his right, in a direct line of sight for his hands, sat Ms. Pentland the world-renown pianist now music teacher. She, of all the people in the house, understood what lay beneath the music. Today, Asher would play a work of his own composing, dedicated to his wife Emma.

Crowded into the front parlour sat their combined families. Jean and Horace appeared younger than their years. The Chisholms were there *en masse*. As always, Hayley and Lindsey had their heads together over something. His mother, father and sister had welcomed Emma into the family.

His beautiful Emma glowed. A small smile played over her lips. Was she thinking of the card from Sondra congratulating and wishing them all the happiness in the world? Or was she thinking of the letter from the fertility clinic stating they were both in good order?

Emma's smile made him the luckiest man on earth. He drew her joy inside himself, bowed his head to clear his thoughts of everything but the joy. Taking a breath, Asher raised his hands and began to play.

Meet Joan

Joan Leacott is skilled in many arts—sewing, knitting crochet, cross-stitch, painting, and piano. The skill favoured by her husband and son is cooking, especially pumpkin pie.

She spends her winters in Toronto, Canada attending piano classes, melting in the hot yoga studio, and writing.

Her summers are spent on the shores of Georgian Bay relaxing on the deck with a romance novel and a glass of wine. After she's done her laps in the bay, she settles down to write more multi-generational stories of people living and loving in today's world.

Joan loves to hear from her readers. You can contact her via her website www.JoanLeacott.ca or on Facebook at JoanLeacottAuthorPage.

See you on the streets of Clarence Bay!

Other Books in the Clarence Bay Chronicles

Instant family: just add daughter.

Three generations of Rossetti women are hoarding secrets.

Cathy Rossetti's secret is Hayley, an outspoken ten-year-old who's about to meet her family for the first time. Sadly, it's taken a terminal illness to bring Cathy back to her hometown.

The elder generation of Rossetti women guards a thirty-year old secret with the power to rock Cathy's world. Will her mother take their secret to her grave, or will her aunt break her punishing vow of silence?

Hayley hates secrets, so she's sleuthing around Clarence Bay looking for her daddy. Is it her new BFF's father or mayoral candidate Ryan Chisholm or Ryan's handsome campaign manager?

Ryan has a secret, too. He's still in love with Cathy, his high-school sweetheart. For a man running his election campaign on a platform of honesty, this could cause problems. Will dumping his popular fiancée cost him the election? And if Cathy still loves him after eleven years absence, she's not telling.

Find *Above Scandal* at your favourite retailer.
https://books2read.com/Above-Scandal-Leacott